GLITTER

AND

SMOKE

BOOK SIX OF THE GEOPOLITICAL TECHNO-THRILLER SERIES

ANDREW B. LOUIS

A major power uses the drug trade and arm sales
to help a terrorist's rebirth.

For information regarding permission, please write to:
info@barringerpublishing.com
Barringer Publishing, Naples, Florida
www.barringerpublishing.com

Cover, graphics, and layout by Linda S. Duider
Cape Coral, Florida

ISBN: 978-1-954396-53-1
Library of Congress Cataloging-in-Publication Data
Glitter and Smoke / Andrew B. Louis

Printed in U.S.A.

DEDICATION

To family and friends who have known how to support and encourage me to keep at my passion and to all those who often work and risk their lives in the shadows to keep all of us safe.

OTHER BOOKS BY THE AUTHOR

Other novels by Andrew B. Louis include:

 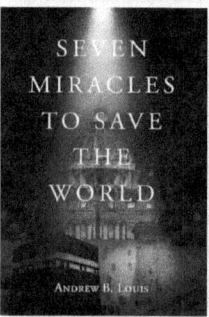 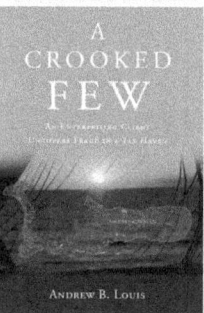 

Operation Kovesh, The Shadow Experts, Below the Surface,
The Crypto Trap, Escaping the Bear, Seven Miracles to
Save the World, A Crooked Few and *Tough Choices*
available at Amazon.com.

www.AndrewBLouis.com

ACKNOWLEDGMENTS

Though all the writing and errors are solely my own doing, a number of people contributed to the creation of the text. I would like to thank the numerous friends and family members who were kind enough to comment on various drafts and led me to make material changes for the better. A special mention is reserved for my wife who labored through so many versions that I am certain she has lost count.

SYNOPSIS

An unmarked cargo plane was hit by anti-aircraft fire as it was coming in for a landing somewhere in the vicinity of Erbil in Northern Iraq. It is believed that the shots originated among Kurdish rebels. A *Mossad* agent, friendly with the local insurgents, gets access to the wreckage and stumbles on a small briefcase; it contains a fortune in diamonds. He assumes that he just happened onto a drug traffic exchange location, where opiates are sold for diamonds.

An important piece of intelligence reached David Heller, *Mossad*'s new Head of *Disruption*. Two ships had transited through the Bosphorus, the Istanbul Strait, that links the Black Sea to the Mediterranean Sea. Someone thought they saw missiles below deck, but the Turkish navy did not want to intervene. The belief was that the two boats were on their way to Syria and, if so, would have to be intercepted.

Mossad designs a plan to infiltrate the drug trade with the help of an invention from a star scientist: diamonds manufactured through a totally novel process. They appear virtually indistinguishable from the real ones. Working with Countess Renate, the founder and head of The Shadow Experts, *Mossad* finds a way to have the diamonds cut and uses them to trade with the smugglers; moreover, it discovers a hitherto unknown Russian activity. Will the Russian ships succeed in making their suspected arms delivery? Could their interception bring about a larger confrontation as both Russian and American navy ships are in the area? Will the worst be avoided? Will the terrorists who were attempting to resuscitate ISIS in Syria be prevented from wreaking havoc?

Disclaimer: The events described here are plausible. In fact, they have been "sampled" from a number of different real-life situations. However, all the parties to this story are totally fictitious. If there was some resemblance with individuals or institutions, it would be purely coincidental.

PROLOGUE

SOMEWHERE IN NORTHWESTERN IRAQ

Josh Steimetz, better known to his local acquaintances as Abu Musa, was a *Mossad* agent whose mission was to find ways to hinder the local drug trade which *Mossad* believed was one way or another starting to benefit Palestinian terrorists. More or less refined opiates would indeed transit out of Afghanistan via neighboring Iran and from there make their way to Turkey or Syria, and then onto their eventual markets.

The route which *Mossad* had recently identified seemed new. Two alternatives were well-known: one, the "southern" route which went from Afghanistan through Pakistan to the Arabian Sea and the Indian Ocean. The other, the "northern" route, involved crossing Turkmenistan and the Caspian Sea, and then moving across Azerbaijan and Georgia into Eastern Turkey. This new route through Iran, Iraq, and either Turkey or Syria seemed to have two interesting advantages, besides the fact that it was new and thus less "policed." First, it offered easier access to Europe via the Mediterranean Sea or even the Black Sea, an important attribute for customers in Northern Europe. Second, it provided a means for local rebels, principally Palestinians, to cash in on the trade, offering their services, particularly in northern Iraq and Syria. Unfortunately, everyone knew that drug smugglers always needed to innovate in terms of routes to "keep the merchandise moving, with minimal interference or hindrance" as they said.

More importantly, ever since *Mossad* had caught a Hezbollah boat red-handed as it was unloading drugs in Massawa in Eritrea[1], painstaking groundwork had indicated that the "middle route"—via Iraq and Syria—may well have been expanded to serve the funding needs of ISIS. Originally, *Mossad* had thought that the drug trade was one of the ways Palestinians financed their arms purchases. That had to be stopped and was one of the major reasons behind Josh Steinmetz's mission. The analysis had however been refined to identify ISIS as a possible principal actor; that was an even more important potential risk, which if real would have to be eliminated.

After its defeat on the field—though it saw it as but a temporary setback—ISIS had regrouped in the north of Iraq and the northeast of Syria. Both contiguous areas bordered Turkey, forcing ISIS to compete with the Kurds. In fact, ISIS's choice of territory should not have surprised anyone given the meaning of the acronym "ISIS;" it stood for "Islamic State of Iraq and Syria." It described very well the geography of the califate which ISIS wanted to recreate. It was thought that besides older and more traditional tribal connections, the fact that the area sat in the middle of routes to bring Afghani opium to the West was a useful dimension.

Jewish from his mother's side with a father of Lebanese Christian Maronite descent, Josh was ideally suited for the mission. With a beard allowed to grow as is traditional within the Shiite Muslim community, he surely could look the part. This was despite his being quite a bit taller than many of the local Arabs. He was helped by the fact many would observe that he had a lot of the traits of the famous "men of the desert" which translate as *"Bedouin"* in Arabic, though a

---

[1] See "Below the Surface" by the same author. Barringer Publishing, 2022.

majority are Muslims, and he was not. He was a shade more than 6'2"
tall and tipped the scales on the high side of two hundred pounds.
Yet, his weight was all muscle; there was little room for fat on a body
shaped by sports such as soccer, cycling, weightlifting, and *krav maga*,
a self-defense system developed for the military in Israel. It consists of
a wide combination of techniques sourced from a variety of combat
sports, ranging from judo to wrestling and boxing to grappling. In
fact, many of his friends said that his stature was enough to earn him
respect quite rapidly, though he normally oozed charm and was in no
way ever aggressive. He was totally fluent in Hebrew, Arabic, English,
and, though a skill acquired more recently, in Kurdish the language
of the land where he had been posted six months ago.

Ever since his arrival in Mosul, Josh had developed "friendly"
links with the Kurdish community. Traditionally, Kurds have been a
majority ethnic group in Kurdistan, a geographic territory comprising
the Upper Mesopotamia and the Zagros mountains—the chain that
separates Iran and Iraq today. The geo-cultural territory had not been
maintained as a separate nation ever since Kurdish-inhabited areas
were split between the Safavid and Ottoman empires, in the 16th and
17th centuries. Now, Kurds find themselves spread into Turkey, Iraq,
Iran, and Syria. However, there remained a strong sense of tribal
identity based on Kurdish culture and languages, not to mention the
remnants of a diffuse national identity. Though more moderate than
the surrounding ethnic groups on political and religious matters,
the Kurds still strived for some measure of political autonomy, if not
outright independence; they unabashedly cited their goal as the re-
creation of Kurdistan as a country.

That evening, Josh had driven a bit further than usual from his
Mosul base, in the direction of Erbil, a smaller town less than sixty
miles away. Erbil claims to be one of if not the oldest cities in the
world, tracing its history back 7,000 years. Josh typically spent his days
catching up on his sleep so that he could go to work from evening

through the night into the early morning. At these times, he would typically go "on patrol," in search of anything unusual. He would then trade any find that he had made with Kurdish militants with whom he had struck up a friendship of convenience: they would help him, if he would help them. They were not terribly excited by the fact that their ancestral territory was being used for the drug trade, though, in truth, many believed that they were willing participants—they needed money to buy arms, just as any and all rebels. They remembered the pain that had come with the conquest of their territory by ISIS and earlier in their fights with the Baath's nationalists. They enjoyed some relative quiet at this point and did not want anyone to come and create trouble or give anyone an excuse for intervening. Thus, officially, the vast majority of the people did not support the drug trade. They worked to earn their living in a traditional manner; yet, known but unsaid was the fact that certain Kurd leaders had to participate in the trade. Without arms, their historic struggle would simply not be possible.

Josh, aka Abu Musa, had told the Kurds he had met that he was somewhat of a bounty hunter. He had said that he specialized in trying to locate drop off or pick up points for drug smugglers. He was indifferent as to whether he could happen on drugs left behind or some payment for drugs that had not been duly collected. However rare, they were usually nothing but very small finds. Occasionally, a Kurdish friend would give him a hint or better a clear pointer. He would go and investigate, and then report. All the work he had done so far had convinced him that the region north of the Mosul-Erbil axis all the way up to the Iraq-Iran border was a prime location for the drug trade. However, he had not been able to identify anything specific that could be useful to his bosses in Tel Aviv or might serve the needs of his "Kurdish friends."

Josh was "prospecting" in a relatively rugged area, though there were still plenty of farms and what looked like legitimate businesses in the immediate neighborhood. Suddenly, he stopped dead in his tracks. He heard gun fire in the distance. It was sufficiently sustained that he identified it as anti-aircraft fire, though, in fairness, he later conceded to himself that it could have been anything else. He immediately thought that one of his Kurdish friends must have seen a plane in a place where it should not have been and started firing at it. As it was quite dark outside, he could not see exactly where the gunfire originated but he did not have the time to ponder the question much longer. Within seconds, he heard the scream of aircraft engines and immediately saw a plane approaching him with fire coming out of the right above-wing propeller. The plane could not be much more than a few hundred feet up when it flew just over Josh's head. The next sound was unmistakable: the aircraft had crashed nearby, triggering an explosion. Josh made a mental note that the explosion was weaker than what one might have expected; he concluded that the plane must have been low on fuel. He thought: *Probably was scheduled to land nearby. I may finally be in luck . . .*" He was also thinking that a plane that crashed while low on fuel had a much lower risk of further explosion; the fire would burn what was left, but there would not be enough for it to explode.

He jumped in his car, a Jeep left behind by American soldiers and repainted to eliminate the military connection and drove toward the site of the crash which he estimated had to be less than a couple of miles away, assuming the typical 5% rate of descent of an aircraft in final approach. The terrain was somewhat rugged and hilly, but still practicable. It principally comprised fields that were cultivated with dirt tracks separating one from the other. With the four-wheel drive firmly engaged, he drove a bit less than two miles and soon saw flames. He kept going until he was able to identify the plane as an Antonov 32, a 78-foot-long twin-turbo prop plane manufactured in Ukraine. He thought: "*this would definitely fit with a feature of the drug trade. Very interesting!*"

The impact of the aircraft on the ground had broken it in two. The fuselage aft of the overhead wing had separated from the cockpit area and appeared surprisingly intact despite a few bits of contorted metal protruding here or there; at any rate, there did not seem to have been any fire there. He thought . . . *not surprising since the fuel tanks are forward.* He would be able to go check what the plane carried. The other half of the plane, comprising the now partially broken wings and what was left of the cockpit was another story; it was still burning and, with the aircraft having come down nose first, its front end looked like an accordion that was fully folded down. As he observed it from a safe distance, it was quite clear in Josh's mind that there could not be any survivor in that front section. On the other hand, knowing as he did that the fuel reservoirs were in the front section of the plane, and seeing that there were no additional external fuel tanks attached to each wing between the fuselage and the engine, he concluded that there was minimal risk of explosion in the tail end of the fuselage. Plus, the distance between the two parts of the carcass was sufficient that he did not feel exposed to the risk of a deadly explosion somewhere in the front half of the wreck.

Proceeding toward the tail section, he was still looking for survivors, as, if there were any, the tail-end of the fuselage is where they would be or would have initially been as they could have been ejected on impact. He did not see anyone. In fact, the inside of the aircraft was totally empty: "*a cargo plane. The connection with the drug trade is becoming increasingly clear*" was his first thought. At that point, there was no longer any desire to save anyone on his mind; he hoped to find something in the fuselage or near it that could point him a bit more directly or precisely in one direction or another. He started his inspection with the aftmost section of the fuselage and was slowly backing up toward where the front of the plane would have been, using regular semi-circular movements of the beam of his flashlight, to make sure he did not miss anything. As he was about to reach the forward end of that aft section, he was a bit disappointed to come back empty-handed; not even a scrap of paper or any material that could point to opiates. He stepped down from the fuselage and kept looking around on the ground nearby, probably more out of habit than conviction. Suddenly, his flashlight picked up something that was reflecting the light, right in the middle of the burned grass. He approached it carefully as he had no idea what it could be though he assumed it had to be a piece of metal. Five steps further, the object on the ground became much clearer: a briefcase with a metallic grey polycarbonate shell. One of the two locks had popped open in the shock, but the other remained shut. He carefully picked the briefcase up, keeping it horizontal to make sure that nothing fell from it. Then, he returned to his car. That's also when he thought he heard voices in the distance.

He jumped into the car, started the engine and drove in the opposite direction from where the voices were originating. That might or might not get him closer to the Mosul-Erbil highway, but it would at least reduce the risk of unpleasant encounters. He worried that the voices might have heard his engine come to life. Therefore, he was careful to rev it up as little as possible, to keep noise to a minimum. A couple of miles on, he slowed down and turned the engine off. He was happy to notice that he could not hear a sound. He thought: ". . . *must have driven far enough away.*" He took the time to deposit the briefcase on the floor in the footwell in front of the passenger seat, moving it from his lap where he had "parked" it as he left the scene of the crash precipitously. Resuming his return trip, he drove in the direction of the nearest road: "*no point driving on dirt tracks if I can be on a real road!*" His pocket GPS showed a divided highway approximately two miles due west from where he was. It would take him to Kawraban, across the Great Zab River, a tributary to the Tigris River, nearby. Once on the highway, he disengaged the four-wheel drive system of his car and proceeded in the direction of Mosul, using the more economical two-wheel drive setup only. Somehow, he expected the briefcase to contain money and was wondering whether it would be real or counterfeit. Yet, despite his curiosity, it was clear in his mind that he would not try to open it now—too much risk that it would be boobytrapped.

Upon reaching the building where he was renting a two-bedroom apartment, he drove into the underground car park. He decided to walk around the car to retrieve the briefcase from the passenger side of the car. In truth, he did that more out of habit than because he had planned it that way. He opened the door and could not believe his eyes: on the floor, right next to the briefcase, he saw a couple of reflections of the ceiling light which had come on when he opened the door. He reached for his flashlight and pointed the beam directly at them. He was sure he was staring at a few small diamonds. He picked one of them up and inspected it as closely as the circumstances permitted. *"Darn it. This **is** a diamond"* was all he could think. He assumed that this one as well as the few others he was seeing on the floor had likely escaped from the side of the case where the lock had popped open. After all, he was not sure he had kept the suitcase totally horizontal as he had transferred it from his lap to the front passenger footwell. He thought: *"Maybe not cash; maybe diamonds?"* He picked the diamonds up, all four of them. He waved the beam of his flashlight across the floor of the car to be sure there was no other straggler. Finding none, he carefully took the case back to his apartment. The odds that the briefcase contained a bomb were receding in a hurry, but there was no point being careless.

Once in the apartment, he set the briefcase on the dining room table. He made sure that all curtains were drawn to ensure that no one would be spying on whatever he was doing and seeing whatever he had found. He first looked at the four diamonds. Josh estimated that they each weighed probably a carat, a couple of grams, and noted that they were all cut and polished: probably a round, brilliant cut, though he was no specialist in the diamond trade. He had never been engaged and thus had not had to learn the basics. He thought: "... *must have lucked upon the payment for some drug shipment which the plane was supposed to collect.*"

His careful inspection of the second lock yielded nothing of note. In fact, the second lock, the one which had remained shut, popped almost accidentally when he touched it, ever so lightly. Josh opened the case. He was now staring at a small fortune, all in small, cut diamonds. He used his bathroom scale to eyeball the weight of the diamonds, first weighing himself carrying the case and then himself without the case. The difference pointed to about eight pounds. Assuming that the weight of the case was around three pounds, he thought: "*Eight minus three is five; five pounds of diamonds equal about 25,000 carats . . . Holy Cow—there's about $100 million in here. Must find a way to send this back to Tel Aviv. Not gonna be easy!*"

Having placed the diamonds safely where no one would find them, he left the apartment. He drove directly to the nearest auto repair shop that sold tires. He asked that his four tires be changed. The owner was a bit surprised arguing:

"But, sir, they still have a few hundred miles in them . . . Though I do see that the front right one is a bit tired."

Josh conceded that he could keep them a bit longer, but still asked:

"Would you have four tires that fit this car?"

"I do, sir."

Josh lied further:

"I need to drive quite some distance and I want to have new tires for that. And isn't it lucky that you have here four tires that fit my car?"

"You are right on that. Normally, I would have to order them, but someone cancelled their order. So, his loss and your luck."

The repair shop owner asked him to come back and pick up the car the next day; he also asked:

"Do you want me to do both a static and a dynamic wheel balancing?"

"Sure, I'll need it with the new tires. And by the way, do whatever you want with the old tires. I'm sure some poor fellow might be prepared to buy them for what little life is left on them."

He added:

"Don't think I need a wheel alignment, but feel free to do one if you decide it's necessary."

The auto mechanic was smiling.

CHAPTER.01

ANKARA AND ISTANBUL, TURKEY

Mehmet Isaac, officially a commercial attaché in Israel's embassy in Ankara, also happened to be the most senior *Mossad* representative in Turkey. Though the military and intelligence cooperation between Israel and Turkey had suffered in the not-too-distant past, both countries were making efforts to get back to their hay days, starting in 1949 when Turkey was the first Muslim majority country to recognize the State of Israel. Recent efforts were focused on military, strategic, and diplomatic cooperation, based on their joint concerns for the general political instability in the region.

Strategically, there are two very important elements of Turkish geography which make it a crucial focus. First, Istanbul is arguably the most important among the five cities that sit on two continents: Istanbul (Turkey), Suez (Egypt), Magnitogorsk (Russia), Orenburg (Russia) and Atyrau (Kazakhstan). All five of them straddle the divide between Europe and Asia, with the last three of them located on the Ural River. Thus, straddling two continents makes Istanbul the crucial transit point for Russian ships desirous to sail in the Mediterranean to reach or to leave the Black Sea. The second important element of

Turkish geography is that it marks the furthest current expansion of Islam on the north coast of the Mediterranean.

■ ■ ■ ■ ■

The critical role of Istanbul is in part due to the Bosphorus, also known as the Strait of Istanbul. It is a natural waterway, about 19 miles long, 2,300 feet wide at a minimum and around 350 feet deep. It forms part of the continental boundary between Europe and Asia. Flowing as it does through Turkey, the Bosphorus separates the country between Anatolia, the westernmost protrusion of the Asian continent and Thrace which is now shared by Greece, Bulgaria and Turkey. The Bosphorus is a notoriously difficult passage for ships to navigate both because of traffic and the relative narrowness of the Strait. A short while after having successfully negotiated the Bosphorus and then the Sea of Marmara, another challenge awaits sailors: one of the world's narrowest waterways, the Strait of Dardanelles, also known as the Strait of Gallipoli, which connects the Sea of Marmara with the Aegean and Mediterranean seas. The Strait is about twice the length of the Bosphorus, but about half the depth, except at its narrowest point abreast of the city of Çanakkale, where its depth about matches that of the Bosphorus. Nearly 50,000 ships transit annually through these two straits from the Black Sea to the Mediterranean Sea and back, about twice as much traffic as through the Suez Canal.

■ ■ ■ ■ ■

Mehmet Isaac had risen to his position in part because of his bicultural heritage. He had always been faithful to the Jewish faith but had a father who converted to Judaism after marrying Mehmet's mother. Mehmet's father grew up in Turkey, near Antalya, on the country's southern coast. He met Mehmet's mother, Ruth, on a trip to Greece and fell sufficiently in love to leave Turkey and move to Israel. He was not immediately accepted by Ruth's family and that may have contributed to convincing him that he should convert to Judaism. He eventually worked as an engineer in Hebron and relocated to Tel Aviv so that Mehmet could benefit from the best possible study environment. Mehmet certainly took full advantage of that, earning a solid engineering degree and serving his compulsory military obligation in the Air Force, where he earned his wings.

In his current posting, Mehmet was spending quite a bit of time in Istanbul, usually at least two days a week. He would drive or fly the 280 miles from Ankara, Turkey's capital, to meet contacts he had made, with a special attention given to those involved in the navigation of the Bosphorus. It was an open secret that Russia was supplying arms to several of the belligerents in the greater Israel-Arab conflict. Though a portion of these arms were shipped by air, the majority came by ship, which meant that they had to transit through the Bosphorus. Mehmet's role was thus in part to warn Israel, through *Mossad*, when he felt he saw something particularly suspect. Israel was not going to interdict any form of arms traffic in international waters; it could not.

Yet, it could make it more difficult in at least two ways. First, any vessel which came too close to the exclusion zone beyond territorial waters was fair game; Israel did not always stop them but would surely do it if there was any indication that the arms cargo was more than small artillery. Second, Israel had enough apparently civilian ships, though in fact many were partially military vessels, that it was always possible to harass suspect boats. As tensions increased in the last few years, Israel had assigned a Dolphin Class submarine, INS *Protector*, to patrol between the Dodecanese islands, at the very south of the Aegean Sea and the northern tip of Cyprus.

■ ■ ■ ■ ■

The Dodecanese are a group Greek islands so named because at one point they counted twelve islands. They are known for their medieval castles, Byzantine churches, beaches, and ancient archaeological sites. The largest of these islands, Rhodes, was once the home of the Order of Malta. The Order was driven from Jerusalem in 1187 and established its headquarters on the coast of Palestine, before moving to Cyprus and then on to Rhodes. In 1530, it moved to Malta where its government stood until it was expelled by Napoleon in 1798. The order then moved to Italy, in Rome, where it is now the smallest "sovereign country in the U.N." Actually, its full name is the *Sovereign Military Hospitaller Order of Saint John of Jerusalem, of Rhodes and Malta.*

■ ■ ■ ■ ■

Mehmet was conversing with one of the deckhands with whom he had struck up a particularly close relationship. They were near the Port of Haydarpaşa, also known as the Port of Haidar Pasha, a general cargo seaport, near the southern entrance to the Bosphorus. Ships reach the harbor after having sailed under the last of the three suspension bridges that cross from Asia into Europe, the 15 July Martyrs Bridge, better known as the Bosphorus Bridge. Berat Demir, the deckhand, surprised Mehmet:

"By the way, Mehmet, I just heard a conversation I'm sure will interest you."

"Really?"

"Yes. This morning, a friend of mine was attending to a ship whose crew was Russian but that was not registered in Russia. The ship needed to buy fuel. My friend climbed onboard to have the captain sign all the papers needed. Routine stuff by the way. Then, as he was walking past a wide-open cargo hatch, he said he saw stuff."

"What stuff?"

"Well, he was not sure, but he said it looked like missiles."

"Missiles?"

"Absolutely. He said they were supposed to be covered by some sort of tarp, but one of the corner ends was not secured properly and had flapped back."

"And?"

"Well, he couldn't linger. So, he kept going and walked off the boat. Yet, he quickly mentioned it to a friend, who then in turn was mentioning it to another friend when I walked by them. I asked a few questions, but they had no answer."

Mehmet thanked Berat profusely. He asked when the incident occurred, to which Berat simply replied:

"As I said, quite early this morning."

"Anything else?"

"I knew you'd ask the question. I was saving the best for last. The first ship has since sailed, but a sistership of the Russian boat is currently at anchor. I'm sure they're doing the same thing as the other vessel: buying fresh provisions and fuel."

"Could you show it to me?"

Berat smiled and then pointed his finger to a boat anchored not more than fifty yards away. With a somewhat contrived theatrical demeanor and a wide smile he said:

"Voila! Here you go my friend."

Berat did not fully understand what Mehmet was doing next. While he had never seen him with glasses, even on days which like that day were quite bright and sunny, Mehmet reached for a pair of sunglasses in his shirt pocket and started walking toward the ship. Berat followed him as he thought his friend was simply moved by natural curiosity. What he did not know was that *Mossad* equips its agents with various forms of glasses which can serve as discreet cameras, as well as several other uses which are not relevant to the story here. Mehmet was thus simply shooting as many pictures of the boat as he could so that they could be forwarded ASAP to David

Heller in Tel Aviv. With any luck, *Mossad* might be able to intercept both this vessel and her sister ship.

Getting closer to the ship, Mehmet noted that the shape of the hull suggested that the ship was not recent and thus that the hull was probably made of wood. He switched to another pair of glasses; while the initial pair looked like sunglasses, this new pair looked like classical reading glasses, except that the nose bridge was quite a bit larger than one would expect. Berat was increasingly baffled:

"What are those? Why do you need such a large nose bridge?"

Mehmet smiled and said:

"They're just reading glasses. But the nose bridge is reinforced because I tended too often to sit on them."

Berat nodded and watched Mehmet who was still getting as close as possible to the ship and looking at a piece of paper that he had pulled out of his rear pant pocket. One of the men on the ship asked from the deck:

"What are you doing here?"

The question having been asked in Russian, Mehmet could only motion that he did not understand. He replied to the sailor in Turkish, wondering what the question was. The sailor clearly did not speak Turkish. Another sailor came around, probably attracted by the noise; he spoke some Turkish. He asked:

"What is the matter, man?"

Mehmet simply and disarmingly replied:

"I was looking on this to see if I could find the name of the ship."

"Do you read Russian?"

"I do not, but I do read English. The ship looks like it's registered in Panama, and I assume that's why you have the name in English as well."

The second sailor sat there, surprised by the reply, which, however, was totally accurate at least with respect to the facts, if not Mehmet's intensions. Mehmet smiled at both sailors and thanked them. He walked back to where Berat had stopped. Berat was surely a courageous man, but he was not about to expose himself to any unnecessary harm.

■ ■ ■ ■ ■

Though he had originally planned to stay in Istanbul for another day, Mehmet rushed to the nearest main street. He hailed a taxi and asked to be driven back to his hotel. He wanted to report his discovery as quickly as possible, as well as forward the various pictures which both pairs of glasses had taken. Mehmet reached out to his laptop computer and connected it to the two pairs of glasses as soon as he was back in his room at his hotel, but not before he had drawn the curtains closed; there was no point offering anyone the opportunity to spy on him. While the photos taken with the "sunglasses" covered every aspect of the one side of the ship that was moored along the quay, those taken with the "reading glasses" were much more interesting.

The reading glasses offered x-ray vision through the hull, which, as Mehmet had observed, was made of wood and fiberglass. The fact that the images were electronic rather than on a traditional cellulose film, meant that the dosage of x-rays was small. Though an extended use of these glasses might be damaging to one's health, the risks to the agents using them in the field were quite limited. The larger than usual bridge was the "gun" that shot the protons. The quality of the images was excellent, quite a bit similar indeed to the x-rays which were routinely found in dentists' offices. The images that appeared on his computer screen left little doubt as to what the cargo was. They validated the earlier comment he had heard, from Berat, about the other ship. Mehmet could see there was a lot of metal inside the belly of the ship, a lot more than should be expected. Of course, there should have been metal toward the aft of the ship—that would be where the twin engines would typically be. Similarly, one would not have been surprised to find some metal near the center of the ship, as fuel tanks can be made of metal, though increasingly often fiberglass is used, as it is lighter. However, the metal that was suspected further toward the stern had to be cargo, and that cargo was totally consistent with missiles or heavy armament.

Mehmet decided he should drive back to Ankara as quickly as possible. He checked out, a day early as it turned out, paid his bill and drove away. He elected to take the Eurasia tunnel which opened at the end of 2016. He thus crossed from Europe into Asia under the southern end of the Bosphorus. Prior to 2016, he would have had to make a detour and use one of the three suspension bridges that cross over the river. Though the route he took was "officially" always classified as Highway E80 on the European directory of divided highways, it did not initially allow one to reach the 75 miles per hour speed limit; the initial miles had to go through the Asian part of Istanbul, with a lower speed limit. Yet, Mehmet could finally speed up when he reached Derince, along the northern shore of the Gulf of Armutlu Peninsula on the coast of the Marmara Sea, fifty-odd miles from the end of the Eurasia tunnel. He allowed himself about ten miles more than the speed limit, hoping that he would be protected by his diplomatic plates. He had already concocted in his mind the excuse that he was late for a dinner hosted by the ambassador.

Once in Ankara, he chose not to drive to his apartment, located in the fancy district of Cankaya-Oran, just south of the center of town, but rather to go directly to the embassy which was in the business district, in a commercial building. He would feel safer using the embassy communication system than any alternative he had at home. He still chose the safe telephone rather than a zoom conference set up, as he wanted to minimize the risk that his communication might be intercepted.

"Mark? Mehmet Isaac here."

The individual he had called was Mark Levi one of the key lieutenants of David Heller, the head of the *Disruption* group within

Mossad. Mark had carried out several quite successful missions, including a particularly challenging one that had seen him travel through Europe and the U.S. masquerading as an ISIS agent.[2]

"Yes, Mehmet. What's up?"

Mehmet let go of a long sigh, adding:

"Quite a story, but time is of the essence. Somebody's gonna have to make quick decisions. Let me cut to the chase."

"You've got my full attention."

Mehmet went through a complete recapitulation of his recent experience in Istanbul, covering both the initial conversation with Berat, and his own stroll alongside the quay in the Port of Haidar Pasha. He had taken the precaution of sending the files containing the various sets of pictures by email, so that Mark could immediately refer to them. He paused to let Mark look at all the various images. Mark whistled and noted:

"Well, my friend, you've definitely earned your keep. Thanks a lot. Let me start the ball rolling."

---

[2] See "The Shadow Experts" by the same author. Barringer Publishing, 2021.

CHAPTER.02

TEL AVIV, ISRAEL, MOSUL, IRAQ AND ANKARA, TURKEY

David Heller, the newly minted head of the *Disruption* group within *Mossad*, was quietly sipping his second morning cup of coffee when the phone rang. His group, probably the most secretive within an already very secretive organization, was generally in charge of activities which many would consider illegal. However, these activities still needed to be carried out in the interest of the state of Israel. They were thus considered within the spirit of Israel's Constitution: assassination of foreign leaders, sabotage of certain installations of which Israel did not approve, internet warfare and the like. His group did not appear on any organization chart—that anyone could procure.

A bit over a year earlier, David had succeeded his former boss, Simon Rabinowitz, who had himself been promoted to Head of *Mossad*, following in the footsteps of his former boss General Ariel Landau who had retired.[3] Simon had been promoted to the rank of general upon receiving the promotion which had been delayed by a couple of years when the wife of Ariel Landau had died suddenly

---

[3] See "The Crypto Trap" by the same author. Barringer Publishing, 2022.

leading him to postpone the retirement he intended to take, precisely to spend more time with his wife.

■ ■ ■ ■ ■

"David here . . ."

"I need to speak to you quickly. Are you free?"

David had recognized the voice of one of his key lieutenants, Mark Levi. Mark was very special to David because of the great work he had done for him in earlier missions. David had in fact told Simon that, if something happened to him, he would suggest that Mark be given his job. Simon's reaction had been a broad smile, followed by a small frown which had made David smile at the time:

"I do agree that he would be excellent, but he still has to be groomed. So, please be careful; don't take any unnecessary risks and make sure to have your regularly scheduled medical checkups. I need you around for a few more years, my friend."

David invited Mark to come straight into his office, which he did less than a minute later. David pointed him to the cream leather sofa with the matching side chair. Mark walked around the glass-top coffee table and sat down. David asked:

"Coffee?"

"Sure, please. No milk, no sugar. Just an ice cube to cool it down a bit."

David asked Mark:

"What's the urgency?"

Mark replied that their original concern had now morphed into two important issues. David looked mildly surprised and motioned to Mark to keep going. He started with a very brief summary, just to make sure that David would have the full picture before he went deeper into details. Thus, dispensing with any unnecessary detail, he said:

"We've picked up a couple of ships transiting through the Bosphorus and likely carrying arms; we need to find a way to locate them among the many vessels plying the Aegean Sea and to tail them until we can be sure they are not bound for the Palestinians."

David interrupted:

"You must be kidding. They've got to be sailing to Syria or Lebanon."

"That's exactly what I fear. Now, for the second issue, I just found out through the same source that our man in Mosul has captured a fortune in cut diamonds, most likely from the drug trade which we know transits, at least in part, through Northern Iraq."

Mark paused. David looked totally focused. Mark added:

"At this point, we are increasingly concerned that the drug trade going through the northern routes may well be for the benefit of ISIS and the Palestinians. We suspect that the profits are used to buy more and more arms. But, obviously, no proof of anything at this time."

David could only add:

"Obviously . . ."

David's reaction was very much in character. Prior to being promoted, he had worked under Simon for a long enough time to incorporate many of key elements of Simon's management style. He was quite proud of his team, though, in fairness, the story Mark just told him surprised him. He asked Mark for some more details, particularly with respect to the diamonds. He smiled internally, noting that dealing with diamonds was a real first for him. He thought: "*I may well need her help . . .*"

■ ■ ■ ■ ■

Josh Steimetz used the classical *Mossad* communication tool to contact Mehmet Isaac. While he certainly knew Mark Levi and had talked to him on prior occasions, he was concerned that the conversation should be as discreet as possible. To him, discretion meant both that the counterparty was as innocuous as possible and that the tool he used was as fool-proof as feasible. The tool he used was a simple implement which could be linked to a regular computer or handheld computer-like device such as a modern phone or even a computer tablet.[4] The agent sending a message would compose that message on the computer and then have the system encode and transform that message into high intensity light pulses. These pulses would then be aggregated into a single signal or at most a few flashes which would be sent via a high-intensity light beam to a satellite, in mere milliseconds. The flashlight-like emitting device only needed to be set on a windowsill or on the ground; it would detect the actual position of the satellite and thus the direction in which the laser must be flashed.

The device looked like any small modern pocket flashlight: a plastic cylinder with a slightly flared front end and a short black strap attached to the back end so that whoever used it could secure it to his wrist; at the front end, the unit seemed to have two types of bulbs. First, there was a white LED crown around the periphery; it lit up when the on-off switch was activated, as one would expect from a regular flashlight. Second, in the center of that crown, there was what looked like the top of a traditional light bulb surrounded by a narrow metallic ring. In fact, this was the source for the high-intensity light beam. After a fool-proof procedure, the agent could transform the flashlight as the metallic ring inside the LED crown would disappear and the center bulb assembly telescoped out of the device about an inch, revealing what looked like the top of a normal bulb which was, in fact, almost a full bubble. This allowed the light source within the bubble to rotate, searching for the most direct line to the satellite. The fact that there had to be a direct line of sight between the instrument

---

4 See "Operation Kovesh" by the same author. Barringer Publishing, 2020.

and the satellite was indeed the only absolute requirement for the device to function.

Once it had received the message, the satellite would forward it to its desired destination; there, a similar piece of equipment would decode and transfer the message onto another simple computer or smart phone. Indoor fixed locations, such as the *Mossad* offices or the Israeli residences of those agents living there, often had a small receiver on the outside wall or window frame of the house, apartment or office complex that allowed the satellite to know the exact direction in which it should shine the laser beam; this receiver was in direct contact with the preferred computer, tablet, or smart phone. Agents outside of their home bases would always be careful to place the receiver in an innocuous place, such on a window ledge or even on the dashboard of a car when they were driving.

■ ■ ■ ■ ■

Josh and Mehmet quickly agreed that Josh needed to find a way to leave Iraq briefly in order to bring the diamonds to him. Mehmet, in his role as an accredited diplomat, would have no difficulty making sure the diamonds made it to Israel. It might involve him flying to Tel Aviv or having David or Mark fly to meet him in Ankara or even Istanbul. But either trip would be absolutely routine and most likely use commercial or military aircraft.

Initially, Josh had been concerned by the need to travel away from Mosul with the diamonds. So, they had briefly discussed the feasibility of having the diamonds picked up in the Mosul area by some drone sent by Israel. Israel was the first country in the world to operate drones in combat operations in 1969 along the Suez Canal. It is also the largest drone exporter in the world, though Turkey was becoming a rising force in the business as well. Additionally, *Mossad* made extensive use of drones, and both agents were aware of the reported recent delivery by Israel of 150 small drones to a yet unnamed

European nation. This had not surprised anyone, particularly as Israeli drones are known to be at the high end of the sophistication range, possibly even more sophisticated than many U.S. competitors.

Yet, Mehmet and Josh quickly agreed that the two operational requirements and the importance of the payload made drones an imperfect solution at best. First, the drones had to be able to fly quite a distance as Mosul was more than 700 miles from Tel Aviv and even further, about 900 miles, from Ankara. Second, they had to be able to land and take off as quickly and discreetly as possible, suggesting a need for vertical take-off and landing capabilities, or as near to it as possible. Israeli drones typically could meet one or the other condition, but not both. They have excellent cargo drones with vertical take-off and landing capabilities, but they usually tend to have much too short a range to be useful. Similarly, drones like the Hermes 900 or even the Heron TP (Eitan) that do have the range that would be required there but they then can unfortunately still be picked up on radar, particularly in the very early or very late stages of flight. As Mehmet concluded:

"Unless getting you to Turkey with the diamonds proves to be even more difficult, drones don't look like the best solution."

Further, when Mark had mentioned the diamonds to David, David had clearly said:

"Make sure you get the diamonds. It's not the financial value. I've got a thought to seed disarray within the opposition . . ."

Mark had dutifully repeated David's admonition to Mehmet. In the end, Mehmet had become convinced: it was crystal clear that the drone route involved many more dangers and challenges than the alternative. Later that same day, after they both had had a chance to research the various options, Josh and Mehmet discussed several possible scenarios and approaches. They finally agreed that the simplest solution involved Josh flying to Ankara, though it required him first to assemble the material he would need for that trip to be uneventful and thus to minimize all risks. The key was that no one could know or find out that he was traveling with a fortune in diamonds. Josh knew and mentioned to Mehmet that Pegasus, a local, low-cost airline, flew to and from Ankara from Erbil, less than 60 miles from Mosul, adding:

"You know. Erbil is near to where the plane crashed."

He paused and went straight on, back to his earlier train of thought:

"Pegasus has two flights, one leaving at 1:50 a.m. and the other at 4:30 p.m. I think the one in the middle of the night is best as that's got to be when they'll pay the least amount of attention."

"Agreed, though a contrarian might argue that they'll have plenty of time and few customers . . . Anyway, I'll pick you up at the airport. Assume you'll stay the day and the night in Ankara and fly back two days later . . ."

"Sounds great."

■ ■ ■ ■ ■

Josh's first order of business after talking to Mehmet was a visit to the local hardware store. The list of the items he bought, though esoteric, would not necessarily draw attention in the local context and circumstances: a hard plastic garden hose, some polyurethane tubing, thin plastic sheets, resin in both liquid and sprayable form, sprayable black acrylic paint, acrylic cement, a piece of cardboard, sticky-back Velcro fasteners, a couple of black rubber tips, three small metallic rings, and a couple pieces of solid wood. The fact that he also bought a power paint sprayer and a power drill that could be used to run a simple polishing tool could have seemed odd, though in combination with the rest of his purchases they seemed to make sense. Ostensibly, Josh was embarking on a small home improvement project and that had to be all. He then went to the pharmacy and bought disinfecting cream, bright red mercury-free mercurochrome, dark orange Iodine tincture, a couple rolls of gauze wraps and a knee brace. Somewhat more surprising a list, but he said that he was buying it for a friend, and everything seemingly became routine.

Josh had decided to reduce the risks of losing all the diamonds by dividing them into two packages. The first would be placed in some hermetic plastic wrapping at the bottom of his soft sided carry-on luggage. The piece of cardboard he had purchased was cut to match the inside dimensions of the carry-on and fixed over the diamonds with six pieces of sticky-back Velcro fasteners. The fact that the cardboard, once spray-painted, was as close as possible in color as the inside of the bag made it highly unlikely that someone would detect anything, all the more so as diamonds are not visible when x-rayed and neither would cardboard.

The more complex work involved the creation of a hollow-center cane that would allow him to walk despite a knee injury, which the paraphernalia he had purchased at the pharmacy was meant to suggest. He cut the garden hose to the right length and placed the solid tube of polyurethane inside, ensuring that the assembly would be both rigid and strong enough to support his weight should it ever be tested by a suspicious security officer. He then created another, shorter tube with the rolled-up plastic sheet covered on the inside with a thin spray of resin. Inside that tube, he inserted the diamonds which had been packaged into a thin cylinder. He used the two pieces of wood to create a believable handle, which he initially placed on the side of his work bench, in this case, his kitchen counter.

He had used the remnants of the wood to create two wooden corks which he would insert and glue in place with acrylic cement. The idea was for the "diamond cylinder" to be placed about mid-height inside the cane and secured with these wooden corks. Resin would be poured into both ends of the cane. The cane handle would fit straight against the resin, which would also serve to hold it in place. At the other end of the cane, the rubber cane tip would also fit right against the resin which would also help keep it in place. Once the assembly was completed, he sprayed the cane with three coats of black acrylic paint. He buffed the last coat to give it a nice sheen.

Josh was aware that there was a risk that an x-ray picture of the cane might look odd in its middle section. In order to mitigate the risk, he had carefully measured where corks marking the end of the "diamond tube" were located within the cane. He slipped the first two metallic rings over the outside of the cane and glued them precisely in the right spot, so that the x-ray would show the dark image of the metal and thus draw the attention away from the inside of the cane. The third, he placed just below where the handle and the body of the cane came together. This would avoid the risk of having anyone ask" "why those two rings?" As placed, the three of them looked like markers, about equidistant from each other: it was almost as if they delineated thirds along the vertical part of the cane.

Josh let his "creation" cure and dry for a full day. He mistreated it the next morning, applying more force on it that it should be expected to withstand, though he was careful to raise the force he applied gradually so as to ensure he did not go too far too quickly and break it. He would have had to redo the work, and, this time, the list of hardware items purchased might look increasingly suspicious! Satisfied with his work, he proceeded to apply a bandage to his right leg to suggest a believable injury, with the mercurochrome and the iodine tincture serving to bring color to the "wound" with some of it spilling on his skin under the bandage. The brace covered any marks but would reveal them if he was asked to remove it.

Josh's careful preparation for his trip paid handsome dividends. He had driven the Jeep and parked it just outside the main terminal, along with a few other cars. He was delighted that no one asked him how he could drive a stick shift car with the leg injury he had. Yet, he had rehearsed a reply which said that he could press on the accelerator with the injured leg and have full control of the clutch with the other.

The terminal was not busy; in fact, it was mostly empty. The few people that were there wore modern dress, although there were a few women with colorful traditional clothes, as there also were a couple of men who wore turbans. He had chosen to wear a simple open neck shirt, khaki pants with the right leg cut off just above the knee, white socks, and light boots. People could not miss the brace that we wore over his right knee; had they looked even more carefully, they would have found gauze bandages under the brace and what could pass as traces of blood to complete the picture. His dark brown, soft-sided carry-on hung from his left shoulder, while his right hand held a black cane with a black lacquered wooden handle.

He could not avoid feeling some anxiety as he approached security at the entrance of the terminal. His training and natural self-control allowed him to ensure that none of his anxiety was visible from the outside. The carry-on bag was the first to go through the x-ray machine and it simply sailed through it. Josh did not take the time to wonder whether the officer had seen nothing or simply not paid sufficient attention. The next hurdle was the cane. He was asked to surrender it before walking through the metal detector. He hopped through the metal detector and was delighted that nothing on his body attracted any question. The final step involved the cane going through the x-ray machine. Josh breathed a quiet but sizable sigh of relief when the officer on the other side of the x-ray machine handed the cane back, with no question and a wide smile. He had the clear impression that people were going through the motions without having their hearts in their work. He justified it in his own mind with the observation that there were not too many terrorists trying to blow up planes in Northern Iraq—though one could always worry that the Kurds would one day.

Nobody had asked any question either when he had checked in for his flight or at border control. He had asked for and received a seat at the very front of the aircraft, as it allowed him to keep his right leg stretched during the flight that lasted just over two hours. His arrival in Ankara was just as uneventful, the airport hardly less deserted than Erbil. Mehmet was there to meet him, just outside the custom area. The smile on Josh's face immediately told Mehmet that all had happened as planned. Looking at Josh's right leg, Mehmet understood why he had asked him to purchase a new pair of 38x34 khaki pants for him. He would leave the pair with the right leg cut off in Ankara . . .

CHAPTER.03

TEL AVIV, ISRAEL

David Heller, Mark Levi and Simon Rabinowitz had elected to regroup, following the two important recent developments. Though such a meeting would not have taken place when Simon had David's job and Ariel Landau had Simon's, everyone knew that Simon would want to remain more involved than his boss had been vis-à-vis him prior to retirement. In fairness, David did not mind it either, chiefly because he trusted Simon and felt that a bit more coaching in the early days of his tenure could not possibly hurt. Simon offered his guests coffee, tea or water and then motioned to them, as usual, to sit on the leather sofa while he sat in the matching wing chair set at a right angle. David waited until Simon's assistant had brought the beverages in. Then, with affected nonchalance, he leaned forward and placed a velvet bag on the coffee table, right in front of Simon, calmly announcing:

"I'm told we're looking at $100 million, plus or minus . . ."

Simon, appreciating the joke, carried it forward a bit more. He looked totally non-plussed as he replied:

"Ah. You got the diamonds. Good. What's your plan?"

David was mildly taken aback though he had worked with Simon long enough to know of his sense of humor. Simon knew full well that David was expecting a stronger reaction, which he might have had with other people, and thus played it "super cool." David decided to respond in kind, feigning not to be surprised by Simon's reaction, moving straight away to what was for him the most important agenda item. He asked:

"Before we start on that, could we first discuss the issue of the Russian boats? I'm concerned that time is very much of the essence there . . ."

"Happy to oblige, my friend. But let me ask you: Do you think the two issues are linked?"

At that point, he started laughing, with David following suit almost instantaneously. Mark was a bit surprised, until Simon explained:

"A bit of an inside joke I'm afraid. It was a case of who would blink first, and David won this time."

Mark pretended to understand, though he was still at best unclear. David answered Simon's earlier question:

"Who knows if they really are? But, to us, I think it's quite likely they're part of the same problem."

Seeing Simon raise his eyebrows, David paused briefly and then conceded that he might have overstated the case. He acknowledged that they might not be **part** of the same problem, though they surely appeared **related**. On the surface indeed, they seemed to have little in common since one related to the provision of arms to Palestinian terrorists, while the other had to do with drug traffic. Yet, he concluded:

"In the end, I believe that, until proven otherwise, they are related. As you know, we strongly suspect that the Palestinians are using some of that drug-money to buy arms. And we're pretty sure that ISIS also uses the money they make from trafficking heroin to buy weapons or plant terrorist seeds in various places. So, they are related without being directly so. Am I making sense?"

"Certainly. So, let's first talk of the Russian ships and the missiles they appear to carry."

Mark interjected:

"One question on the boats for a second; why are the Russian doing it? After all, there are many other ways to supply the Palestinians with arms, what with the connections via Iran."

David replied that he generally agreed that it might seem odd, though a couple of points were worth considering:

"First, we know that Russia supplies arms to the belligerents, in this case the Palestinians, broadly defined. Now, in the past, a lot of it came via air into Syria and was then distributed regionally. So, we are indeed looking at a slightly different pattern. However, and Simon please correct me if I'm wrong, since Russia took Crimea over, it may well be that the Bosphorus route is more convenient. For one, it surely avoids having to fly in Turkey's airspace as well as Georgia's and Azerbaijan if you want to fly further west."

Simon opined:

"Cannot disagree with that, David."

David continued:

"Great. Second, as I'm sure you know, we've been noticing more saber rattling on the part of both Russia and China, most likely testing the commitments of the Americans and the willpower of the Europeans. This could be a part of the same pattern."

David paused for a few seconds and added:

"Simon, how do you read this?"

Simon seemed lost in his thoughts for a few seconds. Then he replied that it did make sense. Going further, he said that he would still prefer to separate the two issues, arms and diamonds though he conceded he could not disagree that they were somehow related. With a mischievous smile, he added:

"In truth, aren't all issues related around here? We want to survive and prosper and most of the people around us would rather see us dead and gone!"

David and Mark smiled back, with Mark arguing:

"From my point of view, I think the Russian boats are the main priority."

He paused and seemingly corrected himself as he had noted Simon frowning at his earlier comment:

"I mean, the first priority strictly from a time standpoint. It's clear that time is working against us. As we speak, they are sailing in our direction. Every hour, they're ten to fifteen nautical miles closer . . ."

Simon seemed to nod and then asked:

"What do you suggest?"

Encouraged by David, Mark replied:

"I'd like to have them under serious surveillance, probably first with aerial drones . . ."

He paused and added:

"However, this isn't a slam dunk. First, we've got to find them. Mehmet told me that nearly 150 ships go through the Dardanelles each day."

Pausing to clarify his point again, he then added:

"The Dardanelles, the strait after the Sea of Marmara. You know the sequence: Black Sea, Bosphorus, Sea of Marmara, Dardanelles and then the Aegean Sea?"

Seeing that Simon and David nodded, he continued:

"Add to those 150 ships the myriad of local vessels plying the Aegean Sea and we'll soon be looking for the needle in the proverbial haystack."

Simon was smiling and asked David and Mark to expand further on the plan. David argued that drones should be able to find the Russian boats:

"Once you eliminate the oil and gas tankers and the containerships, both of which are very large, quite a bit larger than the boats we're looking for, you're left with less than 100 boats a day, which is more manageable if we pick them up close enough after they exit the Dardanelles. We don't want to wait too long because the further south and east you go, the greater the local Aegean Sea traffic and thus the challenge."

David stopped in his tracks and looked pensive for a short while and added:

"Though, come to think of it, we probably still have the time to pick up the second boat while in the Dardanelles Strait, and that's got to be easier."

Simon interrupted and told him to go straight ahead with the surveillance. He added:

"I agree with you, David, and with your earlier point, Mark. We don't want to waste time with the first phase. Once we have found the two boats, it should be easier to track them."

He stopped for a second and apologized for having to get up and go back to his desk. There he seemed to be looking for something on his computer. A long thirty seconds later, he exclaimed:

"Ah. Here it is. It's a message from the Navy, Yael Orbach's world, as you know. They have assigned a Dolphin Class submarine, INS *Protector*, to patrol between the Dodecanese islands, at the very south of the Aegean Sea and the northern tip of Cyprus. Nothing to do with the current problem, but an issue of surveillance to avoid any harassment of civilian ships around there."

He paused again and added:

"You never know with Turkey. One day they're with the Russians, the next day they're against them. That should surely help."

Returning to the current problem with the Russian boats, he cautioned:

"We shouldn't assume that these boats will come anywhere close to our shores. They all know we wouldn't allow it. So, it would be a provocation and I can't imagine why they would even attempt it. Now, on the other hand, we've seen transshipments at sea in various places in the past. In fact, if I had to bet, I would assume that this is exactly what's gonna happen. The Russians wouldn't be dumb enough to come too visibly close to Syria and Lebanon. If they do, it's gotta be a test or worse, a menace."

David asked what he thought should be done. Simon immediately returned the question, though he suggested that he could think of at least two answers. From the point of view of Israel, the first answer belonged to the defense minister, and by extension the War Cabinet. Simon explained:

"I won't prejudge anything. We all know what our position is on any violation or attempted violation of our territorial water extension."

He continued with his analysis, arguing that the second point of view was *Mossad*'s. That clearly fell within his area of responsibility, stating in a calm but determined manner:

"Any and all shipments should be monitored and stopped before they reach their intended destinations. No rush though the longer we allow them to proceed, the more we'll know of what they're doing and whom they're helping."

David summarized what he understood his brief to be:

"We first look for the two boats and from that point onward we keep close tabs on them. We'll regroup when we know better where they're going. Agreed?"

■ ■ ■ ■ ■

They switched to the question of diamonds and the drug trade. Clearly, this was a new one for everyone in the group. Mark briefed Simon on the conversations he had had with Mehmet, who had spent a whole day in Ankara debriefing Josh Steinmetz in some depth.

Mark was categorical: he did not believe that Josh had heard of any similar transaction in the past, though he was virtually certain that there had been deliveries of heroin in the area. Simon asked:

"I read somewhere a while ago that the drug trade did not involve planes but the old-fashioned horseback caravans. How does that fit with this one?"

Mark conceded that this is also what Josh had heard, and in fact added that this was one of the main reasons Josh had been posted there for a while to try and make sense of what was happening. In response to Simon's question as to what might have changed, Mark surprised David and Simon with his reply:

"They, the drug traffickers, may need more money or believe that the market is larger."

David countered:

"I'll buy the more money argument more easily. We know that ISIS is trying to rebuild, and you need a lot of money to create all these cells, leaving alone the money required for training and weapons."

He paused and surprised himself with his next question:

"And what if there is a new counterparty somewhere in the chain?"

Simon thought for a short while. Focusing first on David's earlier comment, he suggested that, if a greater need for money was the real driver, then there should be more attempts to make these deliveries in the near term. Turning to David's curve ball, he simply said:

"You know, David? Everything is possible. In fact, I suspect you're onto something. Yet, until we know better, we don't have a choice. We need to proceed the old-fashioned way."

Mark agreed wholeheartedly and went as far as suggesting that Josh's recommendation was in fact to work as hard as possible to figure out where the actual drop-off point was supposed to be and thus see whether it was realistic to expect another bonanza. Simon interrupted:

"Mark, this makes a lot of sense, except for one element."

Mark was taken aback and straightened up on the sofa. Simon asked:

"What do we think the odds are that anything further materializes until these people find out what happened to the diamonds that we have here on this coffee table?"

Simon's point was very well taken. He was assuming that the dealers had been surprised not to have found any trace of the diamonds. He did concede that they might have assumed that the briefcase had burned, and the diamonds with it, adding:

"Got to guess that the pilots knew what was in the case. They also had to know that they would be exchanging the briefcase and its contents for a load of heroin, usually packaged in things that look like bricks in burlap bags."

He paused and went on:

"You might think that they could have decided to keep the briefcase close to themselves, probably just behind the trim wheel, which typically sits right between the two pilots, behind the throttle controls."

Mark suggested:

"That could well have been what they did. After all, Josh said he found the briefcase between the cockpit and the rear-end of the fuselage. Could well have slipped backwards . . ."

"Could have, though on impact things should have moved forward."

"Fair point, Simon. Though I could nitpick and argue that on impact the briefcase might have moved forward, bounced against the controls and rebounded backward. One thing is odd though: Josh told us that the plane looked like it did not have a lot of fuel on board. If that's true, how did it expect to fly back to wherever it needed to? Would they not be a bit "naked" if they did not have the fuel to leave in a hurry if there was an issue with the smugglers?"

Simon nodded and yet let David reply:

"Grant you the questions are valid. However, what if there was an extra fuel reservoir that did not explode, and Josh did not see?"

Mark conceded the point and simply added:

"I'll have to ask Mehmet to question Josh on that. Anyway, where does that leave us?"

Simon smiled with a wide grin. His first suggestion was to damage the briefcase sufficiently to suggest it had been burned in one way or another and to place it back in the general vicinity of where Josh had found it. He added with the wink of his right eye:

"You've got to burn it up some more on the inside . . . After all that's where the diamonds were . . ."

He paused again and concluded:

"And if they're no longer there, it must be because they burned!"

He took a short sip of his coffee and mischievously added:

"That might give Josh the time to see if he can find an additional fuel tank nearby . . ."

Mark enthusiastically supported the move and indicated that he did not think it would be a difficult effort. Simon surprised him. Turning to David though not losing sight of Mark, he asked:

"Do you remember reading about the invention of the young chemical engineer at the Weizmann Institute of Science at Rehovot?"

David was raking his brain and suddenly jumped up and said:

"You bet I do. Mark, for your information, this guy, whose name I forget, . . ."

"Samuel Eisenstein if I recall correctly . . ."

"You're right, Simon. Samuel Eisenstein. That's it. Anyway, this is the fellow who was working on the climate change project. More precisely, I think he was working on carbon dioxide capture in the atmosphere. Taking carbon out of the atmosphere, starting with carbon dioxide, and transforming it into oxygen and carbon. The trees do with photosynthesis. Right?"

Simon replied:

"Absolutely. We both remember high school science."

David had a brief laugh and returning to Samuel Isenberg replied:

"I think his project was entitled "solidifying" CO2."

"Correct. But because that can only be done at extremely high temperatures, most people abandoned the approach for other solutions. It was too expensive to be industrially profitable. Yet, his idea was to see whether he could bypass the carbon state using both the extremely high temperatures which he needed and extremely high pressures. Rather than plain carbon he might be able to get synthetic diamonds."

Simon added:

"At the time, I believe there were still a few issues. But I seem to remember we were recently told that he thought he knew how to fix them. I haven't heard anything more about it. But, David, I guess it's well worth a call, don't you think?"

"Absolutely. And it may require another call . . . To Countess Renate this time!"

■ ■ ■ ■ ■

Back in David's office, Mark and David finalized their strategy. It was agreed that Mark would first focus on the Russian boats, with one particular step which would help prepare a nasty surprise to anyone planning to come too close to Israel. He would also contact Mehmet and coordinate the subterfuge planned for the drug traffickers with Josh. David on his side would visit with Samuel Eisenstein to learn a bit more about where he was in his research and gauge whether his invention could be used in this case as well. Clearly, David could imagine the several ways in which having access to synthetic diamonds could change the picture in the fight against drug traffickers. In the back of his mind, though, and simultaneously, he could think of what it might do to the market for diamonds in general. He allowed a wry smile on his face when he thought: *Russia, along with Botswana,*

Canada, and Australia, is among the largest diamond producers in the world . . . And they're also the country said to have the largest reserves.

CHAPTER.04

Back home in Mosul, Josh Steinmetz started to work on the next step of his mission. He was to set fire to the briefcase with the polycarbonate shell. Fortunately, polycarbonate has a favorable classification with respect to flammability: the generation of smoke is absent or very slow and whatever smoke develops does not propagate. Additionally, polycarbonate produces very few flaming droplets which could contribute to the spread of the fire by igniting other nearby surfaces. Nevertheless, he decided to stage his effort away from home. However, though his normal routine would have him normally leave the house during the late afternoon, he decided to carry out the burning smack in the middle of the afternoon; he did not want people to see flames from afar and they would not if the flames had to compete with daylight.

He placed highly combustible material, principally paper and cardboard, inside the briefcase and took it to a deserted area about thirty miles from Mosul. The ground in that location seemed generally similar to what was near the site of the crash. That was important as he wanted to make sure that any trace of soil that would still be on the suitcase would not obviously point to it having burned away from the crash site. He doused the briefcase, now opened on the ground, with grain alcohol and set it on fire. As expected, the inside of the briefcase very quickly ignited and the strength of the heat radiation was sufficient to soften the shell, though not enough to melt it. He had to wait almost an hour before the whole case cooled off enough to allow him to pick up the remnants. He was happy to see that nothing other than black dust remained inside the case. He placed the whole thing flat at the rear of the Jeep and drove to the site of the crash.

Once within a mile or so of the site, he changed his driving demeanor. From that point on, he chose to drive slowly and very carefully, his senses totally focused on the possible presence of human beings. He did not want to be seen, or even less to be caught placing the burned briefcase near the carcass of the plane. Still about half a mile away, he stepped out of the Jeep, retrieved the briefcase which, by then was almost cold, closed it as best he could and walked in the direction of the wreckage.

He was quietly walking when, suddenly, he thought he had picked up some activity in the distance. He stopped in his tracks and took what little cover was available in a small group of trees that he found to his right. He was on the lookout for anyone getting closer to him. He waited at least another twenty minutes before the sounds seemed to be going away from him, though he remained as silent and careful in his walking as possible. He thought that it would not be the first time that people would make believe they were leaving when in fact they were not; it was a trap he had used and therefore knew very well. Similarly, if the people he could hear were in fact also searching the surroundings for the briefcase; it would not be surprising if they had left someone to serve as a guard.

In fact, as he approached the site and could see the broken-up plane in the distance, darkness helping, he noticed a bright light in the general vicinity. At that point, he could not discern what it was. Using his night binoculars to get a better look, he smiled, noting that the light he had seen was the burning end of a cigarette. There was someone standing guard in the area and he, or she, was smoking. Josh walked even more carefully in the direction of the person that was there, though he was aiming to approach from the individual's back. He thanked his lucky star that he was now walking on dirt with a bit of dried-up grass. He thus had minimal chances to step on a dead piece of wood or anything which might have cracked.

He was now a few feet behind the guard. He was definitely a man whom he gauged to be of middle stature. The person was in fact sitting down. He carefully deposited the briefcase on the ground and flipped open the top of the signet ring he was wearing on his right pinky. Suddenly, he bounded and fell directly on top of the poor guard who did not have the time to figure out what happened to him before Josh used the ring to sting him on the right shoulder. A few seconds later, the man was sound asleep and would remain so for an hour or so. Mossad had told Josh that the man would not remember what happened to him; Josh simply thought: . . . *hope they're right!*

Once the man, in effect, out of the way, Josh returned to the briefcase and placed it in a relatively hidden location on the general path which the airplane would have taken. On the one hand, he clearly wanted to make sure that the briefcase was not in plain view; had it been, how come it would not have been noticed earlier? At the same time, the hiding place could not be too difficult to find, as he really wanted the briefcase to be found. He chose a spot just under the tail of the aircraft, or what was left of it, near the rear right stabilizer, the one that was closest to the ground. He felt that a search party might have missed the briefcase a couple of times but was still pretty sure that they would eventually find it. They would likely assume that the briefcase had fallen from the airplane when it broke in half.

With the guard still sound asleep, he set fire to the area around the briefcase to complete the setting, ready, if needed, to extinguish any fire that went too far. He walked away and watched for another hour until he was satisfied that the fire could no longer spread. He used that extra time to look for anything that might indicate that the plane had extra fuel tanks. Some distance from the cockpit, and quite a bit to the left of the tip of the left wing, he picked up a smell, which reminded him of aviation fuel. Quickly, he discovered the remnants of an external fuel tank. He kicked himself: *Damn it, they attached the external fuel tanks near the ends of the wings rather than in the usual place.* He then simply completed the thought: *at least it makes more sense from a strategic standpoint. Mark would love to know that.*

Then, just as carefully as on the way to the wreckage, he walked back to the Jeep and drove away. He spent that night in his apartment in Mosul. One of the last thoughts he had before falling asleep was: *how long would it take for someone to find the briefcase?* The absolutely last thought was *I need to stay very close to my contacts and hope that someone tells me if they have found something.* He was specifically thinking of a couple of "friends" who had told him of the plane crash. He had been very careful not to let them know that this was not news to him . . .

■ ■ ■ ■ ■

Meanwhile, David had paid a visit to Samuel Eisenstein, at the Weizmann Institute of Science at Rehovot, about twenty miles, almost due south of Tel Aviv. The institute was founded by Chaim Weizmann, the first President of the State of Israel. It is a public research university offering only postgraduate degrees in the natural and exact sciences. It counts six Nobel laureates among those that have been associated with it. Located in a garden-like campus with a meandering brook filled with water lilies and a few colorful Koi carps, it is noticeable from afar thanks to its vertical particle accelerator—

the Koffler Accelerator; designed by Moshe Harel, it has two towers, one which houses the accelerator itself, and the other which has a winding staircase and the cables, pipes and other necessities of the building. The accelerator is topped with a unique egg-shaped room that houses a laboratory and a visitors' gallery.

Samuel Eisenstein welcomed David in a conference room, named after Arieh Warshel, a biochemist, one of the two latest Nobel Chemistry laureates from the institute. Ironically, one might note that Arieh Warshel is proudly counted as a 2013 Nobel laureate from the institute though he moved to the University of Southern California, in 1976, after having been denied tenure at the Weizmann Institute. The room was light, with enough seats around the oval table for up to eight participants. The wall opposite the window bay was covered with pictures and even a facsimile of the Nobel diploma awarded to Arieh Warshel that throned in the center. Each diploma awarded by the Nobel Institute is a unique work of art, with the various prize-awarding bodies deciding the design and appointing calligraphers and book binders. The diploma on the wall showed the usual calligraphed reddish brown lettering on the right side, with etchings of various leaves in pale almost pastel colors on the left. The leather binding was red with a small amount of gilding. Under the diploma, another smaller display completed the picture; it was a facsimile of both sides of the gold medal awarded to him. It displayed a portrait of Alfred Nobel on the front side, while, on the reverse side, the main inscription is the same for all Nobel prizes: "*Inventas vitam iuvat excoluisse per artes* ('discover and refine life through the arts')" with the name of the awardee and the year in a small rectangle at the bottom.

Samuel explained to David the genesis of his project. He conceded that he did not fully subscribe to the catastrophic elements of the consensus climate change theory, arguing that he saw several flaws in the reporting on the modeling. In particular, he noted:

"It's not that I am what is commonly called a "denier." I'm not. At best, I'm a sceptic. But it irks me to see executive summaries that seem to emphasize the less probable scenarios and ignore or poo-poo the others, simply, I guess, to get some press coverage. Also, as a scientist, I am distressed to see the lack of firm protocols in data collection. I've heard, for instance, that temperature gauges which years ago were miles aways from agglomerations are now right in them; why is anybody surprised that temperatures rise when you get closer to houses? I wonder how they manage to trust any of their quantitative work."

David stayed quiet, aware that he was beyond his depth. He preferred to let Samuel complete his introductory thoughts, assuming that he would then get to the topic which David had come to discuss. Samuel noted that he felt that he did not have the hubris needed to believe that humans could change the earth or reverse the course of history, adding:

"I don't know if you know this, but the current CO_2 concentration in the atmosphere is quite a bit lower than its peak. And, in the past, these CO_2 peaks have not been associated with higher temperatures . . ."

He finally made the point that, to him, the essence of science had to be that scientists should investigate all possible avenues. The current tendency to ostracize and label those who disagree made him suspicious as to the so-called scientists' motives. With a mischievous smile he concluded:

"Remember that the consensus has rarely been right. Galileo was outside the consensus when he made his discovery . . . And now they call people who disagree with this global warming bit "flat earth people!" What goes around comes around. Makes little sense, really."

David told him that his views were quite fascinating, but then redirected the conversation to the current project. Coming to the meat of his topic, Samuel indicated that he had always had an interest in figuring out what he called "human photosynthesis." He noted that photosynthesis takes place inside plant cells in small organisms called chloroplasts. Chloroplasts contain a green substance called chlorophyll. It absorbs the light energy needed to make photosynthesis happen. Plants get carbon dioxide from the air through their leaves, and water from the ground through their roots. In a bit of a professorial mode, he looked at David and said:

"Do you know what the reverse of photosynthesis is?"

David's facial expression convinced Samuel that he would have to answer his own question, which he did with the tone and demeanor of a professor who is almost chiding a student for not knowing some elementary truth:

"The reverse of photosynthesis is known as respiration or breathing. Animals like us need energy which is obtained from sugars. Respiration occurs in the mitochondria of cells. During respiration, sugar is broken down in a chemical reaction with oxygen. So, during the day, plants breathe converting oxygen to carbon dioxide, and use photosynthesis to convert light and carbon dioxide to oxygen. But at night, photosynthesis stops, but respiration continues . . ."

He paused for a few seconds and triumphally added:

"Thus, people are wrong when they say that plants produce oxygen during the day and carbon dioxide during the night. That's an oversimplification."

He paused, realizing that he was nowhere near helping David with the issue he had come to investigate. He changed tack and added:

"So, to bring ourselves back to our topic, I have always wondered how we could do to CO2 what plants do: absorb the gas and produce both carbon, which in passing plants use to grow, and oxygen."

David interrupted:

"But, Samuel, this has become a hot topic, hasn't it?"

"You bet. No pun intended as heat is one of the two ingredients needed to generate diamonds. This all gets us back to climate change.

It is a hot topic because people believe that removing carbon dioxide from the air can reverse the damage which they think we, humans, have caused."

He paused to take a drink of water and returned to the main point. He argued that the process to transform CO_2 into carbon and oxygen is well-known. Unfortunately, it requires substantial external sources of energy to produce the heat required. He concluded:

"Thus, in the end, you find yourself with more carbon dioxide than you started with."

Looking directly at David who still seemed to be struggling with the science, he explained:

"This is because we create CO_2 with the energy that is expended to create the required heat that is needed to transform CO_2 into carbon and oxygen."

David looked like he had caught up, though a trained careful observer might simply conclude that his demeanor was only for the purpose of having Samuel come to the point that was of interest to *Mossad*: making diamonds. Samuel went on to explain that he had experimented with several other methods of converting CO_2 into carbon and oxygen. In particular, he named one that involves burning magnesium metal in carbon dioxide, which yields magnesium oxide and pure carbon. Almost casually, he added:

"There is research indicating that the pure carbon you get is in graphene flakes, which might yield very interesting commercial applications."

While noting he was also working on these, he said that he had decided one day to experiment further:

"I wanted to get beyond carbon. That's when I stumbled on the idea of producing diamonds."

He paused and noted that David had shifted in his chair and seemed to be considerably more focused. He added:

"You must squeeze the carbon under intense pressure, more than seven hundred thousand pounds per square inch. By the way, the high temperature and the super high pressure force the carbon atoms to bond to one another in a way that makes diamonds so hard."

But he quickly added:

"Since I already had the temperature part of the process, I had to find a way to add the pressure element. I'm happy to report that, at this point, we are quite close. My research was all about finding the right catalyst to . . ."

Seeing David's quizzical look, he stopped. David said:

"Catalyst?"

"Yes. I see. In chemistry, we call catalyst a substance which prompts or increases the rate of a chemical reaction without itself undergoing any permanent change."

With David back on board, he continued:

"So, as I said, I was looking for a catalyst which might help me avoid having to apply the pressure that would otherwise be needed. Let me simply say now that I have at least one solution, which cuts the pressure by a factor of 100 and am hoping to be able to do better. In fact, at this point, my, or should I say our "diamond making process," if I can call it that, is already working continuously. In the lab and not on an industrial scale, but still . . . The interesting bit is that my diamond producing process is a part of a larger, continuous effort: the carbon producing process is continuous, as I recycle the magnesium oxide with hydrochloric acid, I can easily get back to magnesium metal, and start the cycle all over again."

He paused again, and added:

"I see that I am probably losing you in the weeds, David. Sorry, once a chemist always a chemist."

"No worries, Samuel. How quickly could you produce about five or six pounds of diamonds?"

"It would take a while, but I already have probably close to four pounds as we speak. Why are you asking?"

"We have a terrorist issue which may require us to procure diamonds. Oh, by the way, am I safe assuming that your synthetic process leads to a much lower cost for your diamonds than anything we could find on the market?"

"Absolutely. If *Mossad* needed help, and I assume that you would be able to sponsor enough of my work to pay for it, I am sure I can generate stones at a fraction of the cost of gem quality diamonds. Now, the flip side of this is that you'd need to have the diamonds cut and polished. My process only produces rough, that is uncut diamonds . . ."

David first replied that he would not have expected anything other than that. Yet, he felt he needed to ask:

"Have you ever had some of your diamonds cut?"

"Sure, let me show you a few samples. I have a friend in the diamond district in Tel Aviv who has a diamond cutting and polishing business. He was the one, in fact, that told me that he could not really distinguish between "my" diamonds, if I can call them that, and others. So, he put a small mark near the crown to be able to tell them apart."

Samuel proceeded to show David about a half a dozen stones, cut and polished in both brilliant and an emerald-cut pattern. He added that his friend had chosen the emerald-cut pattern to show the flawless quality better. The diamonds were all in "D" or "E" colors, the two best grades and only one had a small inclusion, rated VVS1. The smallest was about one carat while the biggest, the emerald-cut, was in fact nearly four carats. Samuel added:

"At this stage, we are going to have to decide what we do with these. But my research continues, both in terms of lowering the pressure needed and of possibly adding some color."

Seeing that he had lost David again, he added:

"Fancy color diamonds, for instance in yellow, red or blue are even more valuable than white. Though blue diamonds are the most expensive, they are not widely used, probably because of their cost. Fancy pink is among the two preferred colors with yellow, and most of them come from the Argyle region in Australia. Our getting into that production here would be timely, as Argyle is said to be running low in potential reserves. Otherwise, the other best-known sources of fancy color diamonds are India and South Africa, with Brazil, Venezuela, Guyana, and Indonesia quite a bit further behind."

He stopped again; suddenly he said:

"By the way, the most challenging task you might have ahead of you if time is really of the essence is to have my current inventory of rough diamonds cut. It takes time and skill; a lot of both in fact . . ."

CHAPTER.05

TEL AVIV, ISRAEL AND SOMEWHERE IN THE AUSTRIAN ALPS

While David was busy with his visit to Samuel Eisenstein, Mark had been working on the next steps that had to be taken with respect to the Russian cargo ships. Though finding the first boat had proven to be quite a bit more challenging than expected, the team had been lucky that the second one was still in the Dardanelles Strait. Once located, keeping tabs on it was simply a matter of coordinating surveillance, which at that point was chiefly the work of the aerial drones.

The pilots of the three drones whose duty it would be to keep track of the ship actually sat in adjoining cubicles at Palmachim Air Base, just south of Tel Aviv. They were thus able to coordinate their relays based on when a drone needed to start on its return voyage to base to refuel. The three drones were set up such that there were always two of them over the likely route of the Russian two-ship convoy. The first drone would start with the ship that was further back and fly forward, while another would fly from the second ship back to the first; eventually, the drone that had started the further away from Israel would continue after flying over the second ship in order to refuel. At that time, the third drone would have reached the second ship flying east and would start on its way to the ship that was furthest east. The ballet would continue until someone noticed something that looked abnormal. Given the relatively small size of the drones, their flying at quite high altitudes and the lack of reason on the part of the Russian ships to scan the sky, the odds were favorable that the process would be able to continue for quite some time.

The first decision point came when the first ship veered to port about two hundred nautical miles from Cyprus. This strongly suggested that she was not going to sail in the direction of Lebanon, but rather would likely aim for the Syrian coast, north of Lebanon. This raised a number of questions in the minds of the team which Mark headed. The principal one dealt with whether the ship intended to dock in Syria, most likely in Latakia or Tartous, or was expected to crawl to a stall and meet with smaller boats in the Syrian territorial waters. These could take over the cargo and dock in a myriad of smaller harbors along the coast. Mark was convinced that the only other alternative made little sense: It would have assumed that the ship was using the long route to get to Tripoli, rather than sailing in a Southwestern direction, abeam Paphos in Cyprus and then almost straight to Tripoli, or Jounieh. He kept asking himself: *Why would they take a longer route, unless they knew they were being shadowed? If that, how would they have found out?*

With David back in the office, Mark went to see him to discuss the various options that were available to them. Mark had already discussed the situation with his two most senior associates and they had come to the same conclusion: the most likely scenario had to be the one that involved some form of transshipment somewhere along the Syrian coastline. That would make the northern route make sense. In fact, it could happen anywhere fifteen miles east of Karpaz, the easternmost point of Cyprus. The key element in their minds is that they did not have a lot of time between the moment the ship left Cyprian territorial waters and when they entered Syrian waters. In short, whatever *Mossad* intended to do had to be planned, if not to the minute at least to the hour, with whatever equipment that would be needed in place. The average sea depth between one and four hours east of Cyprus was about 3,500 feet, which was plenty for a submarine to be able to cruise somewhat undetected, except if expected. David asked:

"Great to see you, Mark. What do you recommend?"

"At this point, it's still a wait and see game, because we've got to see the boat make a move. However, we expect the first to rendezvous somewhere along the Syrian coast."

"Eliminated Tripoli or further south?"

"Well! Everything is possible. Couldn't understand why they would have taken the long route."

"Unless the other ship takes the other route? Trying to confuse anyone that could be observing them . . ."

Mark looked pensive for a second. He was surprised because he had not given any real thought to that option. He and his team had been focusing on a strategy based on the one ship and not considered that the two ships might have sailed almost together for a reason."

"Damn it! Didn't think of that. You mean that would increase their chances of one ship reaching its destination . . ."

"Absolutely. The old decoy ploy."

Mark was lost in his thoughts for a minute or so, but David knew him well. He was aware of the need he had to think things through before replying. He had been caught off guard and now needed to revisit his analysis. David still interrupted him and asked:

"How far are the two boats as we speak?" Mark did not reply directly to David's question. He said:

"Wait, the strategy could be even smarter than we think. It takes about a day to sail the entire length of Cyprus. So, we will not know where the second ship is going before we need to be set up for the first."

David smiled. His associate had figured it out. He asked another question:

"Has the first boat started along the northern coast of Cyprus, or could she still veer to starboard and sail directly toward Lebanon?"

Mark smiled and made a sign of submission with his hands, bowing down low. He replied:

"Still got a lot to learn, sir. Let me try and summarize my thoughts in the light of your questions. First, we still do not know where the first ship is going, though one would have to think that she is more likely to sail north of Cyprus. Right?"

"Not sure. What trajectory is the second ship using? Is she following the same general route as the first or is she already sailing further south?"

"If you don't mind, David, let me get back to you in the next hour or so. I should have better briefed myself. Lesson learned, boss?"

David smiled and as Mark was walking toward the door of his office, he added:

"By the way, don't let this get you down. Been there, done that and got the t-shirt myself. I'm gonna call Yael Orbach to see where the INS *Protector* is. And if she's far, I'll suggest that she should cruise toward the Syrian coastline."

Mark smiled.

Almost casually, David added:

"One element we may not have considered is that the ship is bound for the Khmeimim Air Base. You know, the Russian base which they have been given by Syria to operate. Just south of Latakia."

Mark looked stunned. He replied:

"Hadn't thought of that either. Yet, why would they ship missiles by boat when they could ship them by air?"

"Totally valid. Just a thought."

■ ■ ■ ■ ■

David had asked Simon for a few minutes of his time when he returned from his visit to the Weizmann Institute. He felt comfortable that he could procure rough diamonds at a reasonable cost and had worked out a plan in his mind. Yet, there was one element which would still be problematic: cutting and polishing the diamonds. Indeed, he knew that, depending on the circumstances, it can take between four and eight hours to cut a one-carat diamond, using the brilliant cut pattern. The time it would take to get all the diamonds ready, plus the inherent need to hire many cutters bothered him. He worried that there could be leaks, particularly because the diamond cutting community is quite tightly knit. A sudden order for nearly 25,000 carats was indeed virtually unheard of. And, in his mind at least, one thing was crystal clear: *any question is a bad question at this point.*

He wanted to hear Simon's suggestions to short cut the process if he had any. In truth, way in the back of his mind, he knew that he had already thought that Countess Renate and the Shadow Experts might well hold the key. However, he did not know whether the network of specialties covered by the Shadow Experts extended to the diamond market in general and to cutting and polishing in particular. Simon came straight out asking:

"Any lead? Any thought?"

David understood right away that Simon was giving him a chance to come up with the solution himself, as all good managers would. He simply replied:

"Nothing definitive. However, ever since the beginning, I've been musing about whether Countess Renate might . . ."

He and Simon knew very well that Countess Renate had founded the Shadow Experts to serve the "good causes" which needed help.

She had participated in several of the recent *Mossad* missions and had always provided the needed help and assistance.

■ ■ ■ ■ ■

The Shadow Experts were a secret network consisting of specialists across a wide variety of disciplines who cooperated with and were directed by Countess Renate to defend "good causes." They ranged from micro-biologists to advanced material engineers, to art experts, to cyber engineers, to electronics experts and to many other specialties, each as esoteric as the others. All members knew they were members of the network, but most did not know who the others were. They all knew Renate; most, if not all, had seen her in person or on some video conference call. Yet, no one could claim that he or she had met with her regularly. First, the specialists were all "part time associates" who came into a team to solve a problem and returned to the shadows when they were not needed.

■ ■ ■ ■ ■

Simon smiled broadly and exclaimed:
"You and me both, my friend. It's got to be at least worth a call . . ."
He paused briefly and asked:
"Do you want to call her directly, or should we do it together?"
"She knows you best, although we had quite a bit of interaction in our last adventure. I think we should do it together.[5] I'll be happy to work with her directly afterwards."
"Let's try her now!"
Simon dialed Countess Renate on the one number which he had, knowing full well that the call would first be bounced about around a number of different phone addresses until it eventually got to her. Renate was indeed extremely jealous of the secrecy that surrounded

5 See "Escaping the Bear" by the same author. Barringer Publishing, 2023.

her and worked hard to maintain it as tight as feasible. In fact, to this day, she could proudly argue that no one knew where the family castle that served as her headquarters was, or that she and Princess Alexandra were one and the same person. In fact, this was the most crucial element: anybody could find Princess Alexandra's castle, but would they know that Countess Renate and Princess Alexandra were one and the same person? She picked up the phone and asked in a jovial tone of voice:

"Simon, how are you?"

"Doing great, Countess. Doing great. David Heller is with me."

"Hello, David. Great to hear from you again. Anything I can do for you?"

Simon gave Countess Renate a general rundown of the diamond affair, electing, for the moment at least, to ignore the other developments. He still felt he needed to mention that *Mossad* is pretty sure that the diamonds they seized were meant to pay for some shipment of heroin, adding:

"We know that ISIS is rebuilding itself in northwest Syria and assume that they are using drug trafficking as a means to get financing for arms as well as other organizational expenses."

"Did you check whether the diamonds were "clean?"

"You are asking about conflict diamonds, right?"

"Absolutely, Simon. I know there are several categories that we're not supposed to touch. Sometimes, they are called blood diamonds too. So, I simplify the whole thing and talk of clean and dirty diamonds . . ."

David and Simon both knew that "blood diamonds" typically come from alluvial diamond deposits which are considerably easier and cheaper to mine than kimberlite diamonds which require the construction and maintenance of expensive mining facilities. However, they also knew that the so-called Kimberley Process Certification Scheme, which was meant to cut off the sales of conflict diamonds has never really been terribly effective. Indeed, it relies on the issuance of certificates that the stones are not related to any of the conflicts in Africa. However, between corrupt government officials and the ability to create fake certificates, the process has shown it had limits, to put it nicely. More effective has been the decision by certain governments, including the U.S., to ban the import of diamonds mined in certain countries where the odds were high that the diamonds might be conflict related. Yet, even that has its limits too, as one can just as simply "launder diamonds" as one "launders money" having them transit through different places before reaching their destination.

David interjected:

"In truth, Countess, we don't know. I surely would not been surprised to find out that those we seized were not "clean" in your terminology. However, there is no way to prove it, other than the fact that the briefcase contained no certificate."

The countess smiled and said that she understood. She asked:

"What do you need?"

David replied that *Mossad* had a source which could provide about the right weight of uncut, rough diamonds. At the same time, the issue of cutting and polishing them had to be a time-consuming endeavor, adding:

"In fact, it will either be very time consuming, or it will involve a lot of people knowing what it is we are trying to do."

Renate let go a joyous:

"Ah. Ah!"

Oddly however, she did not follow it up with anything of substance. She replied to David's point that she could easily understand the time-consuming part of the issue but was not sure she understood the problem associated with having a larger pool of diamond cutters. David replied that he intended to ask the cutters to make a microscopic mark on the side of the crown to allow the diamonds to be traced. He explained further:

"Our goal is to find out more about the whole drug trafficking network. At this point, we pretty much know that opium production and refinement into heroin are totally dispersed in Afghanistan, at least for the network we are concerned with. We know that there is additional opium cultivation in the "Golden Triangle" of Southeast Asia with more or less complete refining in the region. But that network really does not concern us, at least with respect to ISIS."

Countess Renate indicated she understood, adding:

"I've got to ask you something gentlemen. Where did you get the diamonds, you need cut and polished?"

Simon interjected:

"Countess, I can assure you that you will eventually know. At this point, for reasons I am sure you will understand, I would prefer for this to remain a secret."

Countess Renate smiled and replied:

"Need to know, Uh!"

"Absolutely."

Renate pivoted the conversation back to its original point: the cutting and polishing of rough diamonds. In so doing, she explained why she had reacted the way she did. She explained that she "had access," as she put it, to a major innovation in the world of diamond-cutting, noting that she could not disclose much either. Simon smiled and muttered:

"Understood."

Renate explained that the innovation relates to a digitally controlled automated machine that allowed the automation of a large part of the cutting and polishing process. She added:

"The big prize is that the inventor of the machine managed to incorporate artificial intelligence to drive the cutting process."

She paused and then explained further:

"If you go back to the late 1970s, you will remember that the Japanese, Fujitsu Fanuc, in particular, made a big splash with numerically controlled robots; they replaced a whole class of machine tools. That gave rise to a whole new industry based on what's now called Computer Numerically Controlled or CNC machines. This innovation works best when tasks are repetitive and regular, and when a high degree of precision is required. Well, we know someone who is the first to apply these principles to diamond cutting . . ."

"Didn't exist before?"

"Not to this extent, David. There are too many small differences between individual stones. That's where artificial intelligence comes in. It allows a qualified operator to make a few almost generic decisions, leaving the actual implementation of the details to the machine."

"Smart, quite smart. And I'll bet you'll tell us that an operator can control a whole battery of machines rather than simply one."

"Got it in one, Simon."

David then asked Countess Renate what the next step should be. She simply replied:

"You tell us what you want to do, and we'll deliver."

She paused for a second and added:

"It might in fact be best for us three to have a quick conference call with our contact and then see. I suspect that he may need to see some sample of the diamonds . . ."

CHAPTER.06

The first of the two Russian boats carrying arms to a yet unknown destination definitely sailed north of Cyprus. She was now abeam Anamur on the Turkish coast and thus only one hundred fifty miles from the tip of the Karpaz Peninsula, the northeast tip of Cyprus. It would then be a question of less than one hundred miles before she had reached a Syrian harbor, or a rendezvous point in the Syrian territorial waters—anywhere between eight and ten hours of sailing.

Following Simon's phone call, Yael Orbach, the Head of the Israeli Navy had organized for the INS *Protector* to cruise full speed in the direction of the northernmost point on the coast line of Cyprus where she would encounter the first Russian boat, assuming the Russian ship did not retrace her step and elect to sail south of the island. The INS *Protector* was equipped with two Orcas submarine drones, and a couple types of innovative marine mines. David, Simon and Yael had worked on at least three different contingency plans, depending upon how events would unfold.

The first involved a "mine screen." It consisted of individual marine mines which were tethered to each other in a sequential manner so that they could be viewed as a chain being pulled along by the Orcas, the submarine drones piloted from inside the submarine, one at the front of the line to provide traction and the other at the back to offer appropriate resistance so that the appropriate distance was maintained between two adjacent mines. The screen would then be set near the bottom of the sea, about ten miles east of where the INS *Protector* navigated. The idea was that the screen would be allowed to float up closer to the surface, with help from the Orcas, if the Russian ship gave any indication of continuing her route toward the Syrian coast. The Russian ship would eventually run into the mines which would explode and sink the ship or at least damage it enough to ensure no further forward progress.

Though this was the most "equipment intensive" plan, David, Simon and Yael did not expect to have to pull the trigger on that one. They were indeed convinced that the Russian ship would rendezvous at sea with anywhere from two to four smaller Syrian boats so that she would not be exposed to the risk of being seen entering Syrian waters, or at least not be seen entering a Syrian harbor. There were other plans in place to deal with the Syrian boats that would shuttle the ammunition to shore, if that was how the situation evolved. They had envisaged a couple of complicating factors for which they could not plan: the case of the two Russian boats converging toward each other and more ominously if some Soviet warship or submarine was detected in the immediate area. They assumed that the chances of such a development were quite low, as the cost associated with such a deployment of forces did not seem to make sense given the value of what everyone believed was an important, but still modest and traditional arms shipment.

■ ■ ■ ■ ■

Countess Renate organized the Zoom conference she had promised to set up and started the conversation:

"David and Simon, meet Albert Hoets. Albert is the scion of a traditional diamond cutting family in Antwerp, going back ten generations, right Albert?"

"That is correct, Countess. In fact, our family goes back even further, as it started in the diamond business in Amsterdam as far back as the early 1600s."

"Wow! Impressive indeed. Now, Albert, I want to introduce Simon Rabinowitz, I should say General Simon Rabinowitz who heads up the National Intelligence Agency of Israel, and Colonel David Heller who is responsible for one of its most secret operations, which, if you don't mind, will remain nameless, at least for the time being."

"Delighted to meet you by Zoom, gentlemen. Countess Renate told me that you might need my services. What may I do for you?"

David answered providing a general description of the Iraqi Syrian drug trade situation, though he intentionally omitted to mention the origin of the rough, uncut diamonds that he needed to have cut and polished. He apologized:

"For the time being, Albert, if I may call you Albert . . ."

"Please do, any friend of Countess Renate is a friend of mine."

"Thank you. As I was saying, for the time being I cannot disclose where we are getting the rough diamonds, but I can assure you first that they are not conflict or blood diamonds and second that they are totally legitimate."

He went on to say that he needed to have them cut as rapidly as possible, explaining:

"We intercepted a substantial quantity of cut and polished diamonds, which we assume were in payment of a heroin delivery. At this point, we do not want to touch these diamonds for reasons that will eventually become quite clear. Our goal is to have these other diamonds, still currently in the rough, cut and polished and in effect place them near where we found the first load in the first place. The catch . . ."

Albert interrupted:

"I was waiting for it. I was sure there was one . . ."

"The catch is that we would like the "new" diamonds, if I can call them that, to bear a microscopic mark on the side of the crown to identify them . . . I'm sure you now appreciate that we are hoping to "follow" these diamonds to uncover the full trafficking network or at least a part of it."

"I understand, but why go through the trouble you are going through. Couldn't you simply have a mark put on the diamonds you collected? You would save the time and expense of cutting the new diamonds."

"Excellent question. At this point, I hope you won't mind my saying that I cannot reply."

"Your new diamonds wouldn't be synthetic by any chance?"

Simon and David literally fell off their chairs. David replied:

"What would make you say that?"

Albert replied that in his business one of the first things you learn is that most diamonds are fungible. Except for special stones, because of their color or size, all investment-grade diamonds between one and three carats are considered equivalent. He concluded:

"So, I understand the idea of the microscopic mark. I've heard of that before. But the only reason that would make your approach make sense is if the diamonds you want cut are a lot less valuable than those you picked up . . ."

Simon interjected:

"Albert, let me make an executive decision here. Let me say that these new diamonds are indeed synthetic. However, I should add that, so far, no one that I know of has been able to tell them apart from diamonds that were mined. Even the International Gemological Institute in Tel Aviv failed to recognize them for what they were . . ."

Albert interrupted:

"Hard to believe, but you're not leaving me with a choice with respect to provenance, I guess. Yet there is no law against dealing with synthetic diamonds except for the always relevant: *caveat emptor—*buyer beware."

He paused for a second to take a breath and added:

"Though in the end, the place where they are "made" does not matter much given your credentials and Countess Renate's recommendation."

Simon replied:

"Thank you. Much appreciated. Eventually, we'll be happy to tell you more, as part of our relationship with Countess Renate. But at this point, I would prefer to keep it at that. Can you live with it?"

Albert smiled broadly and assured Simon that it would not be an issue. At the same time, Simon congratulated Albert for having picked up on the otherwise apparent inconsistency of the strategy. Looking at David, he simply added:

"Validates our strategy to call Countess Renate. Other diamond cutters might not be as perspicacious as Albert, but I have to believe that one or two might have had similar suspicions."

Countess Renate interrupted:

"Thanks, Simon. I would simply suggest that we do not discuss any more the idea of substituting the diamonds you found with those. Nobody needs to know why you are placing these wherever you will place them."

Turning to Albert, she asked:

"Can we talk about your invention?"

Albert smiled and quite freely agreed. He explained to David and Simon that his tool allows him to speed up the cutting and polishing work by an order of magnitude. It uses artificial intelligence to identify the structure of the stone and thus to guide the cutting decisions. Then, it uses numerical controls to work on the facets, as this is generally somewhat of a mechanical process. He added a couple of interesting thoughts:

"Though we do not do it as we speak now, our intention as a family and a company is to open operations in India. India has become the largest cutting and polishing center for rough diamonds. It is said that as many as fourteen out of fifteen rough diamonds in the world are polished there. Surat is **the** hub for cutting, polishing and processing rough diamonds, with 85% of these being eventually exported."

He paused for a second and added:

"I know it might sound inconsistent to you, but we would locate the most sophisticated work in India, where they have great experience, and might retain here in Antwerp the more mechanical process. I am conscious that it might look surprising. But once you realize that the sophisticated work is that which requires the most labor, it becomes obvious that you should locate that in the place where labor is cheapest. Of course, we will keep the work on the most exceptional and valuable stones here; it might cost more, but, as you may know, the price per carat increases as the weight of the stone increases; an exponential function."

He let that thought sink in and added:

"Quite a bit in fact! So, the larger, exceptional pieces definitely deserve the best care we can bring to bear."

"Very interesting Albert. I love your distinction between sophisticated and exceptional; so intuitive and yet I've never heard of it."

"Thanks, David. So, at this point, I think that the best approach, if that is OK with you, would be for at least you and I, with Simon and Countess Renate if they want to attend, to get together here in Antwerp with some or all your rough diamonds. Then, we can make decisions from here. Countess, does this make sense?"

"Absolutely, Albert."

Simon interjected:

"I hope you will excuse me, but I am sure that David does not need me there. This is his baby. But he might in fact elect to bring one of his associates to make sure we always have continuity."

David nodded and added:

"His name is Mark Levi, and he is really in day-to-day charge of this project."

■ ■ ■ ■ ■

A couple of days later, Mark and David found themselves in Antwerp's diamond district, roughly a square mile centered around the old town and St. Mary's Cathedral. They found Albert's workshop in a discrete townhouse on Lange Klarenstraat, less than a mile east of the Hilton Old Town hotel where they had spent the night. From the outside, one would have been very hard pressed to guess the activities carried out within the house, a four-story townhouse. Admittedly, locals who knew about the diamond district might have had less of a difficult time making an educated guess. The very tight security at the front door would only provide an additional hint that the place contained very valuable "things." But, in many ways, this was no different from what one would find in similar places, including a competitor of Albert's whose "shop" was three doors down.

Countess Renate had already arrived when David and Mark rang the doorbell; she was having a coffee with Albert upstairs. A security guard let Mark and David into a sort of antechamber where they were asked to submit to a simple search, going through a metal detector, while their briefcase was examined through an X-Ray machine. From the antechamber, they were taken to the formal entry hall. Albert, who had been told of their arrival, had come down from his office with Countess Renate and was waiting for them in the formal entry hall, complete with its majestic historic copper chandelier. He led the group up a grand staircase with gilded brass bannisters to the second floor. Turning to their right, they entered a large room which seemed to occupy about half of the front of the house; a door seemed to indicate that another room, probably comparable, occupied the other half of the facade.

In the far-right corner, they saw a desk to which Albert pointed them. He had already arranged three small armchairs on front of it, with a larger one, presumably for himself, on the opposite side of the desk, ostensibly an 18th century Dutch antique. It was massive, with four relatively short, almost stubby, cabriole, Queen Anne style legs with the characteristic clawfoot motif. The top of the desk was in a darker wood and shaped like three interlocking ovals. On the right-hand side of the desk, stood a massive copper lamp with a dark green leather oval shade with gilded borders. The desk itself was decorated with flower-themed marquetery, using a variety of fruit-tree veneers. The body of the desk was almost as thick as the height of the four legs. It had two large drawers on either side of the footwell, with a large single and thinner drawer in the middle.

Albert motioned his guests toward the desk and, after they were all seated, asked David to show him a few samples of the diamonds he had brought. David extracted them from a brown felt pouch he had placed in his briefcase. Albert had spread a small, dark green, felt cloth flat on the desk. David rolled the samples out of the pouch and onto it. Albert selected one of the stones and looked at it carefully with his jeweler's magnifying glass firmly planted in front of his right eye. He was holding the stone with a pair of beautifully carved silver tweezers. His observation, involving looking at the stone from virtually every possible angle, lasted a good couple of minutes. Then, smiling broadly he said to David:

"Exceptional stone. Would you mind my looking at it under greater magnification?"

David was happy to oblige. Albert rolled over a small table that sat next to the desk, on his left side. David and Mark noted that it had casters at the tip of each leg, concluding that it was most certainly used quite often. He removed the cloth protecting the instrument from any form of lint or dust. That revealed a jewelry and gemology microscope, routinely used by specialists to grade diamonds. He carefully placed the stone under the lens, which in fact was one of three lenses that could be rotated in place to offer different levels of magnification. Holding the stone with the same tweezers he continued his inspection. He then performed another couple of tests and concluded:

"Really magnificent. This one is a truly beautiful "D" color, internally flawless. I would expect that it could yield a couple of brilliant cut two-carat stones. I rarely see a stone like this. You tell me it is man-made, but I can't tell using the standard tools: the hardness, the density, the brilliance, and the color are all very impressive."

He went back to the small sample of stones and repeated the observation of all of them, always coming back with the same message: he could not tell the difference between them and mined diamonds. Turning to David he asked:

"What do you want to do next?"

Looking to both Countess Renate and Mark for consensus, David said that he would be willing to leave the samples with Albert and let him cut and polish them. He noted that the drug trade seemed to prefer easily marketable investment grade diamonds, which really meant diamonds between 1 and 3 carats, with a brilliant cut, in a "D" or "E" color and internally flawless.

Albert collected the diamonds and placed them in a box which he secured in his nearby safe. He wrote a receipt by hand for the diamonds and handed it to David. David was almost embarrassed to take it, though Countess Renate simply said with a broad smile:

"Europeans have a phrase for this: 'good accounts make for good friends.' You find it in English, French, German, and Dutch, in particular."

David simply smiled. Albert then motioned to the group to follow him. Returning to the hallway with the staircase, which was wrapped around the elevator shaft, he preceded them into a room which occupied the whole floor on the back side of the building. In it, one could see a row of self-standing machines, arranged around three of the four walls, with a couple of individual stations on either side of the door. Proudly, Albert said:

"This is where we cut and polish diamonds. Most of the machines are controlled by computer programs, but the two stations you can see on either side of the door are there to carry out the operations which we judge the machines are either not able to make or at least not able to make well enough. You could say that the two master cutters that work there serve as supervisors or probably better said "master consultants" to the cutters whose desks you can see in front of the machines along the walls. The programs, which are based in part on computer aided designs, are actually composed on the next floor. I'd be happy to take you there, but I'm not sure what I could show you other than cubicles like any other open-plan operation."

Renate seemed to agree that the visit would not be necessary. Mark asked:

"How long have you had these numerically controlled machines?"

"The first was completed a couple of years ago."

Albert paused for a minute to remind his audience of the five steps in the diamond cutting process:

"Sorting the rough, planning for the manufacturing, cleaving the rough into a preliminary shape, shaping the girdle and polishing the facets."

He added:

"In fact, you could argue that polishing the facets is a two-step process, as there are the major fundamental facets and all the others that are in effect superimposed on them."

Returning to his point about the machines set up in groups of four and how they linked up together he explained:

"Don't get me wrong, the machines that you're looking at don't all do the same thing. Together, they carry out all the various stages of the cutting and polishing process. In fact, if you look carefully at the machines, you will see that they represent four groups of four machines each."

As he was saying this, Albert was moving his right hand around himself to illustrate his points. He continued:

"All four groups are the same and the small desk you find in front of each of the four groups is where our cutters operate, verifying that the stones look the way they should, and then taking them from one station to the next as a stone is ready for it. The beauty of the process is that a cutter can work on up to four stones at a time, one at each station."

He stopped and seeing that everyone was following him, he summarized the process:

"The whole thing starts on the floor above where sorting the rough and planning for the manufacturing is carried out, with the final product being the computer programs. The first machine cleaves the rough into the preliminary shape, the second shapes the girdle."

Albert paused again to explain:

"The girdle of a diamond is the outermost edge of the stone, in effect the division between the crown and the pavilion of a polished diamond. It is a very important element, as you want it to be not too thin but not too thick either. The girdle is there to protect the diamond. However, there is an important trade-off. A thicker girdle protects better, but the reflections become more visible, and you don't want them."

Returning to the machine set up, Albert concluded:

"The last two machines take care of creating the fundamental facets and then of polishing them."

David was very impressed:

"Thank you, Albert. I feel I've just taken a master class in diamond cutting and polishing."

He paused for a second and added:

"We better let you get to work with these stones. Let me know when you're ready for the next batch."

Mark could not resist asking:

"Could you eventually do away with the manual transfer of the stone from one machine to the next?"

"Excellent question. We probably can, but the main issue is quality control. So, we would have to imagine a setup where the stone is picked up from one machine, moved to the table of the cutter, who could either send it to the next machine or reserve it on the side for further work, manual or automatic. I must confess that we are not there yet . . ."

Albert paused and returning to an earlier issue asked:

"You said you wanted a microscopic mark on the girdle of each diamond David, correct?"

"Absolutely. We would like it to be the two Hebrew letters for E and W, remembering that Hebrew is read from right to left, so the first letter starting from the left should be W and the second E."

David then asked for a piece of paper and wrote the two letters to be used.

CHAPTER.07

TEL AVIV, ISRAEL

The phone rang on Simon's desk:

"Simon? Yael here."

"What may I do for you, my friend?"

"There are new developments on the Russian boat front . . ."

"Ah! Let me first try to connect David, he ought to hear this . . ."

When Simon had conferenced David, Yael explained that he had just learned that there was a foreign submarine in the vicinity of the south end of the channel east of Cyprus which the INS *Protector* was patrolling. He explained that an Israeli Navy frigate was in the area, precisely to relay any signal that might be sent from the Israeli submarine. The message was crystal clear:

"Sonar signal west and south. Most likely underwater but needs verifying. Has to be a submarine."

Yael further indicated that he had asked that an Eitan surveillance drone be immediately redirected to go take a look. He added that the fact that the drone saw nothing confirmed that the sonar signal had to come from an underwater source. Simon interrupted:

"We had initially thought that a submarine escort would not make sense for the Russian cargo ships; too expensive. Could it mean that the weaponry the ship is delivering is important enough to justify a submarine shadowing the ship?"

He paused and directed his question to Yael:

"Remember, we had considered that option and thought it was the least probable."

Yael conceded the point and noted that the one element they had not considered was that the weaponry would warrant some sort of special surveillance. He added:

"I think it changes the situation. I have ordered the *Charm of the Sea*[6] under the command of Captain Barack Decker to sail in that general direction. It's not armed as the frigate is, but it can get closer to the action, as it will be as usual disguised as a fishing boat."

■ ■ ■ ■ ■

Yael did not need to describe the *Charm of the Sea* to Simon and David, as both were well aware that it was one of at least two spy ships which were much more than the regular supply boats they appeared to be. They did look like regular boats with the bridge toward the front half of the boat and the middle and aft sections above deck suitable to carry many different loads. However, in reality, they were fast boats which could transform into hydrofoils with a couple of simple maneuvers. The foils, which at rest were folded into the hull at the bow of the boat, could be extended; at speed, the boat riding on these foils would rise higher on the water and offer both less friction and thus more speed. To accommodate the fact that the boat could rise higher on the water, the angle and length of the two propeller shafts could also be altered so that they would still operate at full power at top speed. That alone made them quite different from any supply boat and would allow them to outrun virtually any boat, particularly as their twin engines were double the power which boats

---

[6] "Below the Surface" by the same author. Barringer Publishing, 2022.

of that size would normally have. Unfortunately, with the need for more power came the requirement that fuel capacity be substantially raised as well.

Another series of modifications would never be visible except to those who knew where to look. First, the vessels were equipped with an air lock which allowed the boat to pick up or deliver loads underwater. Usually, this feature was used to transfer loads from one boat to another, but it also allowed the boats to be resupplied in food or water from a submarine without the operations being visible to anyone not underwater. Also, the lower level of the front deck, under the bridge tower, hid a full gamut of electronic surveillance equipment; it offered space for a couple of operators to work all the while allowing them to move from that space to the modest living quarters on the bridge without being required to step out in the open.

Finally, the vessels could easily change identity. They had three names on rotating supports on each side of the bow of the ship. Simply rotating the support would allow the ship to change its name. At the same time, each of the names corresponded to a country of registration. Currently, they were using Malta, Panama, and Gibraltar. Thus, the flagpole at the very aft of the ship would display the correct flag through a clever mechanism inspired from the multi-color ball point pens of the past: each flag would roll around its own axis and the whole retract into a sheave. The captain could therefore "dial up" the flag he wanted." The cherry on top of the cake dealt with the color of the middle section of the hull. The top of the hull would always be white, while the bottom, the part most often immersed in the water would always be black. The middle section, however, comprised vertical rotating triangles which could display one of three colors: red, dark green and white. Each color went with a different flag and a different name.

■ ■ ■ ■ ■

Yael added:

"Being closer to the action allows her to relay any message from the submarine without it having to surface to transmit. Doubles up with the frigate."

Simon agreed that the help of the *Charm of the Sea* would be invaluable. Yet, he asked:

"Where did you say the presumed Russian submarine was?"

"Effectively at the south end of the channel we identified between Cyprus and the Syrian and Lebanese coastlines. What are you thinking of?"

David beat Simon to the punchline:

"I'm not sure we know whether the submarine is meant to protect the first or the second Russian ship."

"Exactly" was all that Simon could add.

David then started to think out loud. He mused:

"To me, it looks more and more as if the "two-ship convoy" is a ruse. One of the two must have special cargo, while the other may not. Further, whichever of the ships has the special cargo, I sure as hell would love to get my hands on that cargo. We must assume that one of them is bait."

"Where does that get you?"

Simon's question was very fair, and Yael nodded his agreement. David replied that, at this point, he was not sure, but would venture a guess. He argued:

"The ship which is doing something unusual is the first. It sailed north of Cyprus rather than south as usual."

He stopped to make sure in his own mind that he was correct. He reasoned:

"What if there were not one, but two unusual things? We are implicitly assuming that the unusual bit here is that the armament might be different, more powerful or something. Now that surely makes sense. But there is another possible scenario . . ."

Yael and Simon suddenly seemed to listen even more carefully. David continued:

"What if the unusual element is that the armament is to be delivered to an area where the Russians have not gone before?"

Simon interrupted:

"You mean Syria rather than Lebanon?"

"Precisely. Unfortunately, that doesn't make our guessing any easier. I can't decide which ship is the real danger and which may be just a decoy. We still have to focus on both of them."

Yael nodded and then added:

"Note that we'll know sooner or later. If the first is the real thing, then it should be the one going to Syria, agreed?"

David smiled and replied, while Simon enjoyed seeing his *protégé* come into his own:

"Not necessarily. Assume that the first one remains a decoy. Somehow, we should either see her sail for the Syrian coastline or we should see Syrian ships come to meet her in the open sea. Whichever it is, we have to intercept. However, that would not guarantee that the second ship might not quietly keep sailing, say toward Tripoli and unload more lethal or dangerous weaponry . . ."

Yael had to come to the only reasonable conclusion:

"We've got to monitor them both **and** to intercept them both as well."

Simon agreed but added:

"We do, but there are a couple of complicating factors. First, we need to deal with the boats near enough each other in time, otherwise the second might take evasive maneuvers. Second, we also need to avoid getting in direct conflict with the Russian submarine, if that's really what we're seeing."

David exclaimed:

"Indeed, though I can't imagine who else could have a submarine there. Anyway, I think I know what we need to do . . ."

He paused to give some more theatrical weight to his last comment: "We must add high altitude drone torpedo bombers to the mix."

▌▌▐▌▌

Mossad and the Israeli Army had indeed developed a drone-dropped torpedo to deal with a very specific problem: attacking enemy submarines or ships all the while keeping the source of the attack if not undetectable, at least very hard to identify. They had quite successfully used them in a recent operation and had thus made them a part of their normal weaponry.

While most torpedoes are launched by submarines or torpedo boats, *Mossad* had developed the ability to drop up to two torpedoes from the Kovesh drone, an Israeli modification of the U.S. made Sentinel RQ 170. And the drone could do that while flying at or close to half its maximum altitude of 50,000 feet. They made a torpedo which was half torpedo, half cruise missile, using the same fuel source for the two propulsion systems to save space, although they lost quite a bit of range when the torpedo hits the water. These could only run underwater for five miles at most, whereas regular torpedoes can have a range of 20 or more miles.

Further, their use in combination with a Kovesh drone was crucial. The drones indeed had such a small radar image because the Kovesh was designed to have strong stealth features. So, the drones could fly close enough to the target, from a high enough altitude."

▌▌▐▌▌

David summarized:

"In short, we continue our surveillance. We keep the mine curtain in place but let any Syrian ship approach. We raise the curtain after they have sailed beyond it so that they cannot return to the Syrian coastline. At the same time, we keep the Eitan drones'[7] surveillance of both Russian ships. We must be prepared to have the INS *Protector* move if summoned to do so by the Russian submarine, but we remain ready to torpedo either of the two Russian surface ships and, if needed, any boat they rendezvous on the open sea. Any problem?"

Both Simon and Yael immediately agreed and wished him good luck.

---

[7] See "The Crypto Trap" by the same author. Barringer Publishing, 2020.

CHAPTER.08

TEL AVIV, ISRAEL AND ANTWERP, BELGIUM

David's Israeli Air Force private jet landed at Antwerp International Airport, a small regional airport that serves Antwerp and its region; that the airport exists may on the surface seem surprising in view of the fact that Schiphol, Amsterdam's and The Netherlands' major international hub, is barely 100 miles away, while Brussel's airport is only thirty miles away, and in the same country. However, it still maintained international clearing facilities, as it would routinely receive travelers from Belgium or Germany, when not France. A cynic would add that Antwerp's position as the world's diamond capital had to justify the ability to receive international travelers who did not feel the need to transit through Amsterdam, Paris, Brussels, or Dusseldorf. Interestingly, consecrating the city's important commercial place in the world, Antwerp's harbor is the seventeenth largest port in the world, by tonnage, and second only to Rotterdam in Europe.

David was accompanied by Mark Levi and carried a small briefcase as he disembarked from the plane. They had not planned on staying more than a couple of hours in Antwerp and thus had not brought along anything to change into, other than their customary carry-on luggage that they kept on the plane, just in case. As they usually observed:

"You never know what can happen. A simple change of underwear and a toiletry kit can make the difference between a minor delay and a major inconvenience."

They went straight to the townhouse on Lange Klarenstraat where Albert Hoets was expecting them right after security. Albert took them first to the second-floor room where they met earlier. They sat at the same desk he had used earlier. This time, he added, with some visible and justified pride:

"This is really my desk and my office. The office next door looks a lot like it, but it does not have the same furnishings. Here, almost everything can be traced back to my family's distant members in one way or another. I like to say that they bought as modern furniture what are now antiques. Next door, the furnishings while still quite elegant were purchased more recently."

He paused, hesitated, yet added with a smile:

"Well, more recently doesn't mean last year; I mean in the 19th or 20th centuries. Would you guys like to see it when we're through?"

David let Mark reply:

"Probably another time. We are planning on flying back to Tel Aviv this afternoon. Thank you."

Albert placed the cut diamonds he had produced from the rough diamond samples left by David a short while earlier on the dark green velvet cloth on the desk. The cut stones varied in size, as expected and requested by David, between 1 and 3 carats. Albert added:

"They really all are "D" color, which is quite unusual in a small sample. Anyway, I had all of them cut in a brilliant pattern, because it is the one that sparkles the most. However, as you can see, this one is in a cushion cut and is larger than the others, actually 4.84 carats. I would have had to cut too much to make it perfectly round, but its rough shape was perfectly adapted to the cushion cut. I decided to do that to allow you to see how wonderful these gems can be. And you still swear that they are not genuine . . ."

"Oh! They're genuine all right. But they're genuinely synthetically produced rather than mined. By the way, can you show me the small mark on the girdle?"

Albert brought his microscope around and placed each of the stones in turn under it. David and Mark were able to verify that the mark was there and that the Hebrew characters actually said what they were supposed to say and appeared in the correct order. David could only say:

"Many thanks, Albert. This is first class work."

Displaying what was probably a bit of false humility, Albert simply replied:

"I'm just a simple diamond cutter . . ."

Now it was David's turn to open his briefcase. This time, he had brought all the rough diamonds which Samuel Eisenstein had been able to produce so far. He was about two thousand carats short of the 25,000-carat goal *Mossad* had set, assuming what he called a "conversion ratio" of 75%. Albert gasped discreetly, noting that he had rarely in his life seen that many diamonds in one place, other maybe than at the periodical DeBeers sales (officially called Global Sight Holder Sales and Auctions). David explained:

"We are a bit short of our goal, but it is not the major issue. Can I leave this to you?"

Albert nodded, but noted:

"I would not be so sure you are short by much. The stones here are of quite regular a shape when they are still rough. We may well have a higher conversion ratio, particularly if we vary the cut to minimize the loss of material."

David asked:

"Would the different cuts affect the value of the stones?"

"Not really if the cuts are not overly fancy. It should be OK if we stick to a variant on the brilliant round cut."

David added:

"We still prefer the usual investment grade size, but feel free to improvise if one or two stones deserve a different treatment."

He paused to clear his throat and asked:

"How long will you need to complete the work?"

"Normally, I would reply that it should take us more than a month. However, given Countess Renate's instructions, we can speed up the process, by working almost continuously and using a night shift. How about two weeks?"

"Two weeks? That's fast."

David paused and added:

"Whatever you say. Now, by the way, our plan does not call for all of them to be used at once. So, if that is OK with you, Mark and I would love to come back in a week and collect whatever we can."

"Shouldn't be a problem."

"Great. In fact, it may not be both of us, but rather one of the two of us. Depending on what actually happens in the field . . ."

Albert nodded that he fully understood. He ordered his chauffeur to take his guests back to the airport. With the Israeli jet unmarked as belonging to the Israeli Air Force, the chauffeur most likely believed that he was driving a couple of very important diamond dealers. The chauffeur knew that all tail numbers on all aircraft in the world started with one or two characters indicating the country of registration. While "N" denotes planes registered in the U.S., "4X" denotes planes registered in Israel. The chauffeur had seen his share of Israeli planes over the years, given the role of Tel Aviv in the diamond business.

■ ■ ■ ■ ■

David and Mark called Josh Steinmetz on a secure phone. They conferenced Mehmet Isaac in and started describing their thoughts for the next step. They started, however, with the good news as Mark announced:

"We have managed to replace many of the missing diamonds and will have most of the full lot cut and polished in two weeks at most."

Josh had to ask:

"How did you guys do that?"

"I am not sure I want you to know all the details, because you do not need them, and we do not want any leaks. Let me however tell you that David and I were able to buy a substantial quantity of rough, uncut diamonds and found in Belgium someone who could cut and polish them for us just about faster than anyone else."

Mark went on to ask Josh whether he felt he would be able to play the role of a deep undercover contact for some Arabic speaking group. Josh replied that he certainly could play the role from the point of view of the language but was not sure what else he would need to do. He reminded them with a bit of a laugh that he was known as Abu Musa to people around him, adding:

"They think that I am an Arab. I shouldn't need much effort to make believe I represent some group."

Mark replied:

"Exactly what I expected. Great. You're key in that role."

Mark further explained that he and David had concocted a plan which would involve first delivering a box containing a few diamonds near the crash site in Iraq. He went on:

"We hope that it would eventually be picked up by those that were supposed to receive the earlier payment. We will insert a note, written in Arabic, allegedly from a group which would very much like to get into the drug trade in the area, trying to displace those who were originally going to make the payment for the heroin. It will lament that the safety of the area is such that the use of an aircraft seems imprudent for the time being. That's where you come in, Josh. The note will tell whoever receives it that a very deep undercover individual had agreed to serve as an intermediary, though that would come with conditions . . ."

Josh mumbled an inaudible remark, and Mark promptly outlined the main conditions, to which Josh replied:

"I think I can do this, particularly given the conditions you are setting up, Mark."

"Great. On our end, we will attempt to track the box after it is picked up. No need to add that it will be bugged."

"What if they find the bug?"

"Though everything is possible, Marvin Goldstein, our technology expert, tells me that it is virtually impossible. Again, for your protection, Josh, I don't think you need to know more."

A veteran of the service, Marvin was responsible for all technological development for *Mossad*. He had an encyclopedic knowledge of the capabilities of each of the branches of the Israeli Defense Forces. He also knew exactly what was being planned for the future and even what research directions were emphasized and those which were not. At fifty, Marvin had worked with nearly all the key players in the service. He knew his stuff better than anyone and had a mind that thrived on challenges. He loved innovation, even if this was going to stretch his capabilities nearly to the breaking point. He was a man of vision; his vision was focused on technology. His only well-known shortcoming was that he loved technology so much that, often, he would extend his explanations into levels of detail that many considered unnecessary and often veered away from common Hebrew, or English, to speak in technobabble. Yet, most people still gave him a pass on those, as he was so good at everything else.

■ ■ ■ ■ ■

Josh acquiesced though Mark could have seen that he was still on the fence if he could have seen his facial expression. Mark continued:

"We may need more than one delivery on your part, Josh. It all depends upon what we learn of where the terrorists are and decide how we can get to them. We will provide you with a new telephone with a number working in Iraq and Syria. That'll give them a way to reach you without giving out your real number. The box will also contain another phone which we will tell them will be for them to contact you, without having to disclose your number, or for you to contact them as well."

Josh was gradually coming on board, realizing that Mark and David had surely planned this in a great deal of detail. He still asked:

"But how do I get my hands on all of this?"

Mark replied that it was where Mehmet came in. He added that Mehmet had already agreed that he could make one or two discreet trips to Erbil to deliver packages. He would still have to find a way to create a dead drop box where he could deposit the package and allow Josh to pick it up without the two of them ever meeting. Apparently completely changing the topic he asked Josh:

"By the way, Josh, could the terrorists identify your car by the tire marks that you might have left in the proximity of the plane?"

Josh had a short laugh and said:

"I'm sure they could have at one point. But I changed my four tires after I made the pickup."

"Smart, very smart. Who knows about it?"

"A local auto repair shop owner."

"Might he talk?"

"Everything is possible, Mark, but I would not worry at this point. First, I have known him, bought petrol from him and had him service my car ever since I have been here. Second, and most importantly, my tires were not really dead, but they were surely tired. So, changing them was a perfectly rational request, particularly as I pretexted that I was going on a long drive."

"Perfect."

Turning to Mehmet, Mark asked:

"Would you be able to find a way to drop something in Josh's car if it was parked at the airport?"

Josh interrupted:

"Where would I be if I need to leave my car at the airport?"

"Are there so few flights that it would seem odd for you to be casually loitering in the airport?"

Josh agreed that the scenario was plausible, provided Mehmet arrived in the middle of the day. It would not work if everything took place at night, adding:

"Unless I had fallen asleep in my car, coincidentally in the parking lot of the airport."

Mark interjected:

"Now, you're giving me an idea."

▋ ▋ ▉ ▋ ▋

The phone on Mark's desk rang a few minutes after he had hung up after his conversation with Josh, David and Mehmet. He picked it up and was quite surprised to see that Mehmet was calling him back.

"Hey! Mehmet. What is the matter?"

"I didn't want to say more than necessary earlier. However, you do know that I have a private pilot's license; don't you?"

"You do?"

"Yes. Remember, I did my military service in the Air Force. That's where I learned to pilot planes. I have occasionally rented small planes here in Ankara or even Istanbul to go explore the countryside a bit."

"Could you fly all the way to Iraq on a single engine plane?

"Who said single engine? I am licensed to fly a twin propeller plane and have a full instrument rating . . . In fact, I could easily upgrade to a jet license if I needed or wanted to."

Mark was processing what Mehmet had just said, when Mehmet added:

"And, by the way, there is an airport in Mosul. There is no air service there, but a private twin-prop plane can certainly land there."

"Well, why don't we do this, Mehmet. First try to file a flight plan to Mosul and see if it is accepted. If it is, find out whether you can get someone from whom you could rent a plane."

Mark had been fiddling with his computer and then said:

"Voila! I see here that the Americans had studied the possibility of extending the runway of the airport at Mosul but decided against it because one of its ends was too close to a residential neighborhood. So, we could ask Josh to leave his car in the parking lot and go take a walk in the neighborhood while you land, deposit your package, refuel, and take off again. Makes sense?"

"Absolutely, though I still have my doubts on the refueling front. Would feel better if I knew I could fly out in a hurry if I had to."

"Glad you called back, Mehmet. This is great."

He paused and then, almost casually asked:

"Would you be flying over any dangerous area?"

"Not really. It's generally safe. At worst, you're asked to identify yourself. Plus, I would be where I am officially, having filed a flight plan and turning my transponder on. It should look to everyone as a perfectly innocuous flight."

CHAPTER.09

TEL AVIV, ISRAEL AND SOMEWHERE
IN THE MEDITERRANEAN SEA

The secure phone on Yael Orbach's desk suddenly rang. This indicated a message of utmost importance. Yael picked it up immediately:

"Yael, David Heller here. We just picked up a message from the captain of the INS *Protector*. Quite worrisome."

"What is it?"

David told him that the INS *Protector* had received communication from the submarine, which by now was confirmed to be indeed Russian, adding:

"They're asking him to clear the area."

Yael immediately asked:

"Wait a second. What area?"

Then, without giving David the time to respond, Yael asked the obvious question:

"Hold it, how come you got the message and not Navy headquarters?"

Matter-of-factly, David replied that the message had come via Sonar which had been picked up by Captain Decker on the *Charm of the Seas* which had relayed it to *Mossad* as he assumed they were controlling his movements in this operation. He added:

"I'm sure the message from INS *Protector* was also picked up by the navy frigate nearby. She has to have sent it on to Navy Headquarters . . ."

■ ■ ■ ■ ■

Captain Mike Dayan was quietly sitting in his stateroom. His submarine, the INS *Protector*, had been tasked with the job of patrolling the international waters between Syria and Cyprus. That was in the expectation that one or both Russian cargo ships carrying arms, most likely for insurgents in Syria or in Lebanon, would have to execute a transshipment somewhere outside of the territorial waters surely of Cyprus and most probably of Syria. Two Orca remote pilots were working in a separate area of the vessel, but close enough to the control center that they could coordinate their activity with that of the mother ship. They had set up a mine net that could be lowered or raised, depending upon whether their orders were to allow a ship to cross the line or not.

The complete setup also included a spy ship, the *Charm of the Sea*, under the command of Captain Barack Decker. The main role of the *Charm of the Sea* was to relay sonar signals he received from INS *Protector* to *Mossad* headquarters, and from then to Navy headquarters. Though Yael had ordered a Navy frigate in the vicinity, he and David had preferred bringing a much more innocuous spy ship closer to the action. She could relay messages as well and would seem considerably less threatening, all the more so as she was "disguised" as a fishing vessel in her current configuration. As it was, the Navy frigate could relay a message as well though the *Charm of the Sea* was closer.

Up until then, the scenario which seemed to be unfolding appeared pretty much in line with expectations. The first Russian cargo boat had veered to starboard and started on a southern direction after sailing abeam Cape Apostolos Andreas, at the top of the Karpass Peninsula. In other words, she was on track to come to the point where she could deliver her cargo without infringing on the territorial waters of Cyprus and without being too obviously close to Syria. The team was monitoring her very carefully to determine whether she would sail directly for the Syrian or Lebanese coastlines or would have a rendezvous with one or, more likely, several smaller vessels. The other Russian cargo ship had not yet committed to a clear route as she had not reached the western tip of Cyprus; she could either follow the first vessel or veer to starboard earlier and sail south of Cyprus.

Captain Dayan had been told by his sonar operator that he had picked up a submarine some distance away. Though Captain Dayan had immediately assumed that the submarine was most likely of Russian origin, he had not done anything more than reporting the submarine's presence and asking his operator to shift to passive sonar, rather than active sonar. Shifting to passive sonar meant that the ship would continue to receive sonar signals, but would not be sending any, as it would in an active mode. That would make it harder for her to be identified.

I I ◼ I I

Sonar (Sound Navigations and Ranging) is necessary aboard submarines as it is the only way of detecting the presence of other vessels or of communicating with them. Radio or radar signals indeed do not travel underwater, as the microwaves are absorbed by seawater within feet of their transmission. There are two types of sonar. The first, called active sonar, works just like a radar; it emits signals which can bounce off objects and return to the sender, telling him or her of the presence of the object, providing information on size or distance. The major issue with active sonar is that the signals sent by a submarine can be picked up by another vessel and thus point to the presence of the submarine. The second, called passive sonar, involves navy personnel listening to the sounds around the submarine and determining which ones are trivial and which ones might be another boat. Passive sonar cannot be detected from the outside, as it emits nothing: it is in a strict listening mode. At the same time, it is considerably less potent or reliable.

■ ■ ■ ■ ■

"Captain Dayan?"

The call on the internal communication system within the submarine was from Art Chahouat, the officer in charge of sonar communication:

"The submarine which we identified earlier is closing in. He must either see us or hear us. Permission to switch back to active sonar?"

"Permission granted. Keep me closely posted."

Captain Dayan walked briskly from his stateroom to the control room. He indicated to the Officer in Charge that he would relieve him and thus take control of the operations. His first order was to slow the ship to crawling speed and aim its bow in the direction from which the Russian submarine was coming. First, that would allow the INS *Protector* to present a much smaller sonar image to the Russian submarine; second it would point the torpedo tubes in the correct direction if they were ever needed. He also asked that torpedo tubes 1 and 2 be armed and ready to shoot. Finally, he instructed all sonar communication to be recorded, and sent to headquarters via the *Charm of the Sea*.

Deep down, Captain Dayan had no intention to use the torpedoes at present. In fact, he viewed the preparations he was ordering as nothing more than that: preparations. He could not imagine that the Russian ship would try to force her way, and, from his point of view, was keenly aware that shooting at a Russian submarine without clear and documented provocation was not acceptable. He asked:

"Where are we relative to the cargo ships?"

"No news on number two. Number one is still in international waters, about two nautical miles east-northeast of our bow."

"Any indication of any small craft coming from shore?"

"No, sir. Not yet at least."

■ ■ ■ ■ ■

Captain Decker maneuvered his ship further to port to come closer to where he could see on his own Sonar where the INS *Protector* was now that she had reactivated her active sonar. He had heard the news received from the submarine and at this point did not think much of it. Yet, he had thought useful to connect by phone to David Heller to make sure that he had all the latest:

"Colonel Heller?"

"Yes, let's dispense with titles. What's up, Barack?"

"Just want to check in. Heard the communications from the INS *Protector*. Want to make sure I have all the orders I need."

"Understood. From our point of view, no change. We will allow any smaller craft to approach the Russian cargo ship, cargo ship one as we call it. However, we will raise the mine curtain to prevent any craft that has transshipped anything from returning to shore."

"Makes sense. What do you make of the Russian submarine?"

"At this point, I don't know. I worry that it reinforces the fear that one or both shipments are "sensitive" shall we say. So, please make sure that both your ship and INS *Protector* are as far away from the action as possible if we need to raise the mine curtain . . ."

■ ■ ■ ■ ■

"Captain Dayan?"

"Yes. What's up?"

"Message from the Russian submarine . . ."

"Message from the Russian submarine"?

"Yes, sir. They're asking us to stay clear of the Russian cargo boat. They're saying that we are too close to it."

"Reply that we are in international waters and claim freedom of navigation. Copy that to Captain Decker."

A minute later, the senior sonar operator came back:

"Torpedo ahead . . ."

"Initiate normal counter measures . . . Acoustic jamming. Report track."

"Torpedo still coming, jamming in place."

"Launch anti-torpedo torpedo . . ."

"Message from Russian submarine."

"So?"

"Says that first torpedo was a warning. Wasn't armed. Demands clear passage."

"Tell them to hold off for at least ten minutes . . . Move closer to the surface. Need to establish radio contact with headquarters. They'll see our maneuver and hopefully will comply. If not, be ready to fire torpedoes on my count."

As soon as the radio antenna atop the sail of the submarine was above water, Captain Dayan asked to be patched to Headquarters— the sail or fin of a submarine is the tower-like structure found on the topside surface of submarines. Within seconds, Yael Orbach was on the radio, with David Heller listening in. Mike Dayan quickly explained the situation. Yael was obviously not happy, but he first asked David for his advice. David asked a couple of questions with respect to the relative positions of the various vessels and then concluded:

"I would suggest fully surfacing and being far enough away that the Russian submarine cannot suspect the INS *Protector* fired at the Russian cargo ship one or any small craft. As a precaution, I would make sure that a Kovesh with torpedo bombs is in position to shoot at the Russian submarine if needed. However, that should be the very last resort."

He paused and argued:

"When the next Kovesh lands at Palmachim, make sure it carries both a torpedo bomb and a depth charge."

Yael agreed and relayed the message. As he was speaking, David interrupted:

"News incoming. Two Syrian supply ships are approaching Russian cargo ship one. Make sure the Eitan surveillance is in place and have the mine net raised as soon as the two Syrian ships have passed it."

Yael made sure that all operators were ready to execute the orders. He called Captain Dayan again:

"Be as far from the Orcas as possible, while still retaining full operational capabilities for them."

"Check."

Captain Dayan gave orders to start navigating with just the top of the fin exposed and to move away from the Orcas. Calling his Orca pilots, he asked:

"How're your signals?"

"Just fine, Sir. We can operate up to five miles away from the submarine drones."

Captain Dayan relayed the order to the pilot of the submarine:

"Maintain just under five-mile distance from Orcas."

■ ■ ■ ■ ■

David Heller decided to call Simon as the developments off the coasts of Cyprus and Syria were, in his view, starting to be quite serious. Simon seemed very calm, yet he told David that he would immediately call Aaron Spielberg, Israel's Defense Minister, just to be sure he was in the loop. David hung up, waiting for Simon to call back. Within a couple of minutes, Simon was back on the phone with David:

"Aaron is fully briefed. Predictably, Yael had already reported. We agree that we should not engage with the Russian submarine except if she fires another torpedo. If it does, our response will come from a Kovesh and will aim to disable but not sink the Russian submarine."

"The consequences would be dramatic either way, don't you agree, General?"

"I do, but we cannot afford to let aggression go without a strong response. Note however that our response would be a step down from their action, as we would only look to damage the vessel."

"Understood."

"Now, make sure you're on top of what happens with Russian cargo ship two. Where is it now?"

"Just a second . . ."

David looked on his screen and replied:

"Definitely sailing south of Cyprus. Cannot tell whether she's going to Tripoli or to Syria."

"Fine. Keep me in the loop please. But everything so far is absolutely first class. Thanks, my friend."

■ ■ ■ ■ ■

The plan was working perfectly. The first Syrian boat moored alongside the Russian cargo ship and the Eitan images clearly showed wooden cases, likely containing arms, being moved from one boat to the other. A couple of the cases seemed to be quite a bit longer than the others, but they still fit on the back of the Syrian supply boat, which the team estimated was probably around 200 feet long in total, suggesting that the aft deck probably could hold cargo just a tad more than 120 feet. Suddenly, Mark exclaimed:

"Damn it! We've got to change the plan!"

Seeing the surprised look on David's face, he explained:

"They're loading them one after the other. See the first one is already starting to sail back to shore. The mine net may not stop the second, depending upon where she sails relative to the first."

David calmly replied:

"Thank God, we still have the Kovesh and the torpedo bombs. Let's simply see what happens."

He paused for a second and then still very calmly added:

"My biggest worry is what the Russian submarine does when it sees the first supply boat hit the mines . . ."

The mine curtain was indeed about five miles due east of the Russian cargo ship and covered a channel width of about 250 yards. The screen image available to Mark and the team displayed both the current view of the sea, but also two points which were artificial echoes to show where the mines at each end of the net were. The idea was that the Orcas could still move the net north or south depending upon where the supply ship seemed to be going. Captain Dayan ordered the Orcas to move north "full speed" as there was no doubt: the supply ship was bound for Syria, not Lebanon. Mike Dayan knew that his Orca remote pilots had up to 20 minutes to position the mine curtain as that was about the time it would take for the supply ship to reach it.

The unloading/loading operations of the second supply ship were completed and the ship had started its own return voyage back to shore when three explosions shattered the general silence of the sea. The first supply ship had had an unfortunate encounter with one or several mines. She was definitely sinking, though her sister ship would have no difficulty rescuing the sailors who had had the time to jump into the water. The second supply ship accelerated toward the site of the accident, while Captain Dayan, looking at his own screen, calmly invited the pilot of the southern Orca to move the mine net further north. The northern Orca had lost its ability to move the mine curtain as any mine north of where the first ship hit the mines had been severed from the net; she still had about a dozen unexploded mines attached to it. The northern Orca released them and was returning to the INS *Protector* as fast as possible. Yet, the decision by Captain Dayan to have the submarine visible and quite a distance from "the action" meant that it would be a good ten minutes before the Orca would be close to enough for it to be "collected."

David instructed all team members:

"Be very careful and monitor doubly carefully the Russian submarine and all possible sonar signals. Stay on active sonar; I don't care if they can see us: they know where we are. We are not trying to hide. I want to know where the Russian submarine is and in which direction she is sailing. I also want to know whether the second Russian cargo ship continues its voyage or aborts the mission."

Calling Yael on the other line, David asked whether the frigate could sail a bit closer to the INS *Protector*, adding:

"Just to make sure that the Russians hesitate before doing anything stupid."

"You got it!"

CHAPTER.10

TEL AVIV, ISRAEL

David and Mark had decided to meet with Marvin Goldstein to discuss the plan to help Josh Steinmetz unravel what he could of the diamonds for drug trade in Iraq. Mark started the conversation with the observation that Mossad only had a few diamonds at that point, as he put it:

"The samples which Countess Renate's associate, Albert Hoets, cut and polished to demonstrate his process. About twelve stones."

Marvin had to interrupt:

"I would love to see how he does it, as I have really never heard of that technology before."

Mark calmly replied:

"You might well get a chance. But for now, the main issue is how we get these samples to Josh without attracting too much attention."

He continued with a very short summary of the current plan:

"We want to get the samples to Josh and get them there in a box which will allow us to track the terrorists down and to pass on a message to them introducing Josh, whose local name is Abu Musa as a very deep undercover agent for an unnamed organization."

"How big is the box?"

"Well, Marvin, that will be your first challenge. We have a dozen diamonds, weighing less than twenty carats together. So, volume isn't the issue. I would like the box to be able to contain a couple of cell phones, one for Josh and one for the terrorists, together with a letter purported to be from people who knew that diamonds had been sent in the first place."

"Why not from the organization that has sent the diamonds?"

"We can't say the group was the one that sent the diamonds; we have no idea who they are. Josh could be unmasked in less times than it would take to shoot him. We also can't say we are not because we would immediately be suspect, and the terrorists probably would not take the bait. So, it has to be subtle and yet sufficiently enticing that the terrorists take at least the first step."

Mark paused and added:

"I almost forgot, there should be a few more things with the box. We will need a couple of Russian-issue handguns, at least two extra magazines, and some lightweight tool to change his voice . . ."

Marvin exclaimed:

"That's a lot. But I think I might be able to help. Before I go there, have you ruled out him coming here or meeting someone somewhere?"

David interrupted:

"Not yet, but our concern is that we must vary the means of getting things to him. Erbil is a mid-size airport with only a few flights to places where we can be, though it's a full-fledged international airport. No flight to Tel Aviv, for instance. So, in reality, it's Ankara, Istanbul or someplace in the Arab world, where we would not be officially welcome."

He paused for a second and added:

"I know we might be able to count on Saudi Arabia given our prior undercover work together, but that might too "official" for them.

And even with respect to Erbil, having him show up too often at the airport to fly even to Damascus or Bagdad would appear suspect."

"How many times will you need to get to him in the end?"

Mark replied:

"Guessing three or four times."

Marvin had a broad smile on his face. He repeated:

"I think I can help you."

He started to describe a new tool which his group had developed, borrowing from a variety of current technologies. He said:

"We call it a guided rocket-like delivery."

He paused and was mischievously happy that neither David nor Mark seemed to understand. He explained that they used the technology associated with laser-guided bombs to create the delivery mechanism, which was very accurate and quite discreet. He mentioned that the whole contraption initially measured about four feet in length and nine inches in diameter, not counting the fins and tail, adding:

"We drop these from an Eitan, flying at 40,000 feet!"

David spoke first:

"How do you do it?"

Marvin replied:

"Let me describe the dropping mechanism and what happens when the "rocket" is dropped. Then I'll tell you more about the container itself afterwards."

David and Mark nodded, though they both instinctively feared that Marvin would give more details than they needed. Marvin said that the cylinder dropped from the Eitan has an internal guidance mechanism, which looked for and then locked onto a laser beam. That mechanism was located in the very front part of the nose cone. Once the cylinder had been dropped, the Eitan would move some short distance away and shine a laser beam on the delivery spot, the coordinates of which were provided ahead of time, adding:

"The Eitan has to be some distance from the dropping point so that the slope of the laser beam can be below the cylinder. Once the rocket has locked onto the laser beam its engine stops and the rocket keeps going in free fall until a preset altitude, usually around 3,000 feet. At that point, the engine fires up in reverse thrust to slow it down as much as possible."

He paused with a chuckle, conceding:

"The package still hits the ground with some speed, but that speed is not enough to destroy its contents because of a couple of tricks we have up our sleeve."

David interrupted:

"The reverse thrust, whatever you call it, isn't it noisy?"

"Unfortunately, it is not totally silent. Yet, that's why we start them at 3,000 feet. But if you don't mind, David, I need to give you some more detail."

"Go right ahead."

"Thanks."

Marvin explained that the whole descent of the rocket-package comprised four different phases.

"During the first phase, the rocket intercepts the laser beam. In the second phase, as it is now in free fall, the rocket is slowed by an umbrella-like wing which deploys from along the body of the cylinder. It is forced open by the speed and the air that enters between it and the body of the cylinder and needs to get out, thus pushing the umbrella to open and stay open."

Marvin paused and added with a smile:

"The beauty of the design is that this umbrella is deployed quite high up. As it is less than six feet in diameter, you can imagine that at 25,000 feet or higher it is simply not visible to the human eye, until you're looking for it and know almost exactly where it is going to be."

Returning to his earlier flows, Marvin went on explaining that, eventually, the vertical speed of the package is such that it tears the umbrella off, adding in passing:

"That's good gentlemen. That's energy which is not used to accelerate it . . . The remains of the umbrella will float off and eventually land somewhere but nobody will pay much attention to it. The third phase of the descent begins at 3,000 feet when the engine starts the reverse thrusts. It keeps going until it exhausts all the solid fuel left in the reservoir. At that point, both what's left of the reservoir and the engine in turn separate from the rocket. They keep falling, and one needs to be careful on the ground; you don't want to get hit by them. Their fall is pretty much vertical, except if there is a very strong wind."

He paused again and almost triumphally added:

"The fourth and final phase is for the rest of the rocket to hit the ground."

"Wait a minute, Marvin, isn't the rocket still travelling quite fast then?"

"Quite fast, I wouldn't say so, David, but it is certainly not floating down. Let me now turn to the structure of the whole rocket so that you understand why it works."

David and Mark looked at each other, worrying that technobabble was about to become the lingua franca, but still said nothing as they needed to understand Marvin's idea if it was going to be used. Marvin explained that the rocket was comprised of five parts; from the front to the back, it had the guidance mechanism, the solid fuel reservoir, the engine, a crumple zone and the cargo zone. He continued:

"Once the engine and the fuel reservoir, together with the nose cone with its guidance system have been jettisoned, the whole assembly is much lighter. So, it will still accelerate for the last couple thousand feet, but the speed will be manageable. By the way, I see your eyes wandering David . . . Are you wondering how the rocket can continue without a guidance system?"

"Well, frankly I was. Why?"

"Well, remember, we are now at one or at most two thousand feet above the target. The fall will be nearly vertical and there is no need to guide it. By the way, that's a good thing since we wouldn't have a way to do it: we don't have an engine any more . . ."

"I see. Smart. Quite smart. Anyway, what happens when it crashes to the ground? Doesn't it disintegrate?"

"Well, David, I'd be lying if I pretended that the rocket lands intact on the ground. It doesn't. In fact, you used the right word: it crashes. But it's not the rocket that counts; it's the contents, right?"

David nodded. Marvin continued:

"First, the crumple zone ahead of the cargo area crumples and absorbs a lot of the energy linked to the impact. But there is more, and, gentlemen, that's the *"piece de resistance;"* I'm very proud of it."

He paused to check that David and Mark were still following, and then finished:

"The real key, though, is in what I'll call the packaging. The crumple cylinder and the cargo cylinder are both protected by a substance which is said to absorb 94% of the energy. Sorry for the technobabble, but I must use it . . ."

With his hand, David motioned Margin to continue:

"That substance is a viscoelastic, polymeric solid. It "flows" like a liquid under load, or heat here. It's a thermoset, polyether-based polyurethane."

Seeing that he had lost his audience, Marvin said:

"In plain language, what happens is that the substance, which in its normal state is a malleable solid, is liquified by the energy and the heat that the crash produces. Thus, it can flow wherever it's needed, precisely following the contours of what it is meant to protect."

Marvin then started going into further explanations, but David stopped him mid-sentence clearing his throat and then asking:

"How long have we had this?"

"Oh! It's a brand-new tool. We've tested it in the Negev desert, near Ben Gurion University in Beersheba. That's where the substance was developed."

David asked:

"And?"

"Well, I will not say that I would guarantee that crystal glasses would get there unscathed, but none of what you want to include would be a problem, except, maybe, for the cell phones. However, I must admit that we have not used it in a real-life situation yet."

Mark interrupted:

"So, what's your recommendation?"

"To be honest, we need to take a few steps back. The tool I've just described may well be the solution, but it has its own limitations . . ."

Mark asked:

"Limitations"?

"Yes, the range of the Eitan is over 4,500 miles, so distance between Mosul, Erbil or wherever and Israel does not come into play. So far, so good. The general geography of the area where you would need to make the drop isn't I believe a problem either . . ."

David interrupted:

"So, what's the problem?"

"Well, the only issue for me at this point is one of size. I am almost certain that we could not include everything you want into a single package."

"Why?"

"Well, Mark, take the list that you've rattled off. Now imagine that I can offer you the volume into a cylinder that's about a foot long and, say, eight inches wide. Do you think everything would fit?"

Mark was obviously thinking, adding the various components in his head. He started to count out loud:

"The diamonds are peanuts, almost an afterthought. So is the voice box. Let's say therefore that we can put all these, the masks and two cellphones in one third of the cylinder."

"Beg to disagree. Your phones will take up about six inches."

"OK, Marvin. Grant you that. Would there not be enough for you to slide two disassembled Russian handguns and a couple of extra magazines in the rest of the cylinder?"

David interrupted:

"We should be able to test this easily. Having said that, I tend to think Marvin may well be right. See, the average handgun is about 8 inches long. Even though a bit shorter disassembled, I've got to think that the required diameter might become the binding constraint. Tell you what. Marvin, how would you conduct two drops? Then, we can always revert to one if we can find a way of packaging the whole in one rocket."

Marvin went on to describe the sequence involving a first drop containing what he called the "cheap stuff", which in the current case would involve the Russian handguns and their magazines. Once these have been dropped and reception confirmed from the ground via radio or telephone, they would know that the system was working in the local environment, and they would be ready for a second drop. The package in the second tail cylinder would contain the box with the diamonds and the two cell phones and the voice box hidden in a black N95 mask, just like those worn by so many people during the Covid pandemic. He added:

"I would actually suggest having several masks and a single voice box, as they weigh next to nothing and take even less space, if I can say so!"

Marvin was smiling broadly.

CHAPTER.11

TEL AVIV, ISRAEL AND MOSUL, IRAQ

Josh had listened with a great deal of care to all the instructions that Mark had given him over the phone. His first task had been to locate a place which he could use as a "formal" office where he might receive the terrorists if they desired to meet him in person, which everybody hoped they would. He rented a small store in a shopping mall, five blocks north of University Highway, near the eastern border of Al Shurta, a major neighborhood in the center of Mosul. The shop had two main rooms; the front room was where commerce would be carried out, while the back room would typically be used for storage inclusive of minimal toilet facilities. There were two entries or exists from the shop, one in front through which customers would enter, and the other in the back through which supplies or merchandise would typically be delivered. The front room at present contained virtually nothing, save a counter, shelving along the walls and a door leading to the back room. Josh had determined that the meeting would take place in the back room.

Mark had made it quite clear to Josh that he had to be ready to wear a heavy disguise, even if it did look like a disguise. In fact, he had added:

"Use the very first opportunity in the conversation, if there is one, to apologize for the disguise, arguing that your anonymity is crucial to your mission. You might even add that any attempt to uncover your identity would immediately lead to your suspending any discussion and disappearing back into the crowd."

Josh had decided that he would wear a traditional grey keffiyeh headdress, a square scarf usually made of cotton and kept in place with an agal, a dark head band. He would wear a black robe over a dark brown tunic. Finally, he would have a black N95 mask on, with a voice altering box in front of his mouth. Additionally, he would don dark glasses. Now, the purpose of the dark glasses would be twofold. First, they would of course make it that much harder for anyone to identify him if they met him in different circumstances when he was not wearing them. Probably at least as importantly, the glasses were of the special Mossad-issued recording variety. They would make it possible, afterwards, to see all the visitors and hear the whole of the conversation.

Josh had discussed with Mark the setup he was thinking of for the back room. His first comment struck Mark, but was in fact quite perceptive:

"I must stay seated. I am way taller than average, and I don't want to give them that simple hint."

"Great idea. How will you manage it?"

Josh replied that he would sit on an armchair that would be set behind a table with a short tablecloth, so that his visitors would be able to ensure that there was no trap under the table, adding:

"I will not get up to greet them, pretexting some pain somewhere."

Mark could only note:

"Smart; very smart?"

Josh added that he would place on the table the Russian handguns he was expecting, within very close proximity of each hand, in order for his "guests" to be quite sure that there was no mileage trying anything funny. He noted:

"I'll ask them to place any gun they most likely would carry on the table as well. Note, however, that I think there is very little risk they'll do anything the first time. After all, they will already have received the sample diamonds. Their reason for coming would have to be to get information on what they had to do to get more. So, I can't believe they would shoot the messenger. At the same time, I'll wear a Kevlar jacket under my tunic, just to be sure."

He paused and added:

"It's gonna be hot as hell . . . No air conditioning in simple shops here . . ."

■ ■ ■ ■ ■

Josh had been instructed to rent a car for the operation to be carried out the next day, with Mark clearly suggesting:

"We don't want anybody to get any hint at who you might be. They would recognize your current car."

Josh smiled, but replied:

"Makes sense, but you should know that there are plenty of old American jeeps in town. Mine is just like a couple hundreds of others."

"I would have guessed it. But still better safe than sorry."

Mark had asked Josh to pick up a point where the drops from the drone could be made. He had indicated that the plan was to make the drops at night, adding:

"That way, you should be able to see the rocket as it starts its reverse thrust with your infra-red binoculars. More importantly, you'll see the engine as it separates and drops, so that you can make sure you're in the clear."

He also indicated that the preference would be for a place that was as sparsely wooded as possible, readily accessible from a road, and yet with little or no risk of being seen by anyone up even at night. Josh asked Mark whether he was familiar with the Muslim daily prayer cycle. Mark's answer being not totally convincing, he reminded him:

"There are five prayers whose timing is quite specific and determined by the sun: Fajr is said at sunrise, Dhuhr at noon, Asr in the afternoon, Maghrib at sunset and Isha at night. By the way, Isha is often said before midnight, as it must officially be recited between Shafaq and sunrise. Shafaq refers to the red light in the western sky at dusk. Fajr Sadiq refers to the white light in the east at sunrise. So, the midpoint between the two is generally before midnight."

Mark interrupted:

"Very interesting. So, what time window would you suggest?"

"I would think that anytime between 1:00 a.m. and 3:00 a.m. is pretty safe. People have had an hour to fall asleep after Isha and have still a good two hours before Fajr."

Mark agreed and told Josh that he would clarify the actual window as soon as feasible. In the meantime, Josh was to identify the specific coordinates of the drop off point and conduct at least a couple of dry runs in the area at the correct time to verify his assumptions. Mark asked:

"How close to you want to be from the wreckage?"

Josh replied that he would prefer to stay quite clear of it, adding:

"As you know, I have done a couple of runs there, one to place the damaged briefcase and another to check on it. It seems that they have placed some guard on duty there. I'm not sure whether the guard is there 24/7, but I saw him both of the times I was there in the middle of the night."

"This brings up an interesting question my friend. How are you gonna deal with the guard when you need to place the diamond samples?"

"Not to worry, I have a plan and I will not be doing the same thing as last time. Same principle, though."

"I see. Do you have all the right material? I could easily add a few things to the drop off."

"Well, if you have space, a few more hypodermic needles with a sedative that I can fire by gun through a silencer would be much appreciated."

"No problem. How long do you want the sedation to last?"

"Give me at least an hour. I will load at least two if not three of them in the gun because they might suspect something, and I do want to have to shoot to kill if there is more than one person there."

"Quite sensible."

■ ■ ■ ■ ■

Marvin was with David and Mark when they loaded the two containers and rockets onto an Eitan drone. The last-minute addition of a dozen hypodermic needle bullets had not been an issue. Indeed, those look very much like run-of-the-mill ammunition. The only differences are first that they do not require as much powder to provide the necessary forward progress; the impact on the victim needs to be soft enough not to damage any tissue. The second difference is that the nose of the bullet is made of two parts; inside and at the tip of the usual cone, one finds a thin plastic cover over the needle. When the bullet hits the victim, the tip is broken as the thin plastic gives way and the needle penetrates into the flesh. The needle has a tip coated with a mild poison which brings a rapid loss of consciousness; the needle then discharges the sedative, a known anesthetic agent, a propofol variant, contained just behind it. Propofol has the property of acting very rapidly, and to offer the opportunity to induce relatively short periods of unconsciousness without major subsequent side effects. In fact, the rest of the cone also crumples down to absorb as much of the energy still in the bullet as possible.

The plan was that the first drop would start at about 1:30 a.m. Marvin explained:

"With nothing to slow the rocket down, it would reach a terminal velocity of about 320 miles an hour, if the package was dropped from 40,000 feet. In fact, with both initial and terminal slowdown phases, it will average a speed throughout its descent of less than 60 miles an hour. In short, it should take eight minutes to reach the ground."

He paused, seemingly quite satisfied to have demonstrated his detailed knowledge, and added:

"Allowing Josh ten minutes to retrieve the package, confirm that it is in decent shape and give us the go ahead for the second drop, the Eitan should be able to make that drop no later than 1:50 a.m. and then initiate its flight back to Palmachim Air Base."

About five hours after the Eitan took off from Israel, the three men were in the building from which most of the drones in service in Israel are remote-controlled. Located on Palmachim Air Base, it looked very generic from the outside, but the inside was incredibly impressive. It was a two-story building, with the second floor reserved for offices and resting rooms for pilots; the first floor was the major control center. It was about one hundred yards long and about half that wide. The end closest to the main door had a couple of offices, one on either side of the receptionist area. There were two conference rooms at the far end of the hall, one quite large and the other much smaller, with an emergency exit between them. Other than that, the room was fully open plan, with eight rows of individual cubicles, each of which was a control station for one drone. Each cubicle had enough space for three operators to sit in it. There were a few empty cubicles, suggesting some room for expansion. Typically, each day, operators would work two three-and-a-half hour shifts, separated by an hour of rest. That rest was crucial to keep them totally focused, very much like the practice for air traffic controllers who would be exposed to similar intense stress, possibly even more in places where there was a lot of activity.

The men were in a conference room which had a very large screen that allowed them to follow the progress of the drone, though what they were looking at were computer graphics driven by GPS signals and not real images. With a cruising speed set very near its top speed of 100 miles an hour, the Eitan would take almost six hours to get to the drop zone, which was about 570 miles away, as the crow flies. The pilot would however have to make a detour to ensure that he did not fly over Syria. Mark and David were therefore quite satisfied to see that there remained, as planned, a bit less than an hour before the first drop was to be made. Though everything had been rehearsed as well as could be expected, there was always some tension. As Marvin had carefully said:

"You don't know what you don't know."

Yet, Mark placed a phone call to Josh to ask whether everything looked all right. Josh confirmed that he could not see any light from where he was, suggesting that most people were indeed asleep. He had chosen a spot that was less than ten miles from Mosul somewhat south and east; he chose it because the area was totally deserted. There was a stand of five trees about twenty yards from the target area. Josh wanted to have them to provide some cover in the event the engine's free fall brought it down that close to the spot selected for the drop off.

A while later, which appeared longer to most than it really was, Josh's phone suddenly rang:

"First rocket has been launched . . ."

Josh pressed on the top button of his chronograph to start timing the fall and replied:

"Thanks, Mark. Will keep you posted."

Josh went straight for the stand of trees and scanned the sky in the direction from which the rocket should be coming. A few minutes later, his infrared binoculars detected a source of heat coming at him; the reverse thrust had ignited. He was following the trajectory with a great deal of care until he saw what looked like a small change in direction. This had to be the engine and its forward component detaching and now in free fall. He decided to dispense with the binoculars to have more flexibility to move if and when needed. In fact, he was surprised to see that the engine appeared to be falling in the direction of the other side of the target. The sound of the impact a few seconds later confirmed that it had reached the ground. The rest of the rocket was now falling, though at a lower rate of speed, and hit the ground about twelve feet from the actual target. He first waited to see whether he could identify any sound and hearing none looked around the horizon seeking any light that would have ignited. Feeling reassured that he was still by himself, he ran to the rocket, or rather what was left of it.

The front end, the rocket's crumple zone, was definitively crumpled. It looked like a folded fan—no space between any of the individual folds. The cylinder behind the crumple zone looked in as good a shape as could be expected, though still damaged. He opened it and saw that the guns looked fine. He assembled one of the two and fired a couple of blank shots just to be sure. He picked up his phone and called Mark again:

"Everything in order. Ready for second drop."

As instructed by Mark and Marvin, Josh then set fire to the cylinder where the shock absorbing substance had solidified anew. He wanted to make sure that nobody could identify it, and, in the process, was burning all that he could of the last two elements of the rocket. Running to where the engine and forward cone had fallen, he also set them on fire with some extra gasoline and moved away. Marvin had indicated that there were no markings pointing to Israel on any of the parts of the rocket and the engine was run-of-the-mill and could have been purchased anywhere.

Two minutes later, the phone rang again:

"Second drop initiated. Same target."

Josh repeated exactly the same steps as in the prior drop and was impressed to see that the various elements of the rocket all hit the ground in generally the same area. He collected the contents of the second cylinder and set fire to the two new pieces that had hit the ground. Having satisfied himself that there were no obvious traces of his presence, he went for his car. He knew that someone would somehow eventually find the debris from the rockets, he was satisfied that no one would likely find out what had happened.

Suddenly, he stopped in his tracks and fell to the ground. Though he could not see anything, he could hear the sound of human voices. They came from where he had left his car. Crouching, he retrieved his infrared binoculars; he was hoping that he could get a sense of what was happening. Unfortunately, the trees and the leaves between him and the small area off the road where he had parked were too dense. He could not see anything and was not capturing any sign of human heat. What could possibly have gone wrong? Was he somehow followed without noticing it? Did someone see his car and start looking for whoever should be driving it? He decided to stay on his ground and wait for a while. He checked that his phone was set on vibrate thinking: *the last thing I need is for it to ring*! Afterwards, he would move forward, literally a foot at a time and keep using the binoculars. He had placed the contents of the two rockets into a bag that he had attached to his waist. He had however been careful to place the box with the diamonds and the two telephones directly into the lower pocket of his cargo pants, under his tunic, on his left side, just in case.

CHAPTER.12

TEL AVIV, ISRAEL, ANTWERP, BELGIUM AND EASTERN MEDITERRANEAN SEA

As he did on his previous trip to Antwerp, Mark flew an Israeli Air Force private jet to collect about two pounds worth of cut and polished diamonds at Albert Hoets' s townhouse. Albert was as warm as ever when he saw Mark. As usual, he took him to his large office, and, when reaching the desk on which Mark could see a tray of cut diamonds was waiting for him, he noted:

"There is one stone in there with which I took some liberty. Its rough volume and general shape seemed a perfect fit for a pear cut. I could not resist attempting that. I was able to get this 9-carat pear shape which I think is one of the most beautiful stones I have ever seen. I could have split it into two or three and gotten two or three 2-carat brilliant cut stones. But I feel that you should give the stone to whomever provides you with the diamonds. It will demonstrate the quality of his work."

Mark thanked him profusely. He poured the diamonds cut by Albert and his team into a couple of velvet bags which Albert was handing to him. He opened his briefcase on Albert's desk and carefully placed the two bags inside. He then pulled another velvet bag out of the briefcase. That one which Albert had given to David and him when they last visited contained rough diamonds. Mark declared:

"This is the balance of the rough diamonds that we needed to have your cut."

Albert smiled and replied:

"So, we are nearing the end of the assignment . . ."

"In terms of cutting and polishing, yes. But we're only starting when it comes to tracing where the diamonds go and when they re-appear. Your help will be priceless."

Albert smiled again and nodded his agreement. Mark concluded with a question:

"When should I plan on collecting them and whatever is left from the prior package?"

"Give me another week or two, if possible, though I could probably have it done in a week if we keep going full out. But I'd like to give our cutters a bit of rest if we can afford it."

Mark indicated that the two-week target was perfect. After having thanked Albert, he was happy to accept the chauffeur-driven ride back to the airport which Albert was offering.

■ ■ ■ ■ ■

Meanwhile, in Tel Aviv, David was monitoring progress with respect to the Russian cargo ships. The reaction from the Russian submarine to the sinking of the first, and then the second Syrian supply ships had been immediate. It had formally accused the INS *Protector* of having torpedoed the vessels. Captain Mike Dayan replied that given her location and heading which the Russian captain could verify on his own sonar, she could not have fired a torpedo at either of the two Syrian boats. Whimsically, he added:

"Could the explosion have come from inside rather than outside the ship?"

The reply from the Russian submarine was quick and short:

"Could not have exploded from within."

Captain Dayan then replied that, if the vessel was hit from the outside, she could have hit a mine field. He noted that he was not involved in it, suggesting again to the Russian captain that he should look at his own Sonar to compare the location of the explosions and the location of INS *Protector*, adding:

"I cannot be in two places at once. Submarines usually fire from the bow, and sometimes from the stern. You can't fire torpedoes broadside."

■ ■ ■ ■ ■

The second Syrian ship had indeed followed the same heading as the first after having transshipped the armament from the Russian cargo vessel to her own extended platform aft of the bridge tower. After the first ship had run into the mines and exploded, the second ship was probably not more than a mile away. She had approached the area with great care and first rescued the sailors that could escape the first vessel. The mines which had been placed were all sufficiently powerful to stop a ship, but not enough to destroy her completely. She was therefore going to sink, but every sailor should have a real chance to escape the wreckage, particularly as a supply boat does not have much activity below deck, other than the engines and the fuel tanks.

Meanwhile, immediately after the explosion leading to the demise of the first vessel, the Orca pilots had chosen first to lower the mines to a somewhat greater depth. This would allow them to maneuver without being immediately picked up on sonar by the Russians or even the Syrians. Though the operation was somewhat complex as they no longer had one net with each Orca holding one end of the net; they now had two much shorter nets, with the northern Orca having a much smaller one than the southern Orca as the explosion had occurred about one third from the northern end of the net. As instructed by Captain Dayan, the northern Orca released what was left of its net, which Captain Dayan estimated to be about fifty yards in length and started sailing back toward the submarine, starting in an easterly direction. The southern Orca had a difficult task. Though having no control over the "northern net" which was now floating freely, it needed to bring its own net close enough to the other so that it could somehow recreate a semi-continuous net with what was left of the northern net, as the natural buoyancy of the mines allowed the top of the net to remain relatively horizontal. Captain Dayan estimated that the new net that was supposed to intercept the second Syrian supply boat was probably around two hundred yards. After the mine net was released, he instructed the second Orca pilot to follow in the same direction as the northern Orca, moving eastward, and to remain at maximum depth. Captain Dayan waited for the Orcas to be clear of the area before sending a signal which would "tell" the mine net to rise closer to the surface. Mike Dayan had contacted Barack Decker on Sonar, asking him to relay the information to David Heller on the radio. His message to David and Yael reflected the reality:

"The net is shorter and there has to be an overlap between the two tips away from the drones. I hope we can still intercept the boat, but there should be a Plan B."

Turning to Plan B, Mike Dayan asked whether a Kovesh equipped with torpedo bombs was also available. David confirmed that one was circling at 45,000 feet and would be able to launch a bomb with a delay of less than two minutes. Captain Dayan smiled; he knew that that would be more than enough to hit the second Syrian supply boat.

They were comfortable that the first line of attack would be the mine net now located a mile east of its earlier position, with the Kovesh serving as backup if the second Syrian ship managed to sail through the mines unscathed. With a wink, Captain Dayan added:

"We must all understand that we don't have the same control on the net as before. The two halves are independent, and any maneuver is at best clumsy."

The message from David came straight back:

"Don't worry, you can only do what you can do."

Luck was with the team, however, in that the Syrian ship resumed its trip back to shore after its rescue operation and followed exactly the same heading as she was following earlier. That was in fact the same heading as the first vessel was following before she exploded. Perversely, she hit the two halves of the mine screen with a delay of less than ten seconds and the explosion was thus more powerful than the first. The Russian cargo ship immediately made haste toward the scene of the explosion to rescue any sailor they could pick up. That is when the Russian submarine chose a show of force.

The reaction of the Russian submarine was immediate. She fired a couple of torpedoes in the general direction of INS *Protector*. Captain Dayan was not overly worried as the distance between the two vessels was such that he had more than enough time to maneuver out of the way and launch countermeasures. Yet, after having had a radio conference call with Yael, which he could do as the ship was partially above water, he replied to the submarine:

"Stop all aggressive behavior, failing which we will be forced to respond in kind."

A third torpedo was launched in the direction of INS *Protector*. It was followed by a missile that ostensibly came from an Israeli vessel. It turned out to be the INS *Dragon*, a submarine as well, which was sailing further east than the Israeli Navy frigate which the Russian might be able to see on Sonar. The missile hit less than a hundred yard in front of where the Russian submarine was believed to be submerged. Though no "official reaction" came from the Russian submarine, there were unmistakable signs that she seemed to be retracing her steps somewhat. Seeing that the captain of the Russian submarine seemed to accept standing down, Captain Dayan sent a clear message to Yael and David:

"Russian submarine moving away. Don't think hostilities are over. Believe she is on her way to shepherd the second cargo vessel."

The second cargo ship was by then halfway between Limassol and Mazotos, the last two important towns on the southern coast of Cyprus, before she would come abeam Larnaca International Airport and Larnaca Bay. The fact that the ship had remained on an eastern course after passing abeam Paphos on the western coast of the island was not sufficiently clear to determine with any certainty whether she was eventually going to sail toward Syria or Lebanon. The next major indication would be given as she went abeam Larnaca. There she could veer to port and sail in a northwesterly direction; that would clearly indicate that she was going to Syria or close to it. On the other hand, she would need only the slightest turn to starboard to sail in an east-south-east direction which would suggest a destination of Tripoli and thus Lebanon.

Mossad had planned to follow the same tactic it had with the first ship. First, a mine curtain would be set up by the two Orcas, which had had all the time needed to sail back to the INS *Protector* and resupply themselves. They clearly could not yet move into position, though they were sent in a direction such that they would be appropriately located if Tripoli was the Russian target. If it was not, they could keep navigating in a northern direction and stop wherever it made sense once any Syrian supply ships had been sighted.

■ ■ ■ ■ ■

Mark with him, David called Yael to make sure they had all their ducks lined up properly:

"Yael? David Heller here. I need a few minutes of your time . . ."

"I'm sure it has to do with the Russian situation, right?"

"Absolutely."

David went on to discuss the current plan in its latest details and suddenly came to a halt. He asked:

"What if the Russian cargo ship is bound for Tripoli? It has a submarine escort which had already once shown a measure of aggressiveness."

Yael interrupted:

"Excellent question. I was on the phone with Aaron myself a short while ago. The War Cabinet is actually meeting as we speak. We obviously do not want a major incident at sea, but the ship cannot be allowed to dock in Tripoli."

"What do you expect from the War Cabinet?"

"Not sure. My recommendation to Aaron is that they should try the diplomatic route, letting the Russian Ambassador know that we will intercept the ship if she seems to on the way to Tripoli. I know that these would be Lebanese waters, but, as you know, we are on record with the position that we will not tolerate major arms shipments reaching our shores or shores that could supply Palestinian terrorists. So, at the very least, our initial threat would likely be that we would request permission to inspect the vessel."

"And then?"

"Well, honestly David, that's where I stop because everything beyond that is speculation. As you know, we have the frigate INS *Destiny* in the vicinity, though in international waters; we have INS *Javelin* a missile boat on the way and, but this is obviously not known to all but a small group; additionally, another submarine, INS *Dragon*, is submerged within the same general area. We are ready for many scenarios, but I hope that we won't be forced to use any of that."

David asked:

"One scenario which I have been mulling over involves the Russians trying to get to Tripoli, to test our resolve now that they have seen what happened to the first delivery. They would now sail toward Tripoli though their goal would never have been there but Syria . . . Just as was the case with the other cargo ship. Does that make any sense to you?"

Yael replied:

"Funny you should ask. This is exactly the scenario which I shared with Aaron and which I'm sure he will discuss with his cabinet colleagues . . . Probably among others!"

"Brilliant minds . . ."

"Let's not go too far, David."

"I know. I know. One implication of all we've discussed may well be this: we probably do not need the Orcas where they are. Should they move up the coast?"

"Tough call. We still don't know whether Lebanese vessels will or won't rendezvous the Russian cargo ship . . ."

"Understood. Now, if you don't mind, let me suggest a real curveball . . ."

"What if the Russians are awaiting reinforcements?"

Yael reassured David. He explained that the Israeli Navy was monitoring the movements of all the Russian Navy ships east of Greece. He added:

"As you know, the U.S. Sixth Fleet, which is headquartered in Naples, Italy, is responsible for patrolling the whole of the Mediterranean Sea. Aaron instructed me to get in touch with them to let them know what we were doing. One of my aides actually just sent a message to the Harry S. Truman aircraft carrier strike group. Coincidentally, they are sailing in our general direction."

He paused for a second and calmly concluded:

"Whatever the Russians do, we are ready. There will not be any provocation on our part, or on the part of the Americans, but I would imagine that the Russian submarine captain would think twice before engaging too aggressively. In fact, I would argue that he's already gone a bit too far . . ."

Though it might have appeared that Yael was in mid-sentence, he suddenly stopped and said:

"Just a second, I have an urgent incoming call. I'll put you on hold . . ."

He picked up the other call:

"Yael Orbach here."

"Sir, we have news from the Russian cargo ship front."

"What?"

"The second cargo ship appears to have stopped and to be at anchor abeam the Bay of Larnaca, over twenty miles offshore."

"Anchored in international waters, right?"

"Correct, sir."

"Thanks. Keep me posted if anything changes."

He returned to the conference call with David and Mark:

"David, your crazy idea as you called it may actually be right on. The second Russian ship is now anchored in international waters abeam Cyprus, abeam the Bay of Larnaca."

CHAPTER.13

TEL AVIV, ISRAEL, MOSUL, IRAQ, AND THE EASTERN MEDITERRANEAN SEA

Crawling more than walking, Josh gradually made his way toward his rental car, though he was aiming to emerge from the bushes on the side of the road at least a hundred yards ahead of the vehicle. His progress was made difficult and tedious by the constant need to keep listening for voices or any other sound that would suggest that someone was looking for him. His infra-red binoculars were only helping marginally as the relative thickness of the bushes made it very tough to pick up human heat. He was however encouraged to note that he was neither hearing any voice or noise, nor was he picking up any sign of heat.

Suddenly, he stopped in his tracks as his binoculars had picked up something that was warmer than its surroundings. It was not exactly next to him, but it looked as if it was probably no more than fifty yards to his left. He waited for a while and was encouraged to note that the warm "thing" did not seem to move much. He resumed his progress only to find that the amount of heat appeared to be increasing. His mind was racing. What could that be?

The answer came to him very quickly, though all his technologically advanced equipment did not help. He had just picked up a smell which definitely reminded him of farm animals. He stood up and moved a bit faster though still carefully toward the road. Once there, he was happy to note first that the car was still there and second that there was no one near it. He first checked that the silencer was appropriately mounted on his handgun. He had what he later called a random chuckle remembering a recent discussion with an acquaintance; they had tried to distinguish between a silencer and a suppressor. The friend had argued that a suppressor is for eliminating muzzle flash while a silencer is for reducing the sound. Josh knew that, in fact, the two were virtually interchangeable. He kept thinking: *funny what the mind focuses on when under stress!*

With his right hand on the gun that was still in his right pant pocket, he walked toward the car. As he was less than ten yards from the car, he saw an old shepherd with a small flock of sheep and goats. He was by himself, sitting with his back against a tree while most of the flock was lying down, probably ruminating their last meal. As he was reaching his car, he stepped on a small piece of wood which cracked under his weight. The sound woke the shepherd up. Josh greeted him politely and the man replied with a partially toothless smile. The fact that Josh was wearing the traditional cape over his tunic and had a dark Keffiyeh on his head made the encounter totally natural for the shepherd, who went straight back to his slumber after Josh had wished him a pleasant rest until Fajr when he would turn toward Mecca and say his morning prayers. He thought:

The voices I heard must just have been the shepherd talking to his sheep. They weren't voices, but simply a voice! Need to relax, man! A lot of wasted stress and energy . . .

Josh drove the rental car back to the shophouse he had rented to serve as his local "office" and parked it in front. He was surprised to see that a sign on a store two doors down indicated that it, too, was for rent. Josh made the decision, on the spur of the moment, to call the rental agent as soon as possible to rent it as well. Indeed, though, in theory, there were two ways to get into or out of the store he had already rented, it would not take a terribly ingenious adversary to post people in the front and in the back of the store. Josh or whoever else was inside would effectively be trapped. Josh knew from having been inside "his" shophouse earlier that there were passages from one store to the next, through the attic, despite the fact that there was no floor up there. These passages involved some gymnastics as they required climbing into the attic of the first store, walking on the beams that were a part of the roof support over all the stores and eventually climbing down into the backroom of the second store, having simply passed through the attic of the store in between them. There was also a more complicated escape route that required stepping onto the roof and then running across as many stores as needed, but Josh had thought that the simpler the better—unless one worked in the dark, a man on a roof is not particularly discreet.

Given the "precious cargo" he was carrying, Josh thought it prudent to remain at the store and, in effect, to spend the night there. He needed some rest as he fully expected the challenges of the next day to be quite significant.

■ ■ ■ ■ ■

Yael Orbach and David Heller were sitting in David's officer when Mark Levi came in. He was visibly excited.

■ ■ ■ ■ ■

Earlier, The Israeli Navy had recalled the INS *Protector* to Haifa. There were two submarines "on patrol" in the area of where the first Russian cargo ship had unloaded its freight and the two Syrian supply vessels had been sunk. Yael had decided to recall the INS *Protector* because it had been "seen" by the Russian submarine. Thus, "seeing" her navigate in a southerly direction, which is definitely away from the action, might suggest to the Russian captain that the Israeli Navy was standing down in its local activities. Yael counted on the fact that the Russian had not figured out that INS *Dragon* was close enough to carry out any duty that might have been assigned to her sister ship.

In fact, Yael had a totally different plan in mind. As had been done in other search and rescue operations requiring a high level of discretion, he had decided to have the INS *Protector* tow a deep-sea rescue vehicle to the area where the two supply ships had sunk. He wanted to retrieve whatever cargo they intended to bring ashore. In order for the operation to be carried out in total secrecy, the vehicle was tethered to a submarine while at the base, in Haifa, and the two were then sent to the general area where the two Syrian supply ships had sunk. The whole operation would thus be carried out under water, and could not be seen from above, even with the most sophisticated equipment. The area where the two vessels had sunk was just outside the very top of the Levantine Sea, between Cyprus and Syria. The rescue operation was able to identify a wreckage field about 2,000 feet down. Yael had noted:

"We are lucky the waters are so shallow. The average depth of the Levantine Sea is over 14,000 feet deep, though in all honesty that depth is reached further west, off Crete."

The operation associated with the control of the second Russian cargo ship still needed assistance of both Orcas since they were available. This had required the discreet transfer of the Orca pilots from INS *Protector* to the *Charm of the Sea* captained by Barack Decker and then from there to the INS *Dragon*. Thankfully, everything could be done underwater and thus would likely not have been noticed by the enemy. The equipment needed to control the Orcas had been packed in a waterproof container so that it was not exposed to potential interference by sea water.

Yet, at present, the Orcas were needed in the arms retrieval effort because no human can dive to the depth where the wreckage was strewn. The goal of the operation was to retrieve as much of the cargo as possible, principally to gain intelligence as to what the Russian were supplying to the terrorists. The Orcas were thus used to patrol the bottom of the sea and use a special underwater tool in connection with the deep-sea rescue vessel to capture the cargo. The INS *Dragon* therefore had to sail close enough to the debris field for the Orca pilots to have perfect control. Once the operation was completed, the Orcas would then stay with the INS *Dragon* as the INS *Protector* brought back the deep-sea rescue equipment and the arms retrieved back to Haifa.

The operation took the better part of a whole 24-hour period as the wreckage field was spread over an area of approximately a square mile. The sailors were not surprised as they knew this reflected both the fact that the two boats had been hit by mines in different, though relatively close locations, and the effect of currents on packages of different weight and density. The Orcas effectively followed virtual gridlines, using their onboard cameras to identify anything that might be of value. When any such item was located, the images were first reviewed by Captain Mauri Breyer and the staff of the deep-sea rescue vehicle, after which they were forwarded first by Sonar to the *Charm of the Sea* and then from there by radio to David Heller. Once the decision was made to retrieve or not to retrieve the piece of cargo, the task was split between the Orcas and the deep-sea rescue vessel to pick it up and eventually load it into INS *Protector.*

■ ■ ■ ■ ■

Mark Levi was indeed quite excited as word had come in from Haifa after an inventory of the arms that had been retrieved was compiled. He said:

"As we would expect, there were a number of cases of relatively classical weapons. However, the real surprise is that there were also a number of missiles which were considerably more advanced than anything we've seen so far. The new stuff has to do both with their guidance mechanisms and with their having multiple heads."

Yael interrupted:

"Multiple heads"?

"Yes, sir. We have known for a long time of MIRVs, you know Multiple Independently targeted Reentry Vehicles. A variant on the ballistic missile theme. What's surprising here is that these don't seem to have ballistic range. I wonder whether they're designed to confuse the Iron Dome."

■ ■ ■ ■ ■

Mark was referring to Israel's all-weather, air defense system, which was designed, with the help of the U.S., to protect the country against incoming rockets or artillery shells. Unfortunately, though it might arguably be the world's most advanced missile defense system, it had only been 90% accurate. This meant that 10% or so of the missiles might go through. The good news was that current belief as to the capabilities of the dome was wrong. A few important wrinkles had been surreptitiously added which improved the system accuracy and power.

■ ■ ■ ■ ■

David was the first to react:

"How serious is that, Yael? Do you know?"

"Well, the Iron Dome is obviously not my specialty, but from what I know these missiles would make the job quite a bit more complex, but not necessarily impossible. Having said that, I think we should discuss this with Aaron as soon as possible. He needs to know and, eventually I guess, so does the War Cabinet."

Mark brought back the conversation to the nitty-gritty operational details. He conceded that the news was crucial as it certainly had the potential to alter the balance of forces on the Israeli/Syrian border, particularly in the Golan Heights. Yael and David were nodding. Mark surprised them with his next point:

"My real concern, though, is that we don't know who the intended recipients are. We suspect that the first two loads were bound for Syria. OK. But we know that ISIS is also trying to rebuild its forces in Syria. Could ISIS be the real eventual client?"

Yael interrupted:

"This is an excellent point. My own worry is that it makes little sense for the Russians to take the risk of this operation if they are trying to do is to supply the Syrians. After all, we know they have a base in Syria: Khmeimim Air Base is currently operated by Russia as per a treaty that was signed with Syria in August 2015."

He paused and added:

"But that's not all. Guess what? The base is located south-east of Latakia, the country's principal port and one of the two harbors we had identified as the likely destination for the Russian cargo vessels."

Mark whistled:

"Very interesting."

"Indeed. But on that basis, why have cargo transit by sea when you can fly it in?"

Mark and David were looking at each other. David exclaimed:

"Damn it! That must mean that this is not a standard transaction. What if it meant that the Russians are supporting a rebirth of ISIS and doing it so to speak in the back of the Syrians? I'd love to know if Syria has the same missiles as those we fished from the bottom of the Levantine Sea."

Yael conceded: "I'm afraid you might well be correct. That could very well be. That's why I've given instructions that we keep a very close eye on the area from which we retrieved the missiles. I'm pretty sure Syria does not have deep-sea rescue capabilities, but I'm sure Russia has. So, I wouldn't be surprised if Russia had brought a rig into Syria. I want to know if they go down to look for the stuff."

He paused and added:

"And if they look for it and don't find it . . . I want to know that as well."

CHAPTER.14

Josh had carefully prepared the scene for his meeting with the suspected drug dealers, if there was to be one. When he had rented it, the back room of the store had quite a number of empty cardboard boxes strewn about the floor; Josh arranged them such that they looked carefully packed and placed against the walls. When done, he was happy to note that the whole of the back wall, except for the space around the rear door had been thus "decorated." He had also disposed a few of these cartons on the left-hand wall, reserving the center right of the room for his desk. The desk, which was very plain, came with the space, as did the very basic armchair that he had placed right behind it. There were also a couple of chairs that he had set in front of the desk, and each at a forty-five-degree angle relative to the desk.

Prior to starting his "decoration" he had stopped at one of the nearly two dozen electronic stores in Mosul, most of which were located on the left bank of the Tigris River and, in fact, relatively close to the shopping center in which he had rented his store. He wanted to have a few cameras which would provide him with some degree of advance notice of what was happening around the building. He placed one camera outside over the front door, another outside over the back door and the other two inside: one to capture all that was happening in the front room, and the last one right behind himself so as to film whatever was happening during the meeting. All cameras were connected to his computer and had recording features including sound. The computer that he bought was a powerful laptop which could both link up with the internet and with the local communication networks. The laptop was open in front of him and to his left, though one might question why the external keyboard attached to the laptop seemed so far away from him, and to the side which would either indicate that he was left-handed or that he did not intend to use it. Additionally, he had connected an external secondary screen which he had set up near the front of the desk and to his right. That screen displayed the images from the security cameras he had installed.

■ ■ ■ ■ ■

Josh's next step was to return the car he had rented to receive the packages containing the merchandise that Marvin and Mark had sent. He knew there was no way he would use his own car, nor should he even consider continuing to use a car which had been seen in at least two locations: once parked in front of the store and the other near the place where the packages had been received. He did not think that there was any real reason to suspect the poor shepherd and his small flock of sheep and goats, but why take any risk when you do not have to? He walked to another car rental store, which was quite convenient as it was located within the grounds of the University, near the central library and less than a half a mile from University Highway, which would lead him directly back to the store.

From there, he rented a local four-wheel drive SUV, which, he thought, would allow him to drive closer to the site where the plane had crashed. He went first to his apartment to change into his more traditional clothing: a dark brown tunic, a black cape and a black keffiyeh held by a black agar. He had his own handgun in his right pocket, with the silencer mounted. He had two magazines with him, one with regular bullets and the other with bullets equipped with hypodermic needles. He waited until Isha prayers were said and then took his time driving to the vicinity of Erbil.

Having been there at least three times, since the night when the plane had crashed, he knew the way quite well. More importantly, he had found back roads near the site that allowed him to approach relatively close to it, without running the risk of being seen. As usual, he had his infrared binoculars, more to detect heat and thus likely human beings than to see more clearly what might be ahead of him. The moon was high in the sky and provided good, natural light; yet it was still quite dark on the ground. He parked the car about a half mile away from the site of the crash and continued on foot. He fully expected that there would be at least one, possibly two "guards" near the wreckage. He assumed that the drug dealers had not lost hope of establishing some connection to whomever owed them a fortune in diamonds, and thus that the guards were there for that purpose.

His binoculars picked up two heat sources. The first was clearly taller than the second. He thought: *This must be the guard.*

The second was quite close to the ground. For an instant he wondered whether it could be an animal. He kept moving forward but was increasingly careful. As he was getting closer but still without seeing anything, the heat generated by each target, the central part of the image started to seem very, very hot. That is when he realized he was looking at a wood fire.

He knew that he now had to move extremely quietly so as not to be seen by the guard, as he had by now confirmed that the second heat source was indeed a guard. However, was he asleep or standing? Further, he still did not know whether there might be other guards in the vicinity, though he very much doubted it; he had not seen any on his prior reconnaissance trips and was not picking up any additional heat source. He saw that he could move about ten yards to his right without running the risk of entering the guard's field of vision. However, at that time, one thing was crystal clear: the guard was definitely awake and looking around. Having gotten to that new station, Josh repeated the prior precautions: the infrared binoculars did not signal any additional danger. He picked his next intermediate target, this time slightly to his left, but principally forward another ten feet. Reaching it, he was now less than thirty yards from the guard. He had been careful not to wear any deodorant of any sort, if only to make sure that the guard, if there was one, could not pick him up by his scent.

He weighed the potential benefit of getting closer to the guard versus shooting at him with a hypodermic needle-bullet. He was about to set himself to take a shot when the guard, for some unknown reason, started to walk. In fact, worse yet, he seemed to walk in Josh's direction. Josh decided not to do anything immediately, as he was relatively well-hidden by the tree trunk just in front of him. Additionally, he had his gun at the ready, so he thought:

Why shoot at a moving target if I don't have to? Plus, he's moving towards me. I know he's here and he doesn't know I'm here. At least I hope he doesn't know; or else . . .

He held his fire and soon saw the guard ostensibly getting ready to return to nature some of the liquid, probably tea, that he had consumed earlier. Josh, "as a gentleman," let him finish his business. He saw him seem ready to move back toward the fire and his earlier position. Josh let him get there and pulled the trigger when the guard was close enough to the fire that its heat would keep him warm while he was taking a drug-induced nap, though not too close so that he would not risk falling into the fire either. He allowed him the time to settle on the ground and counted five minutes to be absolutely sure that the drug had to have taken full effect.

Josh then moved toward the guard, but quickly stopped in his tracks. There was a voice calling. He assumed that it was calling the guard, who, he knew, would surely not reply. He retreated ten feet behind the guard and used another tree trunk to hide. He did bring the next bullet up into the firing chamber of his handgun, having already made the decision that the site was going to become a slumber party for at least a couple of the drug dealers. The voice kept coming closer, though Josh felt that it seemed to be moving less swiftly. He thought:

Couldn't have seen anything yet and can't possibly see me, unless they have this echo-system that allows his voice to seem to come from in front of me while he would be behind me. Could they have infrared binoculars as well?

The voice and the man that went with it were now in the clearing, quite close to the fire. Josh waited until the man got a bit further from the fire so ensure that he would not fall in it and then fired. The man had a sudden urge to sleep and fell to the ground. Josh waited another five minutes to make sure that the man would not open his eyes and see him. He then walked to the second "guard" and deposited the box containing the diamond samples, a cell phone and a letter, right next to his right arm. He was sure that he could not miss it when he woke up.

■ ■ ■ ■ ■

David and Mark had worked diligently drafting the letter, first in Hebrew knowing that it would eventually be translated into Arabic.

"Dear friends,

We know that the plane which crashed here was carrying a small fortune in diamonds. Judging by what is left of the plane, we suspect that the diamonds went up in smoke along with quite a bit of the flammable insides of the plane.

Whether we are or not the group who sent you the diamonds does not matter. However, we are quite interested in the goods you are selling. We have access to the same high-quality diamonds and would be willing to entertain a relationship. The few samples we are leaving along with this letter should serve to confirm our credibility and our goodwill.

One of our representatives is currently in Mosul under very deep cover. You can get in touch with him using the cell phone you will see in the box with the diamonds. He is prepared to meet you in a place he has selected. His phone number is pre-programmed into the cell phone. To reach him simply turn the telephone on and press 111.

Please refrain from contacting whomever had sent the diamonds to you, or anyone else about this letter. We have excellent sources within a number of organizations and would find out quite rapidly. Our revenge would be quite unpleasant on the members of your group, and we would show no pity.

Should you decide to reject our offer, we will expect you to give our representative a call indicating to him where he can recover the diamond samples. These samples are for you to keep if you decide to accept our offer.

This offer is valid for the next three days. *ma'a Salama.*"

■ ■ ■ ■ ■

The first guard woke up first, though his friend followed him within a minute or two, in other words before the first guard had recovered his full consciousness. At first, the guard was not surprised to see his colleague as he was well aware that the time for his rotation out of the scene of the wreckage had passed. Yet he could not understand why he and his replacement seemed both to have fallen asleep. Josh's bullet had hit him in the right shoulder area, largely because Josh wanted to be sure he avoided any vital part of the body. The guard noticed some pain in his shoulder and wondered what might have caused it. He had not yet connected the pain and his falling asleep.

With the second guard now awake, they started talking about the incident. The second guard complained of a pain in his right thigh. He raised his tunic and saw a clear bruise. It was still only a small mark, but the blue ring around the point of impact was clear enough that he realized that this was unusual. That was the point where they both realized that they had been shot at, with something that put them to sleep. Looking at their watches, they concluded that they had slept a good thirty minutes.

The second guard saw the box with the diamonds, the cell phone and the letter and opened it. He picked it up and could not hide his surprise as he shared it with his colleague. The letter was on a simple sheet of paper, which was folded, but not sealed into an envelope. He read it aloud and fell silent. This did not compute. The threat was worrisome. The offer might be interesting. Yet, both were on their guard. At the same time, it was crystal clear to them that they were in no position to make a decision. They had to take the letter to the elders and see what they elected to do. Though they hesitated leaving the wreckage without surveillance, they decided to go and carry the letter together. A cynic might suspect that both wanted credit for their effort and also were keen to ensure that the other did not escape with some or all of the loot.

CHAPTER.15

TEL AVIV, ISRAEL AND MOSUL AND ERBIL, IRAQ

Josh's "special phone" rang. He calmly picked it up and listened. The voice at the other end did not identify itself, other than saying that his group had received the letter and would like to talk. Josh was aware that both his and the phone that had been "offered" to the drug dealers contained a geolocation feature which allowed *Mossad* to begin to track where the drug dealers were. He knew therefore that he needed to keep his counterpart on the phone to give the technicians in Tel Aviv as long as he possibly could for them to locate the phone.

He replied that he would be happy to meet with representatives of the group. He had been careful to put on the N95 mask with the voice box adapter which disguised the sound of his real voice. He set out the three crucial conditions that would have to be met for the meeting to take place:

"First, there must not be more than two representatives from your group. Second, they may be armed while outside of the shop, but they will need to deposit their arms on the same desk I deposit mine when we are together. Finally, I will sit at the desk and remain seated for the whole meeting. There will be two chairs for your representatives."

The voice at the other end of the line was ready to accept the conditions though it was not convinced by the requirement of being unarmed. It said:

"How will we know that you do not have another gun hidden some place?"

Josh replied that unfortunately they would not, but neither would he be sure that they did not carry extra arms as well. He brought his interlocutor closer to the main point arguing:

"In the end, what is there for you or me to gain if we get into a shooting match in the store? OK, I can see that we would have lost about $1 million in diamonds, those which were in the box. Not a small sum, but, as you know, in our business, not that much. From your point of view, I do not see any upside. I don't know the value of the diamonds that burned in the accident . . ."

The voice interrupted:

"Had to be $100 million!"

"That's what they owed you? Well, you see . . . The only chance you have to recover any of that is to have a new arrangement. I don't need to tell you that your other counterparty is probably furious that the plane was shot down."

"How do we know your group is not responsible for downing the plane?'

"Again, you don't. Neither do we know you didn't do it either. However, imagine that we knew the plane carried such an amount of diamonds, don't you think that we could have done something smarter than shooting it down if our only goal was to replace that counterparty in your current trade?"

The voice seemed to calm down, all the while Josh was delighted to have been able to hold it on the phone for so long. Assuming that his colleagues in Tel Aviv had all they wanted, he brought the phone call to a conclusion:

"Are you willing to meet? I will not have anything more to give you at that time, but we can begin to get to know each other a bit better . . ."

The voice disagreed:

"We cannot have a meeting if there is no exchange of goods at some point there. You said you will hide your identity, which we accept. But what would we gain meeting you?"

Josh replied that they could establish some rules, agree on pricing and delivery and set the date of the next delivery. The voice was hesitating. Ostensibly, it was attracted by the opportunity to have at best another possible customer, and at worst someone to replace the other. The voice came back with what it said was its last offer:

"Two junior members of our team will meet you where you specified and under the conditions you specified."

"Fine with me, but will they be allowed to negotiate?"

"Will you allow them to use their cell phone while there?"

"No, because I do not want to take the risk that they would shoot any picture of the room or of me."

Josh paused to see whether the voice would react violently. Hearing no immediate reaction, he continued:

"However, they would be welcome to leave the store and call you from the street."

"Will you allow them both to leave to call? I don't want one to be by himself with you inside while the other is outside . . ."

With a chuckle which was dutifully reflected in Josh's "corrected" voice, he replied:

"I see we both do trust each other a lot."

He added:

"Fine with me. By the way, I would prefer but do not insist on the meeting taking place after *Isha*. It will be more discreet for both your people and me."

The voice agreed and they chose two days hence just after midnight as the date for their meeting.

■ ■ ■ ■ ■

Josh immediately called Tel Aviv on his secure phone to report and to find out what they learned. Mark replied and started with profuse congratulations. He added:

"Frankly, we did not expect that your interlocutor would stay on the line for so long."

He said that there was good news and bad news in terms of what they learned. The good news is that they had managed to identify a precise location for the phone the voice was using. The bad news, however, was that the location did not tell them much:

"The caller was probably in a car that had travelled on the road linking Mosul and Erbil. He was just east of the Great Zab River, actually near a village called Kalak. However, though there are isolated farms or small industrial buildings in the area, I would bet that their actual headquarters must be none of those . . ."

"The giveaway has to be the highway, right?"

"Absolutely and the fact that he was on the highway; that's why we think he was in a car."

"Can you keep tracking him?"

"Yes, if he does not switch the phone off, which, by the way, he certainly didn't do right away."

Mark switched to the most important point:

"Are you ready for the meeting? Would you like some backup?"

Josh replied that he was ready and did not think he needed backup for that one. He repeated the rationale he had presented to the voice:

"They have absolutely nothing to gain by killing me, other than the $1 million in diamonds. And, since we know that the $100 million sum the voice blurted out happens to be correct, you'd have to assume that they are looking for a lot more than a mere million dollars."

Mark calmly replied that he respected Josh's view and in fact tended to agree with him. Yet, he told him that a discreet backup would be relatively easy to organize. In fact, almost in passing, he asked:

"Do you know that Mehmet has a private pilot license?"

"He does?"

"Absolutely. So, it shouldn't be difficult for him to rent a plane, file a flight plan to Mosul and serve as a discreet backup for you. Might even come and get a plane from Tel Aviv if he prefers; wouldn't take us more than a few minutes to change the tail code to point to a different country of registration. Could use I for Italy in place of our 4X. The backup wouldn't ever have to appear, but knowing that a gun behind you is pointed at the two representatives of the drug dealers might give you comfort . . ."

Josh was clearly thinking and after a minute came back with a polite refusal. He argued that he had not had the opportunity to see what the drug dealers would do in preparation for the meeting. He told Mark that he had a couple of cameras strategically located outside of the store, both in front and in the back, which would allow him to keep track of what was going on around the store between then and the actual meeting. He added that he also had a couple of cameras inside the store which would allow him to see whether the drug dealers would even attempt to enter the store before the meeting. Mark conceded:

"Looks to me as if you're very well prepared, Josh. Can you find a way to broadcast the cameras to us as well?"

"Sure can, unless someone shuts off my internet access."

■ ■ ■ ■ ■

Josh had kept a close watch on the cameras ever since his conversation with Mark. He was not surprised to see a couple of individuals walk in front of the store on at least three different occasions. They would stop and peer inside, seemingly not fazed by the sign on the door which said: "temporarily closed." Josh had organized for a couple of timers switching lights on or off in both front and back rooms. He did not want the store to look at if it was continually closed, though the sign on the door remained. The same two people seemed quite interested by the alley that ran along the back of the store. They went as far as testing the rear door, which they may have been surprised to notice was metallic. They would also have found out it was locked.

Josh was delighted to see that the same two characters did not seem to be paying any attention to any other store in the small mall, including the one two doors down. This was the store which Josh had also rented to serve, if needed, as an emergency entry or exit. It was also equipped with a similar camera set up, just to make sure that it continued to offer the protection which Josh sought. He had also installed light timers, but, in that store, did not post any sign on the door. Whoever attempted to get in would have immediately noticed the door was locked, yet it did not say when the store would re-open.

In the morning of the day prior to their meeting, Josh noticed some greater degree of animation. The number of unknown characters in the neighborhood had increased and, though they were milling around in the normal crowds, Josh thought it necessary to call "the voice." Josh simply said:

"Hello!"

He recognized the voice at the other end of the phone when it replied:

"Hello."

"Just want to bring to your attention that our agreement calls for up to two people to come visit with me. There are quite a few more of them milling around now and the door to the shop will not be opened and the meeting cancelled if I see that the two associates you nominated are not alone."

The voice mumbled a few incomprehensible words and assured Josh that his two representatives would be alone after midnight. Josh simply replied:

"I sure hope so!"

■ ■ ■ ■ ■

Josh arrived at the shopping mall in the late afternoon. He parked his rental car in the alley behind the second store, two doors down. He retrieved a few small packages out of the trunk and entered the second store through the back door, which he first unlocked. He assumed that he was being observed, though he trained himself not to look around. Once inside the store, he locked its back door and opened one of his packages. It contained a telescopic metallic ladder, which he deployed. He used it to climb up through a trap door into the unfinished attic in the rafters of the store. From there, and after having retrieved the ladder and folded it back down, he walked carefully from one beam to the next, crossing over the store that separated his two rentals. The last time he had left the back room of the store where the meeting was to take place, he had kept the attic trap door opened. He carefully closed it up after having gone through it and climbed down the ladder he had extended anew; he found himself on the floor. He had to be more careful in this store than in the other because he had set cardboard boxes such that there was some space for one person to walk between them and the wall. Once in front of the door to the back alley, he slid three boxes back to hide the space he had created. Nobody seated in front of the desk could possibly guess that the wall was not where it appeared to be.

Once inside the back room, he discreetly used his flashlight to find his way to the door separating the front room from the back room. He closed it and switched on the light in the back room to get it ready for his visitors. Though there were no obvious traps, he was careful to ensure that everything was in the place it was supposed to be. In particular, he took the time to sit for a good five minutes on each of the two chairs and carefully went around the room to check that everything was OK. One thing he had learned over the years was that the best agents had managed to train themselves to notice unusual patterns. They called it diffuse attention, or involuntary observation. Thus, they might be looking straight ahead while their brain would be noticing something in their peripheral field of vision that, somehow, did not look right. He was delighted when the exercise revealed a couple of anomalies he had originally seemingly overlooked; he was quick to fix them. He was now ready to receive his visitors, though they were not expected to arrive for another four hours or so. That would give him plenty of time to monitor the various comings and goings in front or at the back of both stores.

CHAPTER.16

TEL AVIV, ISRAEL AND MOSUL, IRAQ, AND SOMEWHERE IN THE AUSTRIAN ALPS

David Heller called Countess Renate on the phone. He needed her help again with respect to the diamonds:

"Countess Renate?"

"David, good to hear your voice. Please give my best to Simon when you see him."

"Sure will."

Switching to the topic at hand, David explained to Countess Renate that the first few diamond samples had been handed over to the drug dealers. He did not want to go into unnecessary details as to what was going to happen, how, and to whom, but he knew that Countess needed to reach a few people in her network. It was now time to warn the market, but in a very discreet, almost confidential fashion that diamonds bearing a particular mark on the girdle were of particular interest to Albert Hoets who would vouch for their quality. David and Mark indeed, and with Simon's accord, thought that there could not be a better test for Samuel Eisenstein's invention. Albert would then sell the diamonds back to Mossad, which would pay using the real diamonds Josh had initially captured.

They needed Countess Renate because only she would have the contacts needed to make sure that the news reached those people it should without ever being leaked to people that did not need to know. The last thing they wanted was for dealers to start to question the value of diamonds with the tell-tale "W E" Hebrew letters on the girdle. If that happened, the whole plan would collapse, as one could expect that the drug dealers would no longer accept these diamonds as payments. Having, in effect, an ultimate buyer in place who would vouch for the quality of the stones would protect the operation against the risk of someone being more successful than anyone so far and detecting that those were synthetic diamonds.

Countess Renate outlined a plan which really started with Albert Hoets in Antwerp. Once he had finished cutting the last of the rough diamonds supplied by Mark Levi, he would get in touch with a few of his closest friends and clients. She insisted that his reputation was such that she could not and would in fact never ask him to lie to anyone. He would simply tell the story of his recent experience, omitting a few details without making the story definitely false or misleading. She explained:

"I agreed with Albert that he would contact a half a dozen contacts telling him that he had just had the order of a lifetime. He would say that he had cut about 20,000 carats of investment quality diamonds, which come from a single source. He would explain that he had tested the diamonds and had not been able to detect anything that would point to the conclusion they were not genuine. He would, however, also note that he had never seen such a quantity of diamonds in perfect "D" and "E" color, internally flawless, and so relatively homogeneous in terms of size and shapes in the rough. He could honestly say that he was able to cut a few extraordinary stones in sizes ranging up to nearly 10 carats, though the vast majority ended up somewhere between 1 and 3 carats, the sweet spot of the diamond investment market. He would conclude with a cynical admission:

"In murder mysteries or thrillers, you often read that if everything looks too good to be true, it usually is. Well, in this case, the lot does look too good to be true. However, to the best of my abilities, if they're not genuine, I don't know what they are."

David commented that the plan looked excellent, but still had to ask:

"What happens if someone decides to spread the rumor that they are not genuine? You know my worry with respect to Josh in particular . . ."

Countess Renate replied that she would expect the risk to be minimal for two reasons. The first was that Albert would ask his trusted friends to let him know immediately if they found something wrong. She added:

"You have to assume that it is going to take some time for the first of these to get anywhere near any of these dealers."

Turning to the second reason, she surprised David:

"I know from Albert that he has tried virtually every test which he knows how to carry out. I even know that he contacted the International Gemological Institute, the top institution in the world with respect to certifying gemstones. It has an office in Antwerp, near the zoo, and probably not more than a mile from Albert's office. Frankly, if they did not detect the fake, I suspect that we are generally safe, my friend."

David surely appreciated her use of the pronoun "we" to describe the safety which she felt surrounded the experiment. He could not resist asking the next question, though it was at best peripheral to the topic at hand:

"What does that mean for these diamonds? What if nobody can tell they are synthetic?"

"Well, David, my guess is that someone will have to come clean at some point. Your idea of placing a mark on them is surely quite smart. The key is that we have two fail-safe elements."

David looked puzzled, so she explained further:

"Albert offering to buy any and all of the diamonds with that mark on the girdle will, if anything make the diamonds even more expensive. Further, from his point of view, he knows that the more he purchases the more profit he makes since we have baked in a profit margin for him in the rate of exchange between those and the real diamonds."

Back on topic, she concluded:

"My real expectations, for our project, is that we will find out where the diamonds are and through which hands they transit, as people will be looking for the mark. Now, the question remains: at what point in their distribution will people notice the mark?"

■ ■ ■ ■ ■

Josh's instructions to the two representatives of the drug dealers were quite precise. They were to arrive within fifteen minutes after midnight. They were to enter through the front door which was unlocked and to walk directly through the internal door to the back room.

The two smugglers followed the instructions and found themselves standing at the entrance of the back room. Josh said in perfectly accented Arabic:

"Greetings, gentlemen. Please be seated on either of the two chairs on your side of the desk.

The two representatives could not hide their initial surprise. Josh's face was effectively totally hidden. He wore a black keffiyeh with a black agar, a black face mask from which his beard could be seen protruding below and a pair of dark glasses. Some of his black hair was visible also on the side of his face, but, to an unexpecting guest, it certainly was an unusual sight. Noting their discomfort, he added:

"Please, do not mind my appearance. You must have heard that I work under a very deep cover, and I pretty much have to kill anyone who sees my face. With what I am wearing, you are totally safe. Please, as I said earlier, sit down."

He added:

"You can see that my two handguns are on the table in front of me as I had indicated I would do. Please set your own guns on the table, on your side."

More surprised than anything, the two men complied with the instructions. They finally sat down on the two chairs. Josh asked them whether they had a message from the elders for him. The man on Josh's left spoke first:

"We are prepared to offer to you partially refined heroin in exchange for polished and cut investment grade diamonds."

Josh asked:

"Have you heard from your other buyer . . . You know, the one whose plane crashed."

"We have not, but I know that our elders sent them a message telling them about the crash. We also know that they replied something, though nobody told us what."

"Are you prepared to tell me how many diamonds you want per hundred kilos of heroin? Wait a minute, before we go there, how refined is your product?"

"We really do not know how to answer your question, sir."

Josh erupted in some controlled anger to impress his guests saying:

"Really, how do you expect me to agree on anything if we do not agree on price per some preset unit of weight given a minimum level of refinement. Are you selling gum, prepared opium, partially refined heroin or pure heroin, for instance?"

The two men were looking at each other and seemed genuinely not to know how to answer. Josh asked:

"Would you like to go outside, call the elders and come back?"

The two men smiled and jumped up. They walked toward the front room and Josh could follow their progress thanks to the cameras that broadcasted their images onto his screen. He noticed that there was an animated discussion, although he could not obviously make any sense of what they were saying, as he could only see the images, though the sound was also recorded but not available to him in real time. He saw them put the phone back into their pockets and enter the store again. Once seated, the man on the right this time said:

"Our elders will only allow us to say that our product is probably best described as partially refined opium. At this point, they expect to receive about 1-carat investment grade diamond per kilo."

Though the two men could not see it, Josh was smiling as he replied:

"Now we're talking. Two other questions, gentlemen. The first deals with delivery. How often and what quantity each time"?

The man on the right spoke again:

"We can meet your needs however you define them. We do not need to sell a set amount each time. The way we worked with our prior buyer was for him to tell us what they were ready to take, and we would give them a delivery date."

Josh calmly replied that this same approach would work for him. He then asked:

"How does the delivery work?"

The same individual kept doing the talking:

"It has to be away from any town, and we want the exchange of opiate for diamonds to take place at the same time."

"Are you telling me that the plane which we assume had diamonds for you was expected to fly out with heroin?"

"Yes, sir."

"What safety guarantees do you offer? After all, once you have the diamonds, you can also get to keep the opium, right?"

"Ours is a business which requires some ongoing relationship. I fear that our prior customer was in fact scared that we may have shot the plane down to get the diamonds without delivering anything. I suspect this has to be why they don't seem to have come back to us with anything the elders were willing to share . . ."

Josh made it look as if he was deep in thought. However, he had already made up his mind. He would offer them a first deal involving a relatively modest amount of heroin and thus of diamonds, if only to test how the system might actually work. He asked:

"I understand the need for verification. I want to suggest a specific protocol which will allow me to verify that the heroin is what I expect it to be and you to check the diamonds."

The same smuggler replied:

"We'll have to confirm with the elders, but this seems fair."

Josh came back with an offer:

"Could we consider an exchange involving 100 carats of diamonds?"

Josh could see the men process his offer. They would not commit right away but asked if they could again go make a phone call outside. They were back within five minutes:

"We are allowed to accept this offer. However, our elders want to know how they can be sure the diamonds are of the same quality as the samples you provided."

Josh had not anticipated the question. He thought for a few seconds and replied:

"We both have the same problem, don't we. You cannot be sure about the diamonds, and I cannot be sure as to the quality of your merchandise. Our initial local inspection should dispel the most obvious doubts. But we all know that one cannot perceive the exact quality of heroin by just placing a small amount on the tongue or see the quality of diamonds simply through superficial inspection. So, please don't take this the wrong way but why don't we agree that this transaction will be on trust. You will have all the time you need to test the diamonds and I will be able to test the merchandise."

The man on the right still did not appear ready. Josh added a degree of flexibility:

"If it will make it easier for you, I am prepared to cut the size of the order in half or even more. It lowers the risk for both of us."

Josh clearly saw that he wasn't going to get an answer. He said that he was ready to wait a few days if that could help them. He added:

"Your elders have my phone number, and, by the way, I have theirs. Let us bring this meeting to a close and agree that someone will call me with a final response within a couple of days at most. Simply know that I will need at least two, maybe three days to organize my side of the bargain."

With that, still without getting up, but leaning forward from his armchair, he invited his guests to retrieve their guns at the same time he was removing his from the top of the desk. The two men stood up, took their guns and left. Josh watched their movements on the various cameras until he heard that they had closed the front door. He still waited a little while longer until he lost them in the dark of the night.

He immediately stood up and got rid of the mask with the voice box, as well as the dark glasses. He kept the light on in the back room but switched it off in the front of the store. He retraced the steps he had taken earlier in the day until he was in the other store, with the ladder folded. While he was in the second store, he exchanged his black cape and *keffiyeh* for clothing of a much lighter color, though he kept the black agar. He checked on his computer tablet the views from the camera which focused on the alley. Finding it apparently deserted, he carefully opened the back door, closed, and locked it and went to his car.

He had just opened the driver's door when he heard the sound of an engine revving up. He only had the time to step out of the way before the vehicle passed right by the left side of his car and kept going much too fast down the alley. It would have hit him had he not jumped to take cover in front of the car. He swore under his beard:

"Bastards!"

Yet a few seconds later, he calmed down and thought:

Hey! You know nothing of who these people were. Grant you the timing seems too close to be a pure coincidence. But . . .

He was still ruminating when another thought crossed his mind. He made a mental note to himself and drove calmly and prudently toward his apartment, though he was careful to stop some distance away and park the car in a different parking lot. All the while checking he was not followed, he walked briskly until he reached his building and eventually, after having ridden the elevator to his floor, stood at his front door. He noted with some sincere satisfaction that nothing seemed to have been touched while he was out, and that observation covered a couple of traps he had set up so that any intruder would have surely left some evidence of his presence.

Once inside, he got rid of the heavy clothing he was wearing and, though it was still night both in Mosul and in Tel Aviv, he called Mark. Mark did sound as if he was still asleep a few seconds earlier, but he quickly listened quite carefully to Josh's report. The one new thought was the idea which had creeped into Josh's mind after the car incident. Josh rhetorically asked:

"And what if the vehicle actually belonged to the dealer's other customer?"

Mark immediately picked up on the implication:

"You mean . . . You mean that somehow the other customer knows enough about these guys that they have been following them. That led the other customer to what effectively was you. Still, a couple of things don't compute for me."

"Go right ahead. I have my own doubts too. So, we can compare thoughts."

"First, why did they go after an individual coming out of another store"?

"I thought of that as well, Mark, and I don't know. My working assumption is that this was supposed to be a message. What message, by the way, I don't know."

"I can see that, but why would they have not waited for someone to come out of the first store? Does it mean that they know, whoever they are, that you have rented two stores?"

"I bet there were two cars. One in front and one at the back. Whether they were both just conveying a message that one should be careful, again I don't know. Maybe the one at the front was going to follow anyone coming out of the store. As far as the one at the back, we know it wasn't trying to follow me since I was coming out of the wrong store. That one may simply have been confused. In the dark, they may have miscounted the number of back doors."

"Hmmm. Not sure if I buy that, but I'll concede it's plausible. Secondly, why did they not barge into the store after they had seen the two guys leave through the front door? It must have taken you a while to get up and lock the door."

"Honestly, did not think of that. Let me think . . . One possible explanation might be that they wanted to know more about me, as the contact for the two guys, but didn't want to confront me. This gets me back to the idea that this was a warning. Something like "be careful, we don't want competition in our territory" which might make more sense. In short, they may be trying to discourage me."

"Again, Josh. Plausible. What are you going to do?"

"Besides being a lot more careful and establishing a closer surveillance of the store and its surroundings?"

"Yes . . ."

"I think I'm going to ask you for a backup. I'm gonna need a delivery of a few diamonds, and I wonder if Mehmet could be both the delivery man and the backup. After all, nobody knows him here."

"I'll talk to him. You'll need to book your backup into a hotel if everything works. I think you two should not be seen together in any circumstance. You may need to use your classic communication tool to discuss the details before he gets there."

Surprisingly, Josh concluded:

"I hate to seem greedy, but one extra body may not be enough. Remember, one of our working assumptions is that the local drug traffic may be controlled by ISIS. If that's the case, we may need even more support . . . At least, now, we know we're getting somewhere."

CHAPTER.17

Mark and David had asked to meet with Simon. They needed his views on at least three important issues. First, they had to deal with Josh's request for support. Ostensibly, they felt quite comfortable with the idea of having Mehmet Isaac join him for a while, though his position as local head of *Mossad* for Turkey could not be ignored for a terribly long time. This was all the truer as trouble was still brewing in the Eastern Mediterranean, offshore Cyprus. The idea that there were at least one or two additional bodies needed surely made the problem more important and more difficult to resolve.

The second issue had to do with the challenge associated with Josh's probable success in exchanging synthetic diamonds for partially processed heroin. The problem of bringing the diamonds into Mosul had already been addressed and resolved: Mehmet would fly a twin turbo-prop airplane belonging to *Mossad*, though disguised as being registered in Italy. The small physical size of any package made it quite manageable, though one should never assume that going through customs and immigration in a third country would necessarily be routine.

The third issue related to the stalled situation offshore Cyprus. The Russian cargo ship had ostensibly dropped anchor in international waters. One had to assume that she had done that based on instructions received from the submarine, or from an even higher authority. This had to mean that the submarine was in some way requesting some reinforcement. The Russian Navy base in Tartus, Syria usually accommodates only up to four medium-size vessels. However, it has the ability to provide servicing and refueling facilities if needed, even for much larger ships. Having said that, they also knew that a drone overflight had suggested that there were no significant attack ships at harbor at that point. All three men knew that the Russian Mediterranean Squadron, principally supplied and supported by the Black Sea Fleet would never be more than a short, few days from the action if needed. That probably constituted the main risk. Finally, the agreements in place among Black Sea states provide that any such state may transit ships of any tonnage through the Istanbul and Dardanelle straits. Certain permissions are officially required to be obtained from Turkey, but it is not always a really binding constraint.

In answer to Simon's first question, David replied that the highest current priority had to be with the challenges in Mosul, adding:

"Josh has made quite a bit of progress. He will need 100 carats worth of diamonds and should receive 100 kilos of partially processed heroin. The key question has to be: what does he do with the heroin?

Simon asked:

"What's the plan?"

Mark took over and replied:

"We have only made two decisions. The first is that Mehmet should not take the drugs in his plane. Drug trafficking is much too serious an offense, even if he was to use his diplomatic cover. The scandal would be mammoth if he was ever found out . . ."

Simon interrupted:

"Couldn't agree more, though we may have another option, still involving Mehmet. Anyway, it does beg the question: what do we do with it?"

"Well, our second decision is that we do not need to do anything with the first load. The plan is to keep it in the strip mall, although we are thinking of using the second shop rather than the one where the meetings are held."

David interrupted in turn:

"Mark, Simon has not been briefed to that level of detail."

Turning toward Simon, he continued:

"Do you want more on this or are you comfortable?"

"Don't need more at this point. Thanks. I suspect that the risk of keeping some of the drug in Iraq at this point is quite manageable. But it does raise even more forcefully the question of backup for Josh."

He paused for a few seconds, absorbed in his own thoughts and then simply smiled at David and Mark saying:

"You might consider a visit with Marvin Goldstein. He called me to remind me that the old Kovesh drones that could carry people were still operational. I'm sure he's thinking that they might be a part of a possible solution: ferrying agents in and taking the heroin out . . . Personally, I've got my own concerns on that front, but I'd like you all to know the full range of options. Then your decision will be that much better informed."

■ ■ ■ ■ ■

Marvin was as always quite cheerful when Mark and David visited him at Palmachim Airbase. They had agreed to meet there because that was the place from which most of the drones were controlled and where they were stored when not in flight. He greeted David and Mark saying:

"Well, gentlemen, let me show you what might well be your solution . . ."

He paused and led through a double door to a hangar that housed four drones: the Kovesh drones[8] which had started life in the U.S. as a RQ-170 Sentinel. The RQ-170 was like a flying, triangle-shaped wing; it had no tail, and its engine took up the middle portion of the wing. The air intake for the jet was above the wing eighteen inches or so beyond the leading edge; the body of engine made up a good part of the fuselage which protruded mostly above the wing. Israel made a number of modifications to transform the Sentinel into the Kovesh. To make it into a stealth aircraft, the drone was painted in a darkish grey color and its external parts coated with stealth material; Israel had also developed notched landing gear doors and sharpened the leading edges of the wing. Finally, and most importantly, the engineers moved engine exhaust from below to above the wing. On a different note, they had enlarged two bays that sat on either side of the engine, sort of fairings above the wing really, as they still had to preserve the almost flat shape of the underside to ensure stealth. As modified, the drone was capable of flying at about half the speed of a jet fighter, about 700 miles an hour, plus stay aloft for about five hours. Marvin concluded:

"With the distance from Palmachim to Mosul just short of 600 miles, distance should not be an issue, not would there be any need for the drone to refuel while on the ground there."

David showed his delight though he wanted to raise at least two important questions. First, he wondered whether the drone would offer sufficient cargo capacity to bring back the heroin. Marvin replied that the maximum payload in the cargo bays would be about 8 tons, though there were ways where one could trade off total flight range by playing with the amount of fuel taken onboard and cargo weight, adding:

---

[8] See "Operation Kovesh" by the same author. Barringer Publishing, 2020.

"We can of course carry a heavier load if we are prepared to take a lesser amount of fuel."

Mark replied with what looked like a non-sequitur:

"But we would lose a lot of room to maneuver, correct?"

"I'll grant you that but, fully loaded, the drone has the ability to fly the route almost three times. So, I'm pretty sure that we could get you up to 10-ton payload and still have enough flight range to carry out the mission."

He paused for a second and added:

"Clearly, one thing we must consider is density . . ."

"Density?"

"Yes, Mark. Of course, the size of the cargo bays also determines the volume of cargo that we can load. So, with relatively light density cargo, like heroin, we'll have to make sure we have enough space. Volume becomes the issue, not weight."

Turning to David, he asked:

"You said you had two questions; what's the second?"

"We need to figure out how we can land and take off without being noticed."

"That's absolutely the right question. Frankly, we will need to discuss it in more depth. Much more depth in fact. But, before we discuss anything, we need facts, lots of facts. As a first step, I would suggest that we send an Eitan to observe any activity at the airport for at least two or three full days, covering both nighttime and daytime. Can you also get Josh to observe how many people are there, when and for how long?"

"Will certainly do. Our going in assumption is that whatever we plan would have to happen at night. With any chance, they don't staff the airport at night, since we believe there are no commercial flights."

"Sounds reasonable. One thing I'd like to know is where their air traffic control center is."

"As I just said, Josh tells us that there is no scheduled air service there at this point. The Iraqis hired the French group in charge of the Paris airports to renovate the airport in 2020. But things have been moving quite slowly. Yet, we do know that the one runway is operational—it runs almost perfectly north-south."

Mark offered his conclusion:

"To me, subject to some additional reconnaissance work, it would be tempting to think that we should have minimum trouble using a Kovesh, or maybe two of them, to bring a couple of additional agents in and to retrieve them a few days later. The return trips of the drones could be used to get some of the heroin out. Yet, I doubt very much that we could safely plan on organizing ten round trips. Someone would be bound to notice one of the movements and that would effectively make any additional flight impossible. So, I would not want to do anything on the drug front other than a return trip until any and all agents have been successfully lifted out of Iraq."

■ ■ ■ ■ ■

Mark spent the bulk of the next few days making sure he could answer all the questions that had been raised with respect to the use of Mosul airport by the Kovesh. He could clearly see that there was only limited traffic at the airport. As expected, his team in Tel Aviv did confirm that there was no scheduled service. Effectively concluding:

"The airport is a bit of a construction site."

The leader of the team, Omer Feinberg, expanded a bit on that statement:

"We've been able to see a few airplane movements. They involved small crafts, both twin- and single-engine planes. So, people do land and take off. Also, during the day, we saw a number of helicopters using the area. Absolutely nothing at night, by which I mean from sundown to sunrise."

Mark asked:

"Any indication of air traffic control?"

"None to speak of, although there is a fully operating crew in Erbil. They seem to control the airspace in the broad area. Remember there's just a tad more than 50 miles between Erbil and Mosul as the crow flies. We're only assuming that nobody controls the final approach or aircraft moves on the tarmac, if you can call it that. The tower is definitely under repair: it had to have been subjected to shelling during the war. In short, VFR only."

Omer paused and seeing Mark's facial expression added:

"Visual flight rules . . . Sorry. It means that there is no instrument help on landing."

Mark needed something a bit more specific:

"Anything in the immediate surroundings?"

"Nothing to report really. As you know, the airport is smack in the middle of town with buildings pretty much in the immediate vicinity. There's a corridor that used to allow take-offs and landing, and still does, by the way. I would not rate the place any more dangerous than any other, but no more secure either. It's got to be better than the old approach into Kai Tak airport!"

(Omer was referring to the old airport in Hong Kong which required an almost 90 degree turn in final approach as the plane was among high-rise buildings. Passengers on the right-hand side of the plane at times reported having seen what was happening in the apartments they flew by.)

Mark asked again:

"What do we know about ISIS activity in the area? They used to control the town, didn't they?"

Omer summarized their findings:

"Again, there isn't much solid data to report. We know they've been chased out of the area. Yet, we also know that they're trying to regroup. We believe that their camp is further to the west, somewhere between Mosul and Raqqah in Syria, though we think they are still operating in Iraq rather than Syria. There isn't much to the east and north as that's the part of Iraq that's called Kurdistan. Plus, as you know, due north is Turkey which really is not supporting them."

Mark asked:

"What's the conclusion on the use of the Kovesh?"

"I brought all the information to Marvin Goldstein as you had asked. He does not see much of a physical limitation. The major concern though is not with that."

Mark seemed quite interested and asked:

"Where is it?"

"It's the issue of what would happen if things went awry. First, we'd have to make sure David and maybe even Simon are on board with the risk that some lone terrorist might be lurking somewhere. You never know. Second, you've got the whole issue of what you've taught me: plausible deniability. There are thousands of eyes who could see the drone landing or taking off and we know that the finger would be pointed directly toward us."

Mark concluded:

"That was exactly my fear to be honest with you, Omer. Thanks for all the work. I'll talk to David, and we'll move on from here."

■ ■ ■ ■ ■

David asked for a few minutes of Simon's time to discuss Mark's conclusions. He told him that his recommendation was to not use the Kovesh, except as a one-off element of the effort if absolutely necessary. In short, the work which Mark's team had done moved the Kovesh from a primary tool to a secondary solution if all else failed. He repeated the logic which effectively parroted Omer's findings and made the point that there had to be a better solution. Simon smiled and simply said:

"Amazing. That's exactly what I thought you would conclude. The problem, in my view, is not the issue of bringing a couple of agents. As you've told me, they can easily be flown in by Mehmet; after all, if he can fly himself, he can have a couple of passengers, if we can get them to Ankara. You'll have Turkish logistics to worry about, but I'm sure that's not a problem. Plus, in a real pinch, they could fly commercial through Erbil; might be a bit complicated, but surely doable. The real challenge has to be getting the heroin out."

"It may or may not be, sir."

Simon arched his eyebrows. David continued:

"We're not in the drug dealing business and I am not even sure that we need to have physical proof that there's drug trafficking going on . . ."

Simon slapped his right hand on his right thigh and added:

"Hey! I get it. We may simply need to destroy it while still in Iraq . . ."

"Absolutely. We don't want it to hit the market, but we don't need it . . ."

Switching topic, Simon asked:

"By the way, David, any news from the Mediterranean?"

"None whatsoever. Well, let me stand corrected. Virtually none. The first Russian cargo ship is now sailing west and should be nearing the entrance to the Aegean Sea . . ."

"So, she's left the scene of the crime?"

"You could say so. From this, I conclude that she is not armed, or at most minimally armed. The other ship is still at anchor in international waters off Cyprus southern coast. We have to assume that she is just as unarmed as her sister ship. We know that the Russian submarine remains in the area, although she is submerged. The Harry S. Truman aircraft carrier strike group from the U.S. Sixth Fleet is less than twenty-four hours away from the site and proceeding at reduced speed."

David noted that Simon looked quizzical and added:

"We don't want the area to be overcrowded. Plus, we don't want to totally discourage any "transaction" so to speak between the Russians and ISIS if they're really the ones receiving the stuff. We just want the Russians to understand that any aggressive action taken against one of our vessels would likely end up in somewhat of a messy way from their standpoint."

"Surveillance?"

"We still have an Eitan circling above, but we called the Kovesh with the torpedo bombs back to base."

"Well, my friend, it seems to me that as usual you have everything pretty much under control. Thanks."

As he was walking out of Simon's office, David was "smiling interiorly." He was fully aware that his first two years in office had taught him much, but he also understood that learning really never stops. His success in his first major operation as Head of *Disruption* had worked well,[9] though Simon's help had also been quite useful. Feeling that his boss was supporting him the way he did gave him increased confidence that he was developing the way he should. He was thinking: *Do not get cocky. But it's good to know you're on the right track.*

---

[9] See "Escaping the Bear" by the same author. Barringer Publishing, 2023.

CHAPTER.18

Meanwhile Mark had also been working at coordinating Josh's backup efforts. He quickly decided that, in the end, it did not make sense to ask Mehmet to stay on the ground in Mosul. Clearly, Mehmet could be a very strong local support, but Mark had concluded that he was more helpful in a role that did not involve him remaining in Iraq. With his pilot's license, he would be the ideal person to ferry personnel and diamonds into Iraq. Why take the risk that he could be hurt or at least burnt in his official job in Turkey? Further, his conversations with Josh had led him to believe that the "Mosul Team" as they called it needed four members, plus Mehmet as the link to Turkey.

David had thus invited Mark to select the three additional members of the team, after they had agreed that the top three attributes that should be emphasized were all related to the strength of special operations team: marksmanship, the skills needed to be engaged in direct combat if needed and the ability to operate in "enemy territory" without standing out like a sore thumb. That latter requirement clearly meant that the agents, also called *Katsas* had to be fluent in Arabic, and to be able to look like Iraqi tribesmen.

Mark had noted at the time that *Mossad* possessed a number of cosmetic tools that would allow individuals to be made to look the part if needed: blond hair could be dyed black, blue eyes could be dissimulated by colored contact lenses and fake beards or mustaches could compensate for a current clean-shaven look.

Mark first introduced Daniel Strom to David. He was in his mid-thirties and had been with *Mossad* ever since completing his military service. Prior to that, he had studied engineering and, in Mark's words:

"Was excellent when it came to tinkering with anything mechanical."

His greatest strength, however, was his ability to appear to lose himself into any background in which he was operating. Somehow, he had a knack for avoiding attention, probably reflecting his high level of self-confidence. Less friendly or more cynical friends said he simply looked extraordinarily ordinary. Mark told the story of a case where Daniel had been able to operate in plain view while at the same time not being noticed. He simply added:

"He just disappears in any crowd. To me, it's because he is very quick at adopting body moves and behavior that mimic those of the people around him. He is neither too tall nor too short; neither too athletic nor too skinny. He's just right for the job. Importantly, he is fluent in Arabic."

"How about any special ops training?"

"He's been through the paces, just as the other two I'll introduce to you in a minute."

Mark noted that the biggest challenge that Daniel and the other two would be facing had to be a series of complete unknowns, in his words:

"We don't know who we're dealing with, other than the fact that they're drug smugglers. We don't know whether our operation disturbs some existing alliance although we suspect it does. We've reasons to believe that ISIS is somewhere in the mix, but we don't know what role they play. And we have no idea how the drug smugglers with which we hope to deal will behave from one load to the next."

David was nodding, but then asked the obvious questions:

"With all these unknown, what are you asking these guys to do?"

Mark conceded that the question was right on point. He argued that the fact that a plane had crashed with $100 million in diamonds had to indicate that there was some existing arrangement between at least two, possibly more parties. So, it would be perfectly reasonable for the team to assume that they were playing a role of disruption, adding with a smile:

"Right down our alley . . ."

Mark was referring to the fact that the *Mossad* division headed up by David was actually named *Disruption*! Going back to David's point, Mark said that he had set a principal objective for himself and the team. He wanted to learn as much as possible about the various parties to the drug smuggling operation, with the idea, eventually, of finding a way to make the smugglers' jobs increasingly hard and expensive. This would likely require the team to identify both parties to any trade, assuming that the drug smugglers were one and the people to whom they used to sell the heroin in exchange for diamonds the other. He also wanted to see the extent to which he could assist the Kurds in their effort to gain autonomy if not independence, assuming, as he did, that they would cooperate with Josh's efforts. He added:

"That last bit is nowhere near a slam dunk. We must find out who shot the plane down and why. Clearly, it could be the Kurd resistance, but I'm not sure what they gained by doing that since we know they did not collect the diamonds. Having said that, we don't know whether they didn't collect the diamonds because Josh got to them before they did or simply because they didn't know there were diamonds in the plane. But what if there were several groups of smugglers trying to force their way through that route? In fact, the more you assume ISIS is somewhere in play, the greater the likelihood that they would be a client of choice . . ."

David wryly noted:

"You'll have to explain this to me my friend . . ."

"Sure. I think they would be viewed as having almost limitless capabilities to distribute the drug abroad if selling drugs is a major element in their effort to re-arm. We know that they are in Syria, but we also know that there they are only tolerated at best. So, we have to assume that any effort, say by Russia, to provide them with arms must be cautiously managed so that the Syrians do not believe that ISIS is usurping their position . . ."

David agreed that the logic made sense, but, as always, expressed his doubts as, in his words:

"There are quite a few too many unknowns. Too many assumptions. I can't get that warm and fuzzy feeling that we are in control. By the way, Mark, this was a long diversion to your introduction of the team. Who is your second choice?"

Mark smiled and joked that Nathan Spiegel was not his second choice, but his first choice for the second position. David smiled back, noting:

"Touché."

Mark explained that Nathan's greatest strength was his exceptional marksmanship, adding:

"He's the only person I know who can fire a handgun and hit the bullseye, not only using his right or his left hand, but amazingly using both simultaneously. I feel that he could be a huge help to Josh."

David asked:

"I can see why he might be helpful in close quarters as a guardian angel, but how about in wide open spaces?"

He paused and added:

"After all, we've got to assume that the exchange of heroin for diamonds will not take place at the store."

Mark conceded the point. Yet, he argued that Josh would most probably need to be by himself with his three guardian angels hidden when the exchange was actually taking place. This brought him back to marksmanship, arguing:

"Nobody will get too many bites at the cherry. Nathan would be the agent positioned the closest to Josh and best able to take out the enemy if they tried anything funny. By the way, he had been used in a number of commando operations, precisely as "the gun." As you know, agents in these positions may have to operate in awkward circumstances. We're not talking snipers with bipods waiting for their targets to come into view. We're speaking of people holding on to a tree branch with one hand while shooting with the other, or may be something even crazier . . ."

Mark stopped at that point, as he realized that David was lacking one crucial piece of information as to the way the operation was planned. He said that the whole operation involved two different sets of circumstances weaving one into the other as time passed:

"There is a surveillance function when Josh is meeting the drug smugglers at the store. At that time, everyone needs to be prepared to defend an external assault on the store. So, you need eyes inside and outside the store, as well as firing power also inside and outside. And by outside here I mean both in front and at the back. The other function relates to the various exchanges which will undoubtedly take place away from the store, most likely outside of town, probably somewhere between Mosul and Erbil. There, the other agents are in a protection role, protecting Josh against the drug smugglers and both of them against any third party that might want to join in . . ."

Mark paused and seeing that David was following without any trouble, he added that the whole team would have to make very serious reconnaissance missions ahead of time so that they knew as much as possible about the various areas where danger could be coming from. With a wry smile, he added:

"I don't suspect they'll have much time to sleep, at least early on . . ."

"I see. Now, who's you third man?"

Mark replied that Mike Bernstein would complete the team. Also trained as a commando, Mike had in fact participated in a number of missions within *Shayetet* 13. It is a unit of the Israeli Navy and one of the primary *Shayetet* units of the Israel Defense Forces. It specializes in sea-to-land incursions, counterterrorism, sabotage, maritime intelligence gathering, maritime hostage rescue, and boarding. With a wry smile, Mark conceded that there was little in the current assignment that looked directly like Navy-like operations yet added that Mike had joined *Mossad* to use his experience in a broader operational context. He noted:

"Whether it be general awareness, reaction time, marksmanship and the ability to make decisions on the fly, Mike is a huge complement to the other two. Now, the only flaw in the ointment is that his physical appearance is definitely not purely semitic."

Yet, he added:

"He's one of those people with blue eyes and blondish hair that stand out in the Middle East. Blame a Danish mother for that! But remember; we have the tools to change his hair color; we also have the option of having him wear colored contact lenses if we judge it critical."

He took a sip from the glass of water that was sitting next to him and added:

"You'll love the fact that he was once involved in a mission that required the use of the Kovesh drone in its person-rescuing operation. I know we've agreed that we prefer not to use the Kovesh here, but if one of our men was stuck behind the lines, Mike would have no trouble both riding in the Kovesh and, if need be, captaining another agent along with himself."

"I guess that's what we call flexibility, right?"

∎ ∎ ∎ ∎ ∎

Mark, Josh and Mehmet got together on the telephone to plan the details of their next step. They knew that it involved Mehmet bringing diamonds to Josh and ferrying the three additional agents. In the meantime, he would need first to obtain satisfactory papers for the three agents so that they could pass any and all immigration controls they would need to subject themselves to. The first of these would of course be in Turkey, as they would have to fly, separately, from Tel Aviv to Istanbul or Ankara and be officially admitted into Turkey. They probably would not enter Iraq officially, but that should also be something that was covered. The second major step for Mehmet was that he would need to file a flight plan that allowed him to fly from Ankara to Mosul.

Yet, they agreed that Mehmet would make a first roundtrip to Mosul from Ankara with no "cargo" and no passenger, just to see "how things went." One of the first changes Mehmet and Mark made to original idea was that, as suggested by Marvin, Mehmet would not rent a plane in Turkey. Rather, he would fly one from Israel to Turkey and then use it. This allowed him to make sure that the airplane was fully operational, in perfect maintenance order and best suited for the job. It gave him an opportunity to fly a Piaggio P.180 Avanti EVO. The main advantage of this very modern plane is that it is bar none the fastest twin turbo prop aircraft in the world, reaching speeds in excess of 400 miles per hour and still capable of cruising at 41,000 feet. Its range would allow it to fly the roundtrip Ankara-Mosul-Ankara without the need to refuel in Mosul, with more than enough of a safety cushion.

The only argument against choosing it was that the plane is rather unique and looks like virtually no other plane in the world. It is quite slick, with the wings located further aft than normal and a small "mustache" forward wing at the front; its angle of incidence is slightly greater than that of the main wing, so that it stalls before the main wing, producing an automatic nose-down effect prior to the onset of main wing stall. Its propellers are of the pushing rather than pulling variety, meaning that the blades are behind rather than in front of the engine. Its main other weakness was its relatively low luggage carrying volume, limited to about one cubic meter, though some stuff could be placed into the cabin, easily adding two to three cubic meters to the cargo volume if needed.

The main reasons to choose the plane despite its somewhat unusual looks and thus its originality were that it offers a greater range, a faster climb, a lower noise footprint and a reduced fuel consumption, all very important variables in this operation. The cherry on top of the cake is that Mehmet was qualified to fly it, even in a solo-pilot configuration.

Mehmet had no difficulty filing a flight plan, which surprised no one as the trip was going to take place in full daylight. The take-off from Ankara was totally routine, as were the early phases of the flight. About 90 minutes into the flight, Mehmet started its descent. When filing his flight plan, he had claimed he was a film director and that the trip was one of several that would be used to locate potential areas where he might be able to shoot a movie. He thought that it would explain why he would be making the trip once daily in the ensuing few days. Though it was originally recommended that he should consider flying to Erbil whose airport was fully operational, Mehmet argued that he preferred Mosul, particularly since the P.180 could take off or land in less than 3,500 feet. There had been some serious resistance as the Mosul airport was not technically open, but

Mehmet's insistence and a small "present" to the official in charge won out.

For his first landing, the best approach would be toward the north though the winds were in fact quite calm. Less than a mile from the head of the runway he could clearly see the Tigris River running almost parallel to the course he had chosen. He checked for a last time that he was indeed on a 330-degree heading, flaps were fully extended and landing gear down. Thankfully, the weather was quite clear, as the runway was not equipped with any instrument landing assistance. Mehmet set the plane on its gliding slope, ready at any instant to correct the pitch if he should realize that he was coming in too fast or not fast enough, too low or not low enough. In fact, when he was less than 100 feet above ground level, he instinctively added some speed as he judged he was a bit too close to the ground for comfort. The aircraft kept gliding down and made an almost perfect three-point touch down just after the piano keys on the runway, or more honestly on what was left of the piano keys that once were there.

Mehmet guided the plane to the terminal which displayed the obvious signs of being under significant renovations. Looking around, he elected to park the plane with its nose almost toward the head of the runway. He was not surprised that no one was there to greet him, as he had been warned that such would be the case. The plane stood out in the environment, with its modern, almost bullet-like look, its white fuselage and its dark blue tail. It was registered in Italy, the land of its birth, so as to ensure that no one would be able to see its connection to Israel. Leaving the plane on the tarmac, he exited the airport and hailed a taxi asking to be taken to a rental car agency. Mehmet's Arabic was flawless, and he had been told by Josh which agency he was to use. It all seemed pretty routine to all involved.

After having rented a four-wheel drive vehicle, he did not drive in the direction of the countryside, but rather took the time to observe the airport from as many locations as he could. His principal goal was to look for anything that would suggest that the sound, however muffled, of an aircraft landing would have brought people out to see if there was anything to see. He breathed a substantial sigh of relief when he observed two helicopters land and take off in a matter of about an hour. He thought:

At least aircraft movements are not totally unheard of. That's what they had told me. Plus, those choppers are way noisier than my plane.

He avoided making any connection with Josh, knowing that it would always be easier to talk to him from Ankara. He returned to the airport parking lot, if one can call the vague space in front of the construction site a parking lot. He left the rental car there and made his way toward his plane. Suddenly, a voice behind him surprised him:

"Hey, what are you doing here?"

CHAPTER.19

TEL AVIV, ISRAEL, ANKARA, TURKEY AND MOSUL AND ERBIL, IRAQ

Josh picked up the phone whose number was known to the drug smugglers. It rang, and Josh was happy because the smugglers had anticipated his feeling that some renewed contact had been somewhat overdue.

"Yes!"

"We are ready to deliver 100 kilos of processed opium, in fact alkaloid morphine, in exchange for 100 carats of diamonds."

"Understood. That's in line with our bargain. I need about a week to make sure I have the diamonds for you. Where would you want the exchange to take place?"

The voice at the other hand of the line seemed to hesitate, which Josh thought was odd given the fact that it appeared so authoritative on other matters. Josh deduced that the voice did not belong to the most senior individual. At the same time, Josh was concerned that he should try and keep the voice on the line for as long as possible to help the folks back in Tel Aviv refine their analysis of where the phone call originated. Given the lack of reply, Josh made an offer:

"Why don't you all identify a general location? Then, I'll pick a smaller area within that location, and you'll come up with the final meeting point."

He was making the process possibly quite a bit more complex than it should be but did not want to allow the other side to be in control of everything. Having both sides contribute to the decision would appear to offer more protection to everyone. The voice replied:

"I can't reply right now. I'll have to call you back. When did you say you would be ready?"

"I need a week, possibility a couple of days less. I also need the place to be accessible by four-wheel drive, although it can be of course away from a main highway."

Josh paused and asked:

"Will you prefer daylight or night?"

The voice replied:

"I'm sure it will be best at night."

"Excellent. Please note that I will surely have at least one person with me."

The voice sounded surprised and asked:

"Why?"

"Why are there always two of you if not more? Come on my friend, let's skip all these games. By the way, I was nearly hit by a car that tried to run me over the last time we met. I've got to assume that this is not by one of your people . . . Would make no sense, at least until you have diamonds. But if it's not you all, then who is it?"

The voice remained silent, though a couple of guttural sounds led Josh to believe the man on the line was surprised. Josh asked:

"Do you know of any reason why someone would want if not to kill me at least to scare me away from making a deal with you?"

The voice remained just as silent, until it finally said:

"Don't know. I have to ask. Will call you back later."

With that, the voice hung up.

Josh's next phone call was to Mark Levi:

"Mark? D-Day is in at most a week?"

"I assume that by D-Day you mean Delivery Day. Correct?"

"Absolutely."

Mark asked Josh what his plans were, and he simply replied:

"Don't see any reason to change anything. Do you?"

Mark explained that in conversations with Mehmet he had concluded that each of the three additional agents should come on different flights. In fact, he added:

"I've got an ace up my sleeve. If need be, one of them can travel to Erbil by commercial flight."

Josh was surprised, asking:

"Why?"

Mark simply replied that he did not want to have all his eggs in the same bucket, adding:

"After all, I haven't spoken to Mehmet since his first flight. Hope to do it a bit later today."

Josh conceded the point and told Mark that he had arranged for a discreet delivery of inflatable mattresses and sleeping bags at the second store so that the four of them could be there semi-permanently. Yet, he added with a smile he also booked another apartment a couple of streets away so that everyone could take turns to go shower and take care of basic hygienic needs. Mark asked:

"Do you have toilets in the store?"

"Well, there is something that is presented as a toilet, with a sink next to it in both stores. However, I would call this absolutely basic at best. Let's not even talk of warm water . . . except when it's quite hot outside."

Though of course surprised, Mehmet turned toward the voice which had called him. At that time, he was walking around a work fence at the northern end of the terminal, not far from where the control tower was, and meant to return to his plane and initiate his departure checklist. He saw a man wearing what looked like an army uniform, carrying an automatic rifle and at least a couple of extra magazines on his belt. The man was not absolutely threatening, but it was clear to Mehmet that this was not the time to do anything rash. He knew he could probably take the guard out if he had to, but that would kill any chance to carry out the balance of the plan.

He smiled at the man and said:

"As you can see, I am about ready to get back to my plane, start engines and fly back to Ankara."

Though Mehmet spoke in virtually perfectly accented Arabic, the man looked very confused at best. After all, this should not surprise anyone, as there are quite a number of different variants on the pure Arabic language in the Middle East. All the while, Mehmet was walking calmly toward the individual and smiling. The guard asked why he was there in the first place, adding:

"This airport is closed; don't you know that?"

With his best smile, Mehmet replied that he knew that the airport was closed to general traffic, emphasizing **general**, but said that he had received special permission given the nature of his activities. More confused than ever, the guard asked:

"What kind of activities?"

Mehmet replied that he was a filmmaker scouting locations for his next movie. The man still seemed to have difficulty processing Mehmet's answer. Though he was not becoming ostensibly more menacing, his eyes seemed darker and set deeper into their sockets. Mehmet pulled a director's viewfinder out of his pocket and showed it to the guard. Really looking very much like a monocular, it was designed to offer an immediate view of what the camera would hypothetically pick up. It is indeed a well-known truism in the filmmaking industry that poorly planned blocking of potentially unfortunate background elements and camera placements account for more wasted time on set than anything else.

The guard ostensibly did not know that a director's viewfinder would be unlikely to make its way in the pocket of someone scouting locations. Yet, it seemed real enough that he appeared to relax somewhat. Sensing that he was getting the better of the situation, Mehmet even added:

"If you want to, I may well be able to find a way for you to have a small role, maybe even as a guard too."

The man smiled, showing poor teeth, affected by the decay which one finds in several developing areas, particularly those where fresh fruit and vegetables were not always part of the daily diet and dental care embryonic at best. He allowed Mehmet to walk right next to him, ostensibly to show him the director's viewfinder. The man played with it for less than a minute. Suddenly, he stiffened up and said:

"But wait, you haven't told me who gave you permission."

Mehmet lied and talked of an individual in the Iraqi embassy in Ankara with whom he had discussed the idea of the movie. He produced the approved flight plan out of the pocket of his kaki toile jacket. Though the man clearly could not understand any of the words or characters on the flight plan, he seemed to calm down again. Mehmet decided to try a risky tack, but he felt it was his only way to have a good sense of the lay of the land. He said:

"I plan on coming back almost daily for the next few days, with one or two associates to get some initial footage and move forward. Will you be here tomorrow?"

The man seemed surprised, but Mehmet's gambit had paid off. Suddenly, he was taking Mehmet seriously and no longer treating him as someone who should not be where he was. After all, from where they stood they could see the P.180 aircraft parked on the tarmac, which must have impressed the guard. He replied:

"I'm pretty much the only guard on duty here, day in and day out. We don't think there is any need for a guard during the night. What is there to steal here after all? We just want to avoid disruption to the construction effort and prevent people coming here and stealing materials. All the material is locked up for the night and I'm the only one with the key."

His face displayed a sign of pride as he finished his sentence. Mehmet asked:

"You must live close to here . . ."

"Why are you asking?"

"Well, after all, what if there was an alarm?"

The man started laughing:

"An alarm. For a few bags of cement? You've got to be kidding. Plus, everybody knows everything here. It wouldn't take me long to find the thief if someone was dumb enough to try."

"I see. So, you do not live close by?"

The man was starting to feel more and more comfortable with Mehmet and did not hesitate to tell him that he in fact did live relatively close by, but that there was no relation between where his apartment was and where he worked. Mehmet was taking copious mental notes. He waved goodbye to the guard and started walking to his plane, after having told him that he hoped to see him again, the next day or the day after that. Mehmet was surprised when the man asked:

"How far is Ankara?"

Mehmet wondered why he was asking the question. Suddenly, he remembered that he had mentioned the name of the Turkish capital in the earlier conversation. He replied:

"Why do you ask?"

"How long of a flight is it?"

Mehmet realized that he had to reply and simply said:

"Just under two hours . . ."

The man continued his questioning:

"Why do you need to do these roundtrips. Wouldn't it be simpler just to book a hotel room and stay here for the whole process?"

Touché was Mehmet's first thought. Yet he answered:

"That's a good idea, my friend. But the associates that I need with me vary and it would be too expensive to have them all here for the whole time. Plus, when I take pictures or even shoot a few frames, I need assistants to create a mini-movie and that has to be done there. If I wanted to do all this here, I'd have to charter a whole planeload of people and equipment."

That seemed to satisfy the guard who calmly waved goodbye.

■ ■ ■ ■ ■

Having filed and obtained approval of his flight plan, Mehmet flew back to Mosul the next morning. He was happy to note in his mind that the approval of the second flight plan had been considerably simpler than the first; in fact, it seemed like a bureaucratic routine this time. In the meantime, Mike Bernstein had arrived in Ankara from Tel Aviv on a regularly scheduled flight. He was carrying with him both the small lot of diamonds which Josh would eventually need and some movie making paraphernalia which Mehmet would in turn entrust to each of his prospective charges. Mehmet had organized with Mark for everyone on the *Mossad* side to have Turkish passports, although Mike landed in Ankara with a diplomatic Israeli passport allowing him to bring with him stuff which would not be questioned under the protection afforded the diplomatic pouch.

Mehmet was at Ankara Esenboğa International Airport when Mike came through customs and immigration. He steered Mike quickly to the area where private planes were parked, and they both climbed into the P.180. While the camera equipment that Mike had brought was loaded in the luggage compartment of the turboprop, the contents of the diplomatic pouch were carefully loaded inside the plane. Mehmet had made sure that the plane carried a full load of fuel, which was not really an issue as cargo, fuel and passengers did not come close to the total permissible take-off weight.

Though Mike originally chose to sit next to the pilot on the right-hand side of the cockpit, he quickly went back to the main cabin, which was separated from the cockpit by a simple pleated blue and brown curtain. There, he painstakingly unloaded the various guns and ammunition that cleared Turkish customs via the diplomatic pouch. He wanted to make sure that the guns were appropriately oiled and that the ammunition was operational. Of course, he knew that colleagues in Tel Aviv had gone through that very same routine. Yet, commando fighters know that one should always double or triple check everything, as a misfunctioning gun can often be the difference between life and death. Once his inspection was completed, though he had been shaken up by a couple of patches of rough air which Mehmet did not choose to avoid, he replaced everything as carefully as he could. Mehmet had made it clear that the risk was high that a lone guard might be there and that it was therefore important to avoid anything that might arouse suspicion.

As he was starting his descent, Mike, who had returned to his seat in the cockpit, could hear Mehmet mumble something. Probably more out of curiosity than real anxiety he asked:

"What's wrong?"

Mehmet simply replied:

"The last time I landed in Mosul, I had to rev the engines up a bit ahead of the runway, as I was gliding too low. I'm just reminding myself that I have to be a bit higher than my eyes would tell me to be."

"Nothing more serious than that?"

"Absolutely nothing. Ideally, I'd like to glide to the landing with the engines running as low a fuel flow as prudent. I don't know if you know this, but we always land a plane with at least 40-45% fuel flow until we touch down because that's the only way we could take off immediately if something went awry. Actually, we maintain the fuel flow until we're just above the runway and ease off the throttles as we land. That's why the sound of the engines appears to die off as the plane touches down."

"Didn't know that!"

With a noticeable change in his tone of voice, Mehmet added:

"Remember, you're a camera operator scouting locations with me. I wonder whether the guard will be there when we land or later on, but you've got to be ready for him. I think he's no real danger, but we cannot afford any screw up. By the way, the biggest screw up would be something that takes away our ability to land here again. It may be our way in, but much more important it's also our way out . . ."

CHAPTER.20

TEL AVIV, ISRAEL, ANKARA, TURKEY, MOSUL AND ERBIL, IRAQ AND EASTERN MEDITERRANEAN

Yael Orbach called Simon Rabinowitz and asked if he could have a moment of his time. Simon immediately replied:

"Is this related to our current project?"

"Absolutely."

"Should I ask David Heller to join us?"

"Come to think of it, yes. It's probably a great idea."

David walked into Simon's office as he and Yael were already seated in the one corner which had a sofa and two wing chairs facing each other at either end of the sofa. Simon motioned to David to sit on the armchair to his left, thus facing him, while Yael was on the sofa. Yael started the conversation with a general update of the situation in the Eastern Mediterranean. His main point was that though there was nothing terribly new, the various forces had come sufficiently close to one another that it was important to begin to think of the formation which, in his words, "our side" should adopt. He added:

"So far there is no definite move with respect to either the Russian cargo ship or the submarine, though, for the submarine, we can only judge from the Sonar images as she remains submerged."

David asked:

"Nothing in terms of additions to the Russian presence?"

Yael replied that there were Russian Navy vessels near the western tip of Cyprus. However, he also indicated that the USS *Truman* carrier strike group from U.S. Sixth Fleet had positioned itself south and west of Cyprus. He remarked:

"They were expected to transit through the Mediterranean to the Persian Gulf. That was well known. That's our luck. This in no way interdicts the area to Russian vessels, but they would have to pass very near to one or several of their ships. By the way, I should also add that we have seen no indication of any additional Russian submarine joining the first one either."

Simon wondered what this could all mean. Yael explained that there were two possible adverse developments, for which his team was very sharply watching. The first would relate to smaller boats approaching the Russian cargo vessel from the east, which, in his view, would most likely be in order to take delivery of whatever the ship was carrying. He calmly stated:

"We have not seen any trace of that. By the way, remember that the Russian cargo vessel is at most a day's cruising from the Syrian shore, and probably at most 75% of that from the coast of Lebanon."

Simon interrupted:

"In short, things can change quite rapidly."

"Absolutely. By the way, a variant on this theme would be for the Russian cargo ship to start sailing in an easterly direction. Rather than unloading the cargo in the Gulf or Larnaca, the Russians would be doing it the same way as the first . . ."

Getting back to his original point, Yael argued that the second adverse development would have to be some reinforcement coming from the Russian side. He conceded that they did not have much seaborne monitoring to the north and east of Cyprus, but immediately noted:

"Yet it's under Eitan surveillance, so we shouldn't be surprised, unless they're using submarines."

Simon looked pensive for a short while and then asked:

"How about Russian undersea drones or mini submarines?"

"Funny you should ask. They just commissioned the *Belgorod*, the first Khabarovsk class submarine specially designed to house Russia's Poseidon nuclear undersea drone. Now, your intelligence tells us that nuclear capabilities will not be reached until 2027, but the answer to your question on drones, Simon, has to be a resounding yes. The "yes" is ever more emphatic for mini-submarines, as they have at least two families: one which is about eight-yard long and the other, which NATO called the Losos-Class, which is barely short of five yards long."

"That's what I worried about. Can we monitor them?"

Yael replied that though undersea drones or mini submarines were small, they could be detected via Sonar, adding:

"We have a frigate, in international waters, which is listening for them. It's just south of the Syria coastline but should still give us some advance warning."

"What if they don't have any sonar turned on?"

"They should at least have something turned on so that they could communicate with the operators on the mother ship, or submarine here."

Simon returned to the main flow of the conversation:

"So, what are you doing now as we speak?"

"Well, that's what I wanted to brief you about."

Yael went on to explain that he had liaised with the USS *Truman* Carrier group. The strike group comprised one cruiser, the USS *San Jacinto*, along with four guided-missile destroyers, USS *Cole*, USS *Bainbridge*, USS *Gravely*, and USS *Jason Dunham*, and nine squadrons of Carrier Air Wing. He explained:

"All but the USS *Gravely* and USS *Bainbridge* are as I mentioned earlier virtually at anchor abeam the western tip of Cyprus. The two guided-missile destroyers are now on site, and they have been instructed to stay between the Russian submarine and our own Navy."

David had to ask:

"What's the point?"

Yael replied:

"Protection for us. We assume that the most serious risk to our vessels is that the submarine would choose to try and torpedo them . . . Again. By the way, we know that the submarine already fired a couple of torpedoes in the earlier incident. So that's not farfetched, even if it looks foolish. By having U.S. ships in the line of fire makes it quite a bit more costly for the submarine to attempt anything."

Yael paused for a minute and continued:

"I am told that the U.S, Navy had direct contacts with the Russian Navy to explain that their role is not to attack anyone, just to defend their allies, us."

David could not hide his satisfaction, yet had to ask:

"I presume the Americans will not be on site for ever, correct?"

"Sure, you are. But there are a few other steps which will be taken in the next few days to force the situation to move."

"Can you reveal what they are?"

"Suffice it to say that the Russian cargo ship will have to agree to an inspection of her cargo."

Simon calmly added:

"Let's not go too fast as I really want to see who it was that was supposed to take delivery."

Yael simply replied:

"Totally agree with that, Simon. However, we have to assume that the train has left the station. I can't believe the Russians would deliver these arms in full view of the U.S. and Israeli navies. So, I can only envisage one of two scenarios."

Yael explained that the first scenario had the Russians playing the clock, in which case the inspection of the ship's cargo would be a key factor, as they have never delivered multiple warhead missiles to anyone in this region. That could lead them to prefer the second scenario which would have the cargo ship lift anchor and simply sail back in the direction of the Black Sea."

Simon could only add:

"And that would mean that we wouldn't know who was to have them, and what they were."

"True enough, but my own suspicion is that the ship would try again later, for instance after the American ships have gone through the Suez Canal. That's why we will try to force an issue soon."

David interrupted with a wry smile:

"Understood. Yet let's make sure we do not start World War III over this . . ."

Simon could only reply:

"Always the optimist, hey, David?"

■ ■ ■ ■ ■

Mehmet was quietly returning to his plane, ready to return to Turkey when a familiar voice called out:

"So how was it today?"

"Hey! I missed you when I landed this morning."

"You may have missed me, but I saw you and your friend. By the way, where is your friend?"

Mehmet was startled as he was pretty sure he had looked for the guard and failed to see him. He had to ask:

"Where were you?"

"Oh. You mean, this morning? I was having a cup of tea around the corner of the building, with a couple of construction workers. You know, your plane is not very noisy, but its high-pitched, almost grating sound is still quite noticeable. Different from other planes by the way . . ."

"I know. One of its trademarks."

"Now how about your friend, the one which was carrying the camera this morning?"

"Indeed, you saw him . . . Well, he is taking your advice. Since I will need him tomorrow too, he's decided that he might as well spend the night here. He's booked himself in a hotel . . ."

"Which one?"

"Can't remember. But he'll meet me here tomorrow when I come back, with another friend too."

Mehmet was both enjoying the conversation, which he could tell was friendly, and worrying. The fact that the guard had picked up so many details of what had taken place was obviously an issue. That demonstrated a good sense of observation; what else had he noticed that he had not mentioned? Additionally, the guard was asking excellent questions, suggesting that he might well be able to go through a rationale. He made a mental note that he would need to be very careful the next day and be ready for further questions.

He decided there and then to ask Mark to have Nathan fly commercial from Ankara to Erbil. Though it would require Josh to go get him at the airport, it would allow Mehmet not to have to endure two rounds of further questions. Indeed, he knew very well that he was going to fly with Daniel the next day and would in fact make the trip very early in the morning, when it was still dark. Though there was no operational requirement for him to fly so early, he wanted to have tried a landing before sunrise, or after sunset, to check that the bearings which he had carefully established for his visual approach were appropriate. He caught himself wishing that prevailing winds would not change too much, or at least not enough to require him to land in the opposite direction.

■ ■ ■ ■ ■

Josh picked up his drug smuggler phone, as he called it, on the second ring. The same voice as usual was on the line. It was calling to set the details of the delivery. Josh was quite surprised when the proposed location for the exchange appeared to be in fact very near where the fellows in Tel Aviv had thought the voice was when he first called. It was going to take place just after a bridge as Highway 2 passes over the Great Zab River, a tributary to the famous Tigris. The appointment was fixed for 2:00 a.m., on a small road, alongside Happy Park Khabat, which during daytime, was an amusement park. Josh was told that he should drive about a quarter mile due north of the main road and wait there. As he had previewed it in an earlier conversation with the voice, Josh said that he needed to inspect the area before he could accept it. The voice grudgingly agreed and said it would call back at the same time the next day.

Josh and Mike drove in separate cars in the direction of the meeting point to do what they correctly called their initial "reconnaissance work." As they were preparing for the trip, they had looked at the various maps available on the internet and had noted that there was another bridge crossing the Great Zab River barely a half a mile northeast of the bridge on Highway 2. More importantly, they could identify at least four different ways to get to the proposed meeting point, though all converged at either end of the short road alongside the park.

They decided that they should each be responsible for either end of the short road on which the exchange was to take place. Josh, the one the most familiar with the local area, veered left in Aski Kalak right before the Mosque and drove toward the hospital which was only a couple hundred yards from the street leading to the northeastern-most bridge. Mike followed highway 2 until he reached the bridge which the voice had mentioned and veered right almost exactly 2,000 feet after the end of the bridge. The road on which the exchange was to take place was on the other side of Highway 2, the left side, but he had elected to walk the last several hundred yards. He was playing the role of an older man and was thus slightly hunched forward and used a cane in his left hand. For some reason, his right hand seemed to be stuck deep into his pocket. There was no need for anyone to know that he was armed and that his hand was holding the handle of a shotgun, equipped with tranquilizing bullets and a silencer. He was firmly committed not to use it, but as he thought:

Better safe than sorry.

Josh, for his part, also drove beyond the road on which the exchange was to take place, though he found a dirt track, three hundred feet on, which ostensibly separated the park into what seemed like a plain forest on one side and the part where various rides were located on the other. His mind wandered a few seconds and led him to assume that the forest was probably meant to provide potential expansion room for the amusement park. Yet, he thought:

It's really a good thing to have it there. I should provide all the cover we would ever want.

A quarter of a mile down that track, Josh found another road that ran perpendicular to the trail, virtually opposite to what had to be a secondary entrance to the amusement park, since he knew that the main entrance was on the other side, to the east of the park where he had seen a nice parking lot. He made a mental note that this made a lot of sense, as he had seen a fence running on the west side of that earlier trail, while there was none on the east side. He decided to park his car right there and to walk on that road. He was surprised to find that road leading if not exactly to the proposed delivery point, barely fifty feet from it. He thought:

Wonder why they picked that point. It adds one source of uncertainty, both for us and for them.

He retraced his steps and walked around in the forest, noting that there did not seem to be any well-defined trails per se, though there were areas which had seemingly seen more pedestrian traffic than others. He concluded that the forest certainly offered a myriad of locations in which people could hide. He could only observe that many hiding spots would be available to him and his team, but to the other side as well. He pinged Mike with his cell phone. He could not use their helpful *Mossad* satellite communication tool that looked like a flashlight; both sender and receiver would have needed a clear line of sight to the satellite. That would have been much too difficult in a wooded area. They all agreed that their smartphones would do the trick.

They agreed to keep inspecting virtually every "alley" and every corner of the park to make sure that they had identified all possible locations individual members of the team could use. Their goal indeed was not only to exchange the diamonds for the processed opium, but to use that opportunity to place a bug on the vehicle or vehicles used by the drug smugglers. The bugs they had in mind had been yet another innovation from *Mossad*. While, on the surface, they looked like any run-of-the-mill bug, each had an important feature: it contained a minute, but sufficient quantity of aqua regia—a mixture of nitric acid and hydrochloric acid. Once the bug which had been magnetically affixed to its intended support was removed from its location, the container that held the mixture released the aqua regia, which destroyed everything inside the bug. This wiped out any indication that the bug might have been a piece of electronic equipment.

Their hope, in placing the bug, was that it would help them to locate with greater precision where the home base of the smugglers was.

■ ■ ■ ■ ■

The voice called Josh back as promised and asked:

"Any issue with the proposed location?"

Josh agreed that the location was acceptable and offered three days hence for the exchange to take place. He knew that by then Daniel and Nathan would have arrived and was confident that the plan which his reconnaissance with Mike had logically generated would indeed work. Nathan was scheduled to arrive later that day in Erbil, while Mehmet was expected to make a night flight into Mosul to bring Daniel to complete the team. The only remaining step had to be the execution of the first exchange, which still included a number of unknowns, not least of which was how the smugglers would organize themselves. Josh thought:

This is where the challenge begins.

CHAPTER.21

ANKARA, TURKEY, AND MOSUL AND ERBIL, IRAQ

Late in the afternoon of the day prior to the delivery, Josh and his three associates were driving, in three separate cars, to the location where the exchange would take place. Josh was by himself in his car, while Daniel and Mike were riding in the second car and Nathan in the third.

Nathan's mission was to station himself in as discreet a manner as possible near the east entrance to the road where the transaction was to occur. He elected in fact, just as Mike had done for his reconnaissance run, to park the car on the other side of Highway 2. The road off the highway was actually sloping down for the first couple of hundred yards. This would provide, together with the few trees that were around, a perfect hiding place for the car. He walked back to and carefully crossed the highway, and then positioned himself at the southeastern corner of the forest adjoining the amusement park. He spent the first couple of hours initially getting used to his surroundings and secondly looking for any trace of any trap that could have been set in that vicinity. He was happy to report that, so far, he had not found any.

Daniel and Mike went and parked their car at the north end of the trail that bisected the west side of the park. The east side of the park was where all of the rides were located. The team loved the idea that the west side provided such a useful bumper within which they hoped they could be in control. Mike's commando experience allowed him to identify the best ways in which both Daniel and he could operate, combining their desire to stay hidden with their need to be effective in their roles.

Mike's mission was to focus on the northern half of that forest, first inspecting every "alley"—as he called the parts of the forest where pedestrian traffic had seemed the most prevalent—to make sure that he was by himself. All four of the agents had taken an infra-red monocular along, not as a means of seeing better things that were further away, but mostly to detect any human presence through the heat it might emit. Mike's inspection did point to a couple of "heat sources," but he quickly realized that he was looking at stray cats rather than individuals. He then decided to locate himself in the middle of "his" section of the park, to make sure that he would be able to notice any smuggler that would arrive sooner than at the appointed time. He verified that both of his handguns were properly functioning, reminding himself that his right pocket held the gun with the tranquilizer bullets while the gun in the left pocket was equipped with real bullets. Both guns had a silencer just to make sure that a shot would not immediately attract other potential targets.

Daniel, for his part. positioned himself in the northwest corner of the park with the idea that he would be there to take care of any smuggler that might somehow want to prevent Josh from leaving the area after the transaction was completed. Like his colleagues, he was pretty sure that the smugglers would not attempt anything silly at this early point; logic would suggest that they would prefer to sell more of their heroin and receive more diamonds before double crossing Josh, if that even entered into their minds. Yet, he knew very well

192 | ANDREW B. LOUIS

that assuming perfect rationality in smugglers and other criminals was something you only did at your own expense. He passed the time by making a thorough inspection of the north end of the forest and concluded that, at that time at least, he was by himself, with a few feral animals probably taking advantage of the night to look for food.

Josh, for his part, decided to drive into the park through the road separating the amusement park from the forest. He drove there and parked the car near the trail that was almost opposite the western entrance of the amusement park. He went exploring that western half of the park again to make sure that there was nobody waiting for him. He had his gun in his hand as he walked the various "alleys." Finding no one, he returned to his car and remained by the side of the road. His plan was to stay inside the car on that road until the very time of the exchange. Nobody could blame him for that, and it allowed him and his team to be as well-positioned as possible ahead of the moment when he would drive to the exchange point. It had already been agreed that the exchange would follow a pre-established choreography.

He would at no point step out of his car and would have an automatic gun at the ready on his lap. The smugglers would approach his car from the left side to show him a sample of the merchandise. He had reserved the right to ask them for another sample to inspect, just to be sure; if that was the case, he would ask the smugglers to bring a number of packages among which he would pick one randomly. He was fully aware that the additional verification was not fool-proof, but he felt that it would, at a minimum, guarantee that a few more packages would contain the "real thing." After having verified the few samples, he would, if satisfied, pop his trunk open. The merchandise would be placed in the trunk by the smugglers who, when finished, would close the trunk and walk back toward the front of Josh's car, but this time on the right-hand side. One of them would remain behind the car with a gun pointed toward the car's rear wheels. This was meant to ensure that Josh would not drive off with the merchandise without paying. Josh would lower the right window and hand over a small wooden box which contained the diamonds. The smugglers would be expected to verify its contents either on the spot or walking back to their vehicle, though an armed member of their team would stay near Josh's car. Assuming that all was OK, the armed guard would rejoin his associates and both parties would drive away.

Josh knew from the start that the risks were the highest after the exchange had been completed. In particular, the risk was unquestionable that the armed guard might choose to shoot Josh through the right window or windshield once the diamonds had been inspected and accepted. He also knew that there was the risk that the smugglers might shoot at one or several of the tires of his car, to slow his ability to leave and potentially follow them. Finally, there was always the risk that other associates of the smugglers might try to prevent Josh from leaving from either end of the road on which the exchange had taken place.

■ ■ ■ ■ ■

Late the prior night, Mehmet had landed in Mosul, bringing Daniel with him. He was only going to drop him, with some additional equipment and then fly straight back to Ankara. He could certainly have chosen to stay in Iraq, but two important reasons prevented him from doing so. The first was the strong desire to protect the plane. He wanted to make absolutely sure that the plane would not in any way be attacked. Mark had agreed with him that his almost daily ballet might have been observed by someone other than the guard who seemed to have become friendly; there was no point taking the risk that such someone would decide to come closer than warranted.

The second reason was more important. His next flight was to take place so that at least one or two of what he now thought as the local team would meet him at the airport. There he would take delivery of the heroin that Mossad had just "bought" and fly it back to Israel. Mark indeed wanted to see what the merchandise was, after having initially agreed that bringing any of the merchandise to Tel Aviv was not crucial. Now, the fact that the P.180 could easily fly from Ankara to Mosul and then to Bagdad and Palmachim Air Base in Israel was an opportunity that he did not want to miss.

On the surface, this looked like a radical change from the earlier decision that Mossad did not want to appear to be involved in the drug trade. However, Mehmet's idea to take a *Mossad* plane in Tel Aviv had allowed him to accept the mission of flying from Mosul back through Tel Aviv rather than directly to Ankara. The trick would be for the plane to appear initially to fly to some other destination than Tel Aviv and to switch arrival location en route. Then, a *Mossad* plane, piloted by a *Mossad* agent, eventually landing at an Israeli Air Force base pretty much eliminated the risk of being caught "trafficking drugs."

After having landed, Mehmet had remained in the cockpit, as he was planning to start his return trip immediately. As Daniel was stepping down from the plane using the forward door on the left-hand side, he heard a voice:

"You must be a friend of my friend Mehmet? What's your role in all this?"

Daniel immediately called Mehmet, being careful to speak only in Arabic to maintain the appearances, which his dress following the traditional Iraqi customs would reinforce. Mehmet came to the top of the stairs and was stunned to see the guard, asking him:

"What are you doing here in the middle of the night, my friend?"

The guard explained that he varied his patterns to make sure that nobody tried anything funny. Mehmet did not buy that line as the guard had told him that there was nothing to steal during the night, with all the valuable stuff being locked away. He still decided not to argue with the guard and to accept the reply. He would need to be very careful with the next landing which was planned for just about twenty-four hours hence. Turning to Daniel he said:

"Don't worry. He is a friend."

Turning to the guard, he said:

"We're moving a bit more material. We're going to expand our scouting area. In fact, when I come back tomorrow, I plan to fly to Bagdad to look for a few more sites."

"But why do you have to do this at night?"

"A lot of the movie will take place outside of the hottest hours. So, we need to see light conditions both around sunset and sunrise."

Mehmet must have been convincing as the guard did not say anything and just smiled. Mike, who had met the guard when he had arrived, had taken his rental car and had come to pick up Daniel. He was standing a hundred yards away and could see the whole scene developing. He had taken his right handgun out of his pocket ready to tranquilize the guard if needed, observing the situation with his monocular. He detected the smile on the guard's face. He placed the gun in his pocket all the while keeping his right hand on it and walked in the direction of the plane. The guard recognized him and said:

"How was the hunt?"

Mike made a vague comment meant to impress, talking of many locations and a few that would cast interesting shadows at sunrise. This seemed to satisfy the guard who waved them goodbye and walked away. Daniel and Mike retrieved the "luggage" that was in the hold and closed and locked the door. Mehmet started the engines, starting with the right and then moving to the left and both friends could see him taxi to the end of the runway and take off. Daniel noted:

"Quite a bit noisier from the outside than from the inside."

Mike totally changed the topic in reply:

"Do you really believe that the guard is a friend despite what Mehmet said?"

■ ■ ■ ■ ■

The first of the four Mossad agents to hear something was Nathan. It was about one thirty in the morning, thirty minutes before the transaction was to take place. He saw a car turn into the "road of the exchange" and park on the right-side shoulder less than fifty yards on. He noted that the driver had attempted to park the car where it might believably be called "hidden." He openly wondered why the precaution, why would he want to hide. Yet, for the time being at least he decided that solving the riddle was not going to be his first priority. The car eventually parked in a small clearing; it was no larger than a couple hundred square feet, but the driver went straight for it. Nathan thought:

They definitely know the area . . . Let's watch what they do next.

He sent a quiet SMS message to Josh to keep him informed and shared with him the observation that the smugglers seemed to know the area quite well. Josh replied that he was not surprised and that he would forward the message to the other members of the team.

Nathan kept watching the car. Eventually, he saw two men get out of the car. He could not miss noticing that they both carried what looked like an automatic rifle. An additional SMS and he was sure that Josh was aware. As the men started moving away from the car, though they did not look like they were going to go very far, he crawled out of his current hiding place. He first placed a bug on the car, sticking it to the inside of the steel bumper and switched it on. Returning to the inside of the forest which provided him with a convenient cover, he proceeded to track the men. He saw them stop about a hundred yards short of the road on which Josh had parked. He sat down and asked Daniel whether anything was happening at his end, to which the reply was simply: "not yet."

A few minutes later, it was Mike's turn to see a car coming from the direction of the entrance to the amusement park. He immediately noted that it was a pickup truck. He could see that there were two people in the cabin. Messaging all of the team, he told them that he would try to get as close to the truck as he could. Using the cover of the forest, he was able to get quite close. He was getting ready to put a bug on it, when the truck started going forward again. It passed the place when Josh's car was parked, in plain view, and turned right at the end of the road. Mike and Josh immediately had the same thought:

They're the ones with the heroin.

Josh started his own engine, pulled the automatic gun from the floor and placed it quite visibly on the passenger seat. He drove slowly and followed the pickup truck. He stopped a few yards behind the truck, just so that he could drive straight out if there was trouble. He kept his eyes firmly on his rearview mirror as he could clearly see two shadows moving toward him from behind. From Nathan's earlier message, he assumed that these were the guys that had stopped near the corner with Highway 2. He therefore assumed that they were armed as he had been warned, though, in the dark and given the distance, he could not see the guns.

Daniel sent a message to the team:

"Another car in coming toward you two. Couldn't see too much from here, particularly as the headlights were blinding me . . ."

CHAPTER.22

Simon was surprised when Yael Orbach called him on the telephone:

"Simon, a couple of developments in the Eastern Mediterranean that you should be aware of."

"Can we discuss those on the phone, or do we need to meet?"

Simon knew that it would be a short one-mile car ride via Shlomo Ibn Gabirol Street for him to go to Yael's office. Yael's office was in the Matcal Tower, a 17-floor building at Camp Rabin military base in the HaKirya district of Tel Aviv. It is a very impressive building, seemingly made of steel and glass. It was built in 2003 and houses both the Israel Ministry of Defense and the offices of the IDF General Staff. It is quite near to another IDF building, the Marganit Tower and across the road from the civilian Azrieli Center.

"I'm calling on a secure line. No need to be in the same room . . ."

"Can David listen in?

"Sure . . ."

Yael proceeded to tell Simon who had been joined by David that the operations off the coast of Cyprus were actually warming up.

Two small boats had been seen sailing in the direction of the Russian cargo ship. They were still a couple of hours away, but the decision had been made to prevent them from reaching her. This had involved moves by the two Israeli frigates which had been patrolling the area. They placed themselves one behind the other and were sailing toward a point where they would send a warning to the two approaching smaller crafts. The plan was that they would message the boats to stop and wait for further instructions. If the need arose, the INS *Protector*, which had returned after having "dropped" the deep-sea rescue vessel in Haifa, was prepared and ready to use torpedoes first as a warning and then if needed to sink one or both boats.

David asked:

"Where is the Russian sub?"

"She is still in the same general area and should not be able to reach either of the frigates. An American ship is still positioned in the way. That should ensure that the Russian sub does not attack either of our boats?"

Simon nodded, but followed on David's question:

"What if they decide to move?"

"I have talked to the Americans, and they will back us up. In the meantime, INS *Protector* will surface and send a message to the Russian submarine inviting them to do the same, officially to avoid anybody making an uninformed move. We'll tell them that we don't want to transform a small issue into a big one but added that we would be contacting the cargo ship to ask permission to come aboard and inspect their cargo."

Simon countered:

"What if they don't oblige?"

"We'll ask again, but this time might use more forceful words. We'll call it an issue of legitimate self-defense."

David asked:

"Is INS *Dragon* still in the area?"

Yael replied:

"Sure is, but she's far enough away and "hidden" behind other boats so that we think the Russians haven't noticed her."

David still had another question:

"Do we know where the two small boats come from?"

Yael had only a partial answer:

"We still don't, but they do not look Syrian. So, we assume that they're ISIS until we know better. That's why we're aiming at them first. I know it's nothing but a fig leaf, but Syria is a sovereign country while ISIS has been branded a terrorist organization by many authorities. That gives us the right to go after them."

"Any other weapons in the area?"

"Excellent question Simon. We have a couple of arial drones equipped with our guided torpedo bombs."

David followed on:

"And the Americans?"

Yael's reply was totally clear:

"We've agreed that the Americans will only fire if fired at. They would rather not attack a Russian vessel directly, which I totally understand. They are there to dissuade attacks on us. But we have ample fire power to defend ourselves. I'm glad to report that the other Russian Navy ships are within sailing distance, but not close enough to intervene. We read that as a sign that they are also playing a sort of intimidation game."

Simon replied:

"I bet you that they never anticipated that the Americans would enter into the picture."

"Absolutely. In fact, as I told you before, the Americans were on their way to the Persian Gulf. Now we would have certainly planned other tactics if their support was not available."

Yael paused for a second and added:

"We would probably have discreetly attacked the ISIS boats using INS *Protector.* That would not necessarily have allowed us to see what was being delivered, but beggars can't be choosers."

■ ■ ■ ■ ■

Josh and his team were smack in the middle of the ritualized exchange. After he had been passed by the smugglers' pickup truck and started to drive and follow them, he saw the truck turn right toward the meeting point, as expected. It stopped when it reached it. Josh, as instructed, drove past the pickup truck and parked right in front of it. The occupants of the pickup truck started to unload the heroin which was packaged into brick-sized blocks, each weighing about five pounds. Josh inspected the first block which was shown to him, made a small longitudinal incision in the package and confirmed on his tongue that he was indeed dealing with heroin or at least processed opium. After all, it would not have made sense for the smugglers to carry raw opium from the paddy fields. The processing process shrunk the total volume of useful morphine alkaloids down to 12% of the original size of poppy gum: a reduction from 100% to 12% of total volume surely helps handling and transactions . . . He told the smuggler that was standing by his window that he would accept the merchandise and invited him to place the packages in his trunk, which he then popped open.

After the smugglers had transferred the forty-four packages, it was Josh's time to show the diamonds to the smugglers. They took the box in which they were placed and carried it back to the car. Both of them got into the car and, Josh assumed, proceeded to inspect the diamonds. Mike, who had walked through the forest and was now right behind the truck, chose the moment to move from the dark of the forest to the dark of the night on the side of the road, his dark clothing helping keep him virtually invisible. He carefully placed the bug he intended to place earlier under the bed of the truck and returned as quickly as reasonable into the forest where, even with full headlights on, most people would not be able to locate him. His *Shayetet* 13 training was very handy. He positioned himself opposite the passenger door of Josh's car and waited. He did not have to wait long. One of the two smugglers got out of their truck and walked to the driver's side of Josh's car. He indicated to Josh that the deal was satisfactory. Ominously, he warned him:

"We will leave first. Wait a minute or so and then you can leave. Do not try to follow us. You cannot see him from here, but we have another car parked on the road before the intercession. It will wait there until you come out of this road. He'll verify that you turn left as you should if you're going back to Mosul. We will have turned right, as you will easily see. He will come after you and shoot at your car if he sees you following us."

Through his face mask and with the voice box still dissimilating his voice, Josh simply responded:

"Your menace is totally unnecessary. Why would I try to follow you? I know you will have more merchandise to deliver. I also know that I have more diamonds for you, somewhere. One menace deserves another. Do not try anything funny near the store where we met in Mosul. We are not stupid enough to store our merchandise in a place which you know."

The smuggler looked almost contrite and walked back toward his truck.

That is when all hell broke loose. The two men whom Nathan had seen exit their vehicles near the intersection with Highway 2 raised their automatic weapons and started firing in the direction of the pickup truck and Josh's car. Fortunately, Nathan had followed them into the forest as they walked along the road. He shot two tranquilizer bullets at the two men who fell to the ground immediately. He drew them back to the side of the road, retrieved the needles that were still sticking out and calmly returned to his car. He sent a message to

Josh to tell him he was safely back in his car. Josh told him to wait for Mike who was running in his direction and then to drive back to Mosul. He reminded him that they would eventually need to be in the vicinity of the airport where Mehmet would take the merchandise onboard his plane.

The pickup truck drove rapidly alongside Josh's car and as expected turned right when reaching the end of the road. The car which Daniel had seen coming toward the group, on what everyone thought was an unused road during the night, drove past Josh's car and turned left in the direction of the amusement park. Josh was surely surprised, not thinking that people would be working in the park that early. Yet, as the car did not seem to be any menace to anyone, he ignored it.

While waiting for the required time after the departure of the pickup truck, Josh sent a message to Mehmet giving him the all-clear. Mehmet who had landed in Cizre, Turkey, to await the signal knew that he had less than an hour's flight to Mosul. He had taken advantage of the stop to top up his fuel reservoirs, as he knew that there was going to be a long flight after leaving Mosul. The stop had been planned so that the team would have about as long a trip back to Mosul as it would take Mehmet to reach Mosul airport by plane. The idea was that the three cars would arrive at the airport. Mike would run to Josh's car and ride with him into the airport, near the plane which should have arrived on the tarmac. Both Josh and Mike expected Mehmet to park the plane with the nose facing almost due south, which would allow them to transfer the merchandise through the front left door. Thus, no one in the nearby buildings could possibly see any of the action.

As expected, Josh started his engine when Mike had joined him in the car and drove away, turning left on the highway, ostensibly to return to Mosul. Daniel had by that time returned to his own car and was ready to follow the truck for a while until he would receive confirmation from Josh that he had the truck's bug on his GPS.

The relatively high-pitched sound of the plane landing was the signal everyone was waiting for the next action to begin, as the three cars had in fact arrived within a half mile of the airport before Mehmet's plane and had parked with their engines running waiting for him. The plane taxied exactly to the place that had been selected. As he was turning left to bring the nose of the plane facing in the right direction, he saw a couple of headlights coming his way. He assumed, correctly, that these belonged to Josh's car. The car parked right next to the plane. The three men started the ballet: Josh was taking the packages from the trunk of the car, handing them to Mike, who in turn handed them to Mehmet at the top of the stairs. Nathan had positioned himself near the entrance to the tarmac and had both guns at the ready should anyone try to disturb the proceedings. Daniel, for his part, had also left his car and was standing about 150 feet from the plane.

The men had loaded all but four of the packages in the plane when the guard whom Mehmet had befriended irrupted onto the scene. Josh rushed the last four packages into Mehmet's plane and motioned to him that he should depart. Josh was surprised to hear two gunshots ring out, particularly as they seemed to have been fired by the guard. Josh called out to him and started walking toward him. The guard was not looking as friendly as usual, yet Josh elected to behave as if he was acting normally. When he was close enough to the guard, Josh asked:

"Hey, what's wrong? Mehmet had told me that you two were friends . . ."

The man replied:

"He and I are friends, but what are you all doing here?"

"We're all part of his movie team. We've just loaded a few packages containing initial videos. Mehmet is taking them back for processing . . ."

He was managing to keep the man's attention focused on him and motioned discreetly to Mehmet to start moving. The man became nervous again, but Josh kept talking to him as if nothing special was happening. The guard was decidedly turning toward the plane and watching as it was taxying to the end of the runway. Josh made an instant decision that he had to take the risk and tranquilize the man. He could not afford for the plane to be stopped or damaged. With the man's back temporarily turned to him, Josh fired a single shot which hit the man in the right thigh. He fell to the ground. Josh calmly walked toward him, removing any trace of the needle.

The three men returned to their respective cars and drove back to the place where they had agreed to meet . . .

■ ■ ■ ■ ■

Mehmet was about forty-five minutes into his flight, effectively overhead Tikrit when he called Bagdad approach on the radio:

"Must change my flight plan. I am asked to divert to Amman. Emergency request."

Nonchalantly, the air traffic controller replied:

"Permission granted. Flight plan amended and Jordanian authorities informed. Contact Amman approach when you are thirty minutes out. Over"

"Will contact Amman approach when I am thirty minutes out. Thank you. Over."

Mehmet had no intention of doing exactly as requested and neither was there any thought of landing in Amman. The fact that Bagdad had informed Jordanian authorities meant that no one would be surprised when he crossed from Iraq into Jordan. He preferred to fly into Jordanian airspace, as the alternative, though more of a direct line, would have required him to fly through Syria. He expected Amman control to contact him, probably expressing surprise that he had not started his descent. He would again argue that he had to make another stop first, emphasizing *first* so that the Jordanians did not assume that the final destination had changed. He would inform Amman approach that the extra stop was in Tel Aviv and would coyly request permission to start his descent. While the Amman air traffic controllers there might not be as happy to oblige, he would by that time be so close to Israeli air space that he would not worry. In fact, he had decided that he would switch off his transponder so that Amman air traffic control would seem briefly to have lost him on their radar; by the time he would switch it back on, arguing if asked that there was technical malfunction, he would be about to cross into Israeli airspace. He would proceed directly to Palmachim Air Base with a steeper than usual descent angle where David Heller was to greet him.

Mossad had planned the detour precisely because they wanted to find out more about the nature of the opiate alkaloid, which was being offered for sale. They would afterwards sell the merchandise to the local pharmaceutical industry, with alkaloids such as morphine or codeine one of the main classes of painkiller drugs.

■ ■ ■ ■ ■

A few hours later, after they had been able to catch up a bit on their sleep. Josh and his three associates called David Heller and Mark Levi at *Mossad* headquarters. The four of them were staying in the second store, a couple of doors down from where Josh had met with the smugglers. He immediately started the conversation:

"The bugs which we placed are working very well, thank you. Yet, they reserved a surprise for us. The pickup truck went, as I guess we expected, south and east of where we took delivery of the heroin.

On the other hand, the car with the two guys which Nathan had to tranquilize went to the northeast of Mosul."

He paused for a few seconds and added:

"That and the fact that the two guys in the car shot at us convinces me that they were not working together with the smugglers, which I guess is now obvious; but more than that, we figure they probably were competitors. Now, if our thesis about ISIS is correct, the guys that shot at us might be ISIS operatives . . ."

CHAPTER.23

MOSUL, ERBIL, KAWRUGOSIK AND TAL AFAR, IRAQ

Josh and his team initially smiled when they looked at both of the locations indicated by the bugs. The most striking element was that the two spots were almost diagonally disposed relative to Mosul: one to the west and the other to the southeast. This reinforced the view that the two groups were most likely not related and most probably competitors, if not direct adversaries. The second was that, with the benefit of hindsight, the locations were totally logical once one had concluded that the car whose occupants fired in the direction of the spot where Josh and the smugglers were conducting their exchange quite possibly belonged to ISIS.

That bug, indeed, had pointed to the region of Tal Afar, a city in the Nineveh Governorate of Northwestern Iraq, about thirty-nine miles west of Mosul. Tal Afar was a convenient staging point if one assumed that ISIS would have its headquarters in a general area extending west all the way to Al Raqqah which had been known to be their control center during the war and north to the Turkish border less than 100 miles away. Josh and Mike chose to go investigate that area.

At the same time, the second bug pointed to Kawrugosik just shy of forty-five miles from Mosul, though it was about eighteen miles from the point where the exchange had taken place. This is where the team believed that the smugglers might camp out even if it was not their prime location. It was almost due west of Erbil and, more importantly, it was in the general vicinity of where the plane that carried the diamonds had been shot down. Daniel and Nathan decided that they would focus on that region.

Both sub-teams had noted that the bugs had not stayed where they had initially stopped after the exchange. In the case of the smugglers, the bug was back at the point where it had initially stopped, but in the very early morning it had moved before coming back. Daniel and Nathan had carefully noted where the bug had gone on that trip and had decided first to look at the area where it had returned after the delivery. Doing so, they recognized that they may well not be focusing on the most important point: one could easily imagine that they had gone to report to headquarters and probably delivered some or all of the diamonds and then come back to their staging point. Yet, that was where the car was then; so, in the minds of the agents, that was where they should start.

They would still eventually go and visit the place where the car had gone in the early hours after the exchange. What if the group in Kawrugosik was but a minor part of a larger network? In that case, would it not be logical that the Kawrugosik group would have been required to deliver the diamonds to "headquarters?" At any rate, the key point was that whether a sub-group or simply a local contractor, the Kawrugosik crowd would not be keeping 100 carats of diamonds laying around. If a sub-group, they would need to deliver them to headquarters. If a local contractor, they would have to pay for the heroin that was delivered. Daniel had, however, made the point:

"Note that we don't know whether they pay before or after they have in turn sold the merchandise."

Nathan had simply replied:

"Totally fair. Don't want to interrupt your train of thought, but, as you're driving and I'm navigating, let's concentrate on the short term. My GPS App says that we are less than five miles away from where pickup truck with the bug initially parked."

In fact, a road sign was telling them that Kawrugosik was three miles away. They had driven in a generally southwestern direction on Highway 80 and Nathan made his observation as the sign announcing the exit pointed to both Kawrugosik and Kani Qirzhala, the huge municipal garbage dump for the city of Erbil. As they exited the highway, they could see the dump in the distance. There, piles of rubbish were stretching out far into the distance, with the attendant noxious fumes emanating from household waste as much as from the queuing garbage trucks waiting to dump their own contents. Nathan had to note:

"Flies must be the national bird here . . . Look at those sheep carcasses, or maybe they were goats, all in various stages of decay."

He then quickly added:

"That poor lone tree clings precariously to whatever it has found in lieu of nutrients in this uninspiring depression of a landscape. Thankfully, trees don't have noses; the stench must be unbelievable."

They had ignored the first exit which pointed solely to Kawrugosik as the map was showing them that this first road would lead them to the north of the town, while the second, at Abo Saeed, would take them into town, although still at its north end. Nathan pointing to the dump remarked:

"Had we taken the first road, about half a mile ago, we would have missed this sight of a lifetime."

Daniel could only chuckle.

Though not totally unusual, the center of town looked like it was designed on a grid, with eight streets running basically east-west and eleven running north-south. The town itself sat next to a camp which was created by the Kurdish Regional Government to shelter refugees from Syria. Though the camp was a godsend for many refugees, it was not hard to see that the two communities, the locals and the refugees, had so far at least failed to integrate. Locals explained that the area still included barriers supposedly designed to prevent refugees from being exploited by the local population. Yet, there were clear signs that refugees did not enjoy the best and most lucrative positions. Daniel and Nathan had read that the barriers to getting decent jobs had led to casual and exploitative labor among the refugees, as well as gender discrimination and even sexual exploitation. As Daniel had noted:

"This is exactly a type of environment where you would expect smugglers to prosper."

To which Nathan had simply replied:

"Or just revolutionaries . . ."

As they were getting quite close to where the car with the bug had originally stopped and was likely still parked, Daniel noted that they had arrived at the Noor Grand Mosque. It was surrounded both by many homes and by a large unused piece of land that covered nearly two thirds of the block. Pointing to a pickup truck at the back of the parking lot, Nathan suddenly announced:

"Hey, look . . . There . . . That's where the car is."

He paused and added:

"Not surprising in effect; it has to be where I would park my car. By the way, it's not alone . . . Plenty of cars there. It's got to be the parking lot for the Mosque."

Daniel replied:

"Seems like a totally logical conclusion. Let's go walk around and see if we see anything odd."

They parked their own car in an area which contained both beat-up vehicles and what seemed like relatively new cars. They found a place as close as they could to what they knew was the pickup truck driven by the smugglers: their buzzers were definitely confirming it was the vehicle with the bug in its bumper. With Daniel attempting as best he could to hide Nathan as he was pretending to tie up his shoe, Nathan was in fact discreetly inspecting the rear bumper of the pickup truck to ensure that there was no error on the vehicle. Standing back up next to his associate he casually declared:

"This is it. No question. I could feel the bug."

Daniel added:

"And we know it could not have been switched to another car as lifting the bug off the bumper would have led it to self-destruct, or at least to its electronic insides to self-destruct. It could surely not be sending any signal."

They walked in the direction of a pair of small, attached houses which stood just next to another group of three generally similar places, near the southeast end of the piece of land. Unfortunately, they could see next to nothing from the back of those homes. However, as they kept walking toward the second group of what looked like three homes, they noticed that there were in fact only two homes separated by what appeared like a common, roughly rectangular courtyard. Daniel observed:

"This group of homes looks a lot nicer than anything in this city block. Let's continue our walk though I think we may well have found what we were looking for . . ."

As they walked further east on the street at the south end of the plot where the cars were parked, they came across a number of other homes that appeared nicer than others. Daniel almost sadly announced with a fake disappointed look:

"Well, so much for my theory. These could just as easily be those we're looking for."

Nathan nodded when Daniel added:

"The smugglers could be just about anywhere around here."

Nathan with a faint hope in his voice noted:

"Could be, but I'm still going for your first theory."

"May I ask why?"

"Yep. The place where the car is parked. Look, in this area, cars are parked along the road, in front of homes. On the other hand, near the mosque, there was no place on the street. Much too narrow. So, the cars are on the parking of the Mosque."

"Quite correct, however, one could assume that they might have wanted to get just this bit more of safety—park the car away from the house."

"Don't disagree, but why there, where it sits next to another house, when there are many places nearer to where they live on that same lot?"

"Fair question. I guess we'll eventually find out, but probably not today . . ."

■ ■ ■ ■ ■

Meanwhile, Josh and Mike were driving to Tal Afar. Josh was particularly careful not to wear any of the elements of the disguise which he used with the smugglers. Both he and Mike were pretty convinced that ISIS rather than the smugglers were behind the second car, the one which drove to Tal Afar after the exchange. Yet, he felt there was no point taking the risk that he might be recognized. The second largest city in the Nineveh governorate, Tal Afar was still wearing the scars of the wars which had beset Iraq since the early 2000s, if not since much further back in this part of the world that saw the Ottoman Empire fight the Persian Safavids to the east, the Tsars of Russia to the north and the Habsburgs to the west. After the fall of the Ottoman Empire, Tal Afar was included in Iraq, though it kept being used as a base of operation against the British forces in Turkey. It was the center of another major battle between 2003 and 2011, as it was first taken by the U.S. army in a bid to control the violence which opposed local Turkmen against Iraqi nationals. Dissention continued as Sunni and Shiite Muslims battled for control, which eventually saw the area fall under the control of ISIS. Yet, almost four years after the liberation of the town from ISIS control, violence continued reflecting sustained tribal and religious animosities. Finally, in 2017, the city was reconquered by the Iraqi forces. The physical damage which all of these conflicts caused was still visible, although serious reconstruction efforts had been carried out. Yet, there were rumors here and there that some small area remained under some ISIS influence, if not its control.

Josh and Mike had driven on Highway 47 when they passed the east end of Tal Afar. The signal from the bug clearly suggested that the location they were seeking was on the west side of town. In fact, they found the location as they were starting to ask themselves whether something was wrong. Housing density had come down significantly, and they were ostensibly approaching the western limits of the town. Suddenly they came across a road on their left with a supermarket at the corner. They veered left and then, a thousand feet down that road and on their right, they happened on a large compound. It comprised at least three different homes and a substantial amount of land around it. This unmistakably was the spot where the car initially parked. In fact, it had not moved; it was still parked there according to the GPS signal. They first turned right on a poorly sealed road and, a couple of hundred yards later, they found another trail. The map showed that they could drive near the home at the end of the trail and then turn right alongside the north end of the plot of land and return to the original road. Yet, they decided to stop the car, park it along the right side of the road, in the shade provided by a double row of large trees and continue their observation on foot. Casual observation from a car might work, but not the careful inspection they were carrying out. They would rather walk around the neighborhood, though they thought it would be smarter for each of them to go their own way.

Josh followed the road south and, when reaching the trail that ran alongside the north end of the large house's property, turned right.

He walked along the trail trying to see as much as he could over the low hedge that ran all the way along the side of the property. He could see first a small, only partially cultivated vegetable garden with two rows of trees, one on its east side and another on the west side. He could not see any activity, though the place definitely looked inhabited when he walked directly abeam the house. Reaching the end of the trail, rather than turning right again to go back to the road they had driven by car, he decided to keep walking, entering an area that looked totally undeveloped. Penetrating further into that piece of land, he saw a group of six houses at the back of this plot. He kept walking in a southerly direction, as he did not feel it would be terribly prudent to return to the car simply retracing his steps. He found a few additional homes which initially did not seem terribly interesting until he reached the next corner when he found another home that was quite large.

He noted at that point that the signal he was receiving from the bug was increasing in intensity. He turned left on the road that ran on the south side of the home and confirmed that the signal was still getting stronger. He kept walking in a westerly direction and suddenly noted that the strength of the signal appeared to be decreasing. Looking more carefully at the big house he had just passed; he could not help but notice the garage door. Though he initially thought that the car he was looking for had to be inside the garage, he cheered quietly when he saw a car parked alongside a wall there and exclaimed:

"That's it."

He reached out to Mike who was patrolling the other end of the broader site to let him know both what he had found and that he would have quite a long walk to return to the car. Mike told him that he had not seen much that could be of interest on his walk. Yet, suddenly, as he was still talking on the phone, he said:

"Josh, I know this guy . . ."

"Which guy?"

"A guy that just walked by me. He had come out of the larger house we initially identified. He looked like he was going to another house along the road I had just walked. Couldn't turn around to do more. But I am sure I've seen him before."

He paused a short time while he was desperately trying to remember when he exclaimed:

"The guard at the Mosul Airport! That's him. The guard at the airport."

"The one Mehmet thought he had befriended?"

"One and the same."

"Hold it right there. This must mean he is in cahoots with the fellows around here."

He stopped for a few seconds and then said:

"Wait a minute, if this area is some ISIS camp, using several, maybe all of these houses, the fact that he is here rather than at the airport must mean both that he is ISIS as well and that they are planning something."

"Do you think he could have realized that he was shot and tranquilized?"

"Not sure, because I'm certain I removed all traces of anything I could find. However, these things often leave a bruise . . . Assume that he had bled and saw a needle mark, and everything is possible. At any rate, he could not miss the fact that he had been sleeping on the tarmac; that was bound to be a surprise."

They decided to pause the conversation, meet as discreetly as they could back at the car and then drive back to Mosul and discuss their findings with Mark or David, or both. Mike had indeed added that if he was able to recognize the guard, it was totally possible that the guard might have recognized him. Mike was the first to arrive near where the car was parked and was decidedly unhappy to see a few people milling around it. It was a bog-standard rental which should not have impressed anyone. He started wondering whether the guard had indeed recognized him, decided to call a few friends and possibly place a bomb in it or sabotage a crucial mechanical element. He called Josh again:

"Trouble in paradise. There are a few people surrounding our car. We have to assume the worst. Don't come back here. Walk in the direction of the center of town, due east. I'll walk on the road we took for a while as well and let's meet when we are both at least a mile away from here. I don't like the way this is shaping up. By the way, as I was walking, I had another thought: could there be a mole within the smugglers' ranks? That would surely explain why those we call ISIS were there at the exchange . . ."

■ ■ ■ ■ ■

Though still sure that they had found the correct location for where the smugglers had parked their pickup after the exchange, Daniel and Nathan decided they still did not know what really was in Kawrugosik: was it "the" center or was it just "a satellite?" They concluded that there was not a lot more that they could do there. They thus proceeded to look at the place to which the pickup had made a quick round trip that morning. They knew that the smugglers had gone to Erbil, though they were not totally sure what they would find where they got there; in fact, they did not even know whether the pickup trip did or did not have had anything to do with the delivery. Yet, at that point, this had to be the next logical step.

Erbil, which was known in ancient history as Arbela, was the capital and most populated city in the Kurdistan region of Iraq. Though smack in the middle of Kurdistan, Erbil was quite a diverse city from both ethnic and religious viewpoints. In fact, certain people within the city tended to feel that trouble or strife had always been brought to the city by "foreigners." And, by "foreigners," they meant people who did not live there and had not lived there for at least a generation, though they could well be Iraqis. The historical heart of the city was a citadel which has stood on a mound about 100 feet higher than the surrounding plains for millennia. It has been claimed that the site is the oldest continuously inhabited town in the world, with the earliest evidence of population in residence dating back to 5,000 years before Christ.

Daniel and Nathan had noted that the location of the point the smugglers had visited was within the walls on the citadel. They knew that they would have to drive past five ring roads loosely following the contours of the walls of the citadel before they got to the main gate. They approached it and could not miss that it was guarded by an immense statue of a Kurd reading. The houses of the citadel behind the statue were built into the stony ground of the mound and looked down on the streets and the tarmacked roads that circled them. Once inside the walls of the Citadel, they quickly found a whole maze of streets going seemingly randomly in every possible direction. Nathan observed:

"Well, we expected a labyrinth, and we should be totally satisfied."

Daniel deadpanned:

"They didn't know of grids then!"

"Guess not."

They immediately noticed that the main road effectively bisected the citadel into two almost symmetrical sections, both of which were very busy, full of medium to small size houses. They had no difficulty finding the tower that stood at the center. They noted that the pickup truck had parked very close to it. However, just had been the case in Kawrugosik, they noted that the tightness of the streets was such that parking near the tower was most probably the only available option, even if the ultimate destination was some distance away. They looked at half a dozen homes that looked quite a bit larger than others, fully recognizing that the house they were looking for might just as much be small as large as they had assumed. Yet, somehow, they believed that the only reason why the pickup truck might have traveled to

Erbil for a purpose related to their hunt had to be the delivery of diamonds to some senior figure in their organization. Thus, it was logical to assume that such an individual might enjoy some privileged position. However, there was no way they could then identify any one of these larger homes as the one that was suspect, any more than any other.

They were about to turn back toward their car when something attracted their attention. Was that going to change anything?

CHAPTER.24

MOSUL, IRAQ, ANTWERP, BELGIUM, TEL AVIV, ISRAEL AND SOMEWHERE IN THE AUSTRIAN ALPS

Josh and his team had returned to the store in Mosul and decided it was time to have a conference call with Tel Aviv. They swept again the near neighborhood to make sure that there was no device around that would allow anyone to eavesdrop on their conversation.

Mark picked up the phone when it rang and seeing its origin immediately conferenced David on. Josh started his report:

"Our inspection of the various points identified by the bugs seems to have been fruitful, but not to have resolved anything in a definitive manner. Unfortunately, it is also making our lives more difficult."

Mark replied:

"Thanks for the cryptic introduction my friend, but we're going to need more."

"I know, just wanted you to appreciate that we have quite an agenda for you."

Josh started with the most recent discovery made by Daniel and Nathan. He explained that as they were ready to return to their car, to drive back to Mosul, they noticed some unusual activity at the entrance of one of the larger properties near the tower in Erbil's citadel. Nathan explained:

"We saw a couple of fellows who seemed to be carrying small packages from inside a house to a small car parked just in front of it."

Mark could not resist interrupting:

"Processed opium?"

Nathan replied:

"I don't know for sure, but it certainly could have been that."

Mark asked:

"Talking about the place you were looking for, the place where you saw that activity . . . It was signaled by a trip made by the pickup truck after returning to Kawrugosik just after the diamond/heroin exchange, correct?"

Daniel replied:

"Almost. First, it returned to Kawrugosik and stayed there a couple of hours at most. Then, very early this morning, it drove to Erbil. Less than an hour later, it returned to Kawrugosik. That's where we saw it today."

David interrupted:

"Could it be that the house where you surprised the two guys loading packages into the trunk of their car belongs to the head of a smuggling group?"

He paused and explained that he was wondering whether the smugglers as they knew them were operating independently or were a part of some larger organization. Daniel interrupted:

"That's exactly what we were discussing among ourselves earlier today. We're still not sure how "our smugglers" relate to this new place. Could be some headquarters. But could also be a wholesaler from whom they buy the heroin which they then sell."

He paused and realizing that David seemed quite interested in their thoughts, he added:

"We're still unsure also whether they brought the diamonds to pay for the load of heroin which they just sold us or to pay for the next batch of heroin they will then seek to sell."

David interrupted:

"So, whether they picked up another load of opium or not at that time is still a complete unknown."

Nathan replied:

"Am afraid that's pretty much the conclusion we reached."

He paused for a second and continued:

"Now, having seen people maybe loading heroin into their car, still does not tell us enough. They may just be reloading for their next delivery or might have brought whatever they received in payment for the prior delivery and reloading."

Mark interjected:

"There's probably no mileage in our speculating further. We'll eventually find out."

Daniel added:

"But then why did the pickup truck first stop in Kawrugosik? Why didn't it go straight to Erbil?"

Mark suggested that there were at least a couple of different explanations within the set of assumptions governing the current scenario considered:

"One thing we don't know is whether the smugglers pay for the opium first or bring the payment after they have received it. If they pay first, they might have stopped let's say "at home" to decide how much opium they would buy that time. If they pay later, they might have stopped to take their cut, however you call it . . ."

The group jumped on that second option, as it raised a new and interesting question as Josh expressed it:

"If they first stopped home to take their cut, we have to assume that the diamonds may well reach the market through two different channels. One for the head smugglers if we can call him that and the other for his local operatives . . ."

Mark interrupted again:

"That's certainly something to consider. In fact, it could be more than two. What if the head smuggler as I shall call him used some of these diamonds to pay for the opium he then distributes? You might have three different diamonds sellers . . ."

He paused for a second and concluded:

"We'll need to wait and see where and when the diamonds show up in the marketplace. At any rate, the more sellers, the more we shall find out about the network."

Mark paused again and then added:

"We should carry out a second exchange as fast as we can just to have more diamonds in the market . . ."

Josh took the opportunity to discuss their own discovery when visiting Tal Afar, starting with an ironic note:

"We also found out something quite interesting. Our discovery caused us to have to rent another car . . . It may well be causing another challenge. Possibly a major one, I should add."

He went on to relate the fact that Mike thought he recognized the Mosul airport guard near the group of properties they were both visiting in Tal Afar. Mike jumped into the conversation:

"I've been thinking a lot about that one. Assume it was indeed the guard for a second. Then three people from that group fell suddenly sleepy in the middle of the mission. What if it was not the guard who chose to return to Al Afar, but someone in Tal Afar who summoned him there?"

Daniel interrupted:

"How would the people in Tal Afar know that the guard had been tranquilized?"

They all stayed silent for a short while until Mark offered:

"What if it was the guard that "reported to headquarters" what had happened to him?"

Mike cut him off:

"Why would he do that? First, he should not remember that he had fallen asleep and second even if he did wouldn't he worry that he would be punished for sleeping on the job?"

Everyone on the call agreed that they could not fully understand what the exact circumstances were, though Josh observed:

"I hate to be the idiot here, but I don't buy that logic. First, he should not remember that he slept, but he surely would know that he woke up somewhere where he was not supposed to be seated. Second, with that observation, he should not have been worried that he would be punished for sleeping on the job."

Mike added:

"OK, agreed. Well, headquarters might have called him to discuss the problem with his two colleagues that suddenly woke up by the side of a road. That could have triggered his memory, and he would then have been OK to report it."

Josh concluded:

"Whatever the reason why he was in Tal Afar, the fact is that the Mosul airport guard seems to be either part of the group which we think is ISIS or at least an informer. Shouldn't that make the use of Mosul's airport no longer reasonable? Anyone disagree?"

Mark and David wanted to be absolutely sure that they had heard all the opinions. They asked a number of additional questions, as they were simultaneously delighted that the team was making progress and upset that they might well have to change an important element of the current plan. In the end, Mark agreed that he needed to find another location where Mehmet would land, adding:

"I agree that Mosul Airport had a number of positive attributes, but we can't take the risk any longer. I need to talk to Mehmet. I know that Erbil's Airport is considerably busier than Mosul's. There are many flights every day, both internal to Iraq and international. So, whatever we do will have to be much more in the open . . ."

Daniel, the one who always seemed to be able to disappear in a crowd, added with a smile:

"Hide in plain sight?"

Mark picked up on Daniel's point and conceded that it might well be a case where the activity around them might help. However, he added:

"For instance, I don't think we can count on that location to bring any more opium out of the country."

Daniel replied:

"Reasonable, but who knows?"

The conversation might have continued in that direction a while longer, but Josh had at least one other issue he wanted to discuss:

"Before we go any further on this, one question bothers me: How did ISIS find out about the delivery spot?"

Mike added:

"Don't know the answer to the question, but let's all remember that Mehmet, Daniel and I were supposed to be a film-crew. Now the guard did see all of us at one point or another. However, no one saw any of us with Josh at least until the exchange of the diamonds for the drugs. And there, given the light situation at that time in the night, they may not have recognized anyone, least of all Josh given his disguise."

Josh interrupted:

"Darn right. But there is more. We had the surprise incident when the car almost ran me over on the street at the back of the store. Now, I know that we've agreed that it might have been a case of mistaken identity. However, I have to ask myself if there isn't a spy working for ISIS within the smugglers' network."

Mark jumped on the thought:

"Obviously, that would explain everything."

He paused for a second and asked:

"How do we find out?"

Mark answered his own question:

"Leave this one to me. Let me first talk to Mehmet and see how our plans for the next delivery must be changed. I'll then turn to the issue of a possible ISIS informer within the smugglers' organization. That will likely involve higher risks and I need to think about those before asking you to take them."

■ ■ ▨ ■ ■

Meanwhile in the Mediterranean, south and east of Cyprus, the two suspected ISIS boats had gotten close enough to the Israeli vessels that some action could no longer be avoided. INS *Protector* which was not submerged took the lead. She sent a radio message inviting the two smaller boats to stop and turn around. It stated that it would not be advisable to proceed as the area was under Israeli control and no transfer from the Russian cargo boat would be permitted. The two ISIS boats slowed down but did not stop. A blank torpedo launched by INS *Protector* passed a hundred feet in front of the bow of the first ship. A sailor on the INS *Protector*, Elihu Leitner, called Captain Mike Dayan on the internal communication system:

"Captain, important message exchange between suspected ISIS boats and Russian sub. They're asking for help . . ."

Captain Dayan called Yael Orbach on the radio as the submarine was not submerged:

"Chief, we have an issue. The suspected ISIS boats are asking the Russian sub for help. Any instruction?"

"Let's not be trigger happy. Has the Russian sub surfaced?"

"No, at least not yet. She is still underwater. We know almost exactly where she is; we have it on Sonar . . ."

"Can she threaten you?"

"No, American ships are in the way."

Yael thought for a second and suggested:

"I'd invite them again to come to the surface. At the same time, I'd share with them the message you've sent to the two ISIS boats earlier. Make sure you do not sound directly threatening to the sub, but don't hesitate to state that any adversarial move made by any of the two ISIS boats or by the Russian cargo ship will be viewed as deserving a strong response. They should understand we mean business."

"Aye, sir."

Captain Dayan drafted a Sonar message that was both firm and precise, while avoiding any direct threat to the Russian submarine. A few seconds after it was sent, Sailor Elihu Leitner called out again:

"New message from Russian sub to ISIS boats. It says: 'no change in plan.'"

Captain Dayan looked disappointed and yet ordered:

"Release Orca 1, stand by for release of Orca 2."

He was indeed not going to attack either of the three possible targets from the submarine. Rather, sending the two submarine drones, each of which had two smaller but quite effective torpedoes, he gave himself the option of incapacitating or even sinking any of the two smaller boats without providing any excuse that his submarine had fired at them. He asked:

"Com officer Leitner, any further message?"

"Just from the response from the smaller boat, which simply said 'OK.'"

Captain Dayan asked:

"Any sign of communication with the larger cargo ship."

"None so far."

A message from Yael informed Captain Dayan that he had just ordered one of the two frigates to sail in the direction of the cargo ship and to inform her that they wanted to inspect her cargo.

■ ■ ■ ■ ■

Albert Hoets called Countess Renate. He had indeed picked up the first indication that at least a few of the synthetic diamonds had hit the market. She looked at her watch and seeing that the time zones still allowed it, she asked Albert if she could call him back on Skype and have David Heller join in the conference. After a few seconds of banter among the three of them, she invited Albert to repeat his earlier message:

"As I just told Countess Renate, we have just heard one report of a few diamonds that you asked me to watch for being offered for sale in Beirut."

David asked:

"Did your contact identify them as synthetic?"

"Absolutely not. He affirmed that they were of excellent quality."

"Any information as to how many of them?"

"Funny you should ask. I was told there were twelve stones."

"Twelve? That's exactly what the first sample comprised!"

"Precisely. In fact, I knew exactly what they were as I had a written description of the stones in my records. So, I asked him to describe them. I am virtually certain that these are the sample diamonds."

David congratulated Albert and Countess Renate first and then asked:

"Anything further, such as provenance and the rest?"

Albert replied:

"You can be assured that I probed, but my contact could only tell me that a jewelry confrere had called him to show him the stones. Apparently, he had been surprised they were all "D" color, flawless and perfect cut. He had never seen such a sample . . ."

David interrupted:

"Did he say "sample" or was that your own inference?"

"He did call them a sample, as his seller told him that there would soon be more."

Turning the conversation to Countess Renate, David then argued:

"Could we find out more about the other jeweler without arousing suspicion? It seems to me that we have perfect match on this small exchange."

"We certainly can try, David; wouldn't you agree Albert?"

Albert replied that he would suggest offering to buy the stones from the contact."

David asked what he meant. He simply replied:

"It would be quite normal for me to ask for my contact for his source, though I would need to commit not to go directly to whomever he named. Remember, when I reached out to a few reputed and reputable diamond dealers, I had to commit that I would buy the diamonds from them."

Countess Renate added:

"I remember that well. And I committed on David's behalf to buy these diamonds back from you with 125% their carat weight in investment grade stones."

David confirmed that this was also the way he understood the agreement and was ready to hold his side of the bargain. Countess Renate, with a wide smile, concluded:

"Well, Detective Hoets, we are in your hands."

Albert simply smiled back.

■ ■ ■ ■ ■

David Heller immediately brought Mark into the picture. They were ecstatic that the first important test of their strategy had been successful. David asked:

"How quickly can we organize the next diamond drop?"

"Well, that's just become a bit more complicated. As you know, we decided that Mosul airport was no longer acceptable. I talked to Mehmet. He has no trouble flying into Erbil; the extra distance between Erbil and Mosul is almost insignificant in terms of flight time or fuel consumption. The issue is that he will have to spend more time over Iraq, which increases the risk that the plane could be identified or simply randomly shot at."

"But Erbil has quite a few daily flights, right?"

"It does, but Mehmet feels that the same plane landing or taking off a few too many times could appear suspect."

He paused and added:

"I should be clearer. Mehmet's point that a private plane making a few too many appearances might be suspect. They're of course used to the commercial traffic."

"What do you make of that?"

"Well, we're going to deliver all the diamonds on the next trip and use lockers at the airport to store those we do not immediately need. The issue is with the processed opium which the smugglers deliver. I can have Mehmet fly to Palmachim as he did the last time once or twice, but not more than that. Somebody is bound to notice a pattern?"

David seemed to think for a few seconds and then said:

"Should not be a huge problem, right? We may not have to deliver all the diamonds we have made. After all, we captured 25,000 carats from the downed terrorist plane. That means that we have enough to buy back 20,000 carats which is about what Samuel Eisenstein made and Albert had cut for us. Wouldn't you think that Josh would have a good enough relationship with the smugglers after a couple more exchanges?"

Mark conceded that they were both on the same wavelength, though he still had a simple concern:

"Mehmet's plane cannot carry more than a ton of cargo at a time and still be able to fly the route it will need to fly, even if we assume that he can refuel at Erbil."

David simply replied:

"Let's cross that bridge when we get there."

CHAPTER.25

MOSUL, ANTWERP, TEL AVIV, SOUTH OF CYPRUS AND SOMEWHERE IN THE AUSTRIAN ALPS

Yael was back on the phone with Captain Mike Dayan on the INS *Protector*:

"Could you urgently redirect one of the Orcas to dive toward the Russian Cargo ship?"

"Of course. What's the mission?"

"I need as good as possible a picture of the ship's external propulsion system. David Heller tells me that their technological wizard has a possible trick up his sleeve."

"No problem. I'll have those sent to you as soon as possible."

Yael added:

"Oh! I forgot to tell you that Captain Aaron Gratzinger and the INS *Dragon* are sailing in your direction. Do not worry if you see her on your Sonar. The plan is that she would surface if the Russian sub surfaces when you ask her and stay submerged if she does not."

"Aye, sir."

Mark had indeed shared with Marvin the problem they faced just south of Cyprus. He described the quandary in simple terms:

"We would rather not attack what we believe are ISIS boats too early. The risk seems too high that we could be lighting a fuse we sure as heck don't want to light. Similarly, we don't want to board the Russian cargo ship too early. Yet, we definitely want to know what she carries and, assuming she carries the same cargo as the other, we know that we don't want the cargo to reach the shore."

"Understand all that. Tell me: what would be a bad outcome?"

"Bad outcome?"

"Yes Mark, the kind of outcome which would make you feel we have all failed?"

"I see. I see."

Mark paused and thought for a second and then simply blurted out:

"I'd hate to see the cargo ship abandon the mission, turn back and return to the Black Sea and Russia."

Marvin simply replied:

"If that's the case, I'm sure I can help you."

Mark smiled with anticipation. Yet, he still wanted to hear Marvin explain what his solution would be. Marvin proceeded to describe his approach, adding that the only data he needed was whether the Russian ship had one or two screws and the way these propellers were attached to the driveshaft. He concluded:

"It's much easier to prevent the propellers from rotating than to deal with the rudder."

"Why?"

"Blocking the rudder means that the ship would run in a circle. That's doable, but it is not easy for technical reasons you probably don't want to hear. Blocking the propellers simply means the ship cannot move, period."

"Makes sense. How would that work?"

"Very simple. We can manufacture a piece of metal which effectively locks the screw in place."

For once, Marvin may have overly simplified his discourse. Mark simply did not follow, something which Marvin immediately picked up in his facial expression. He explained in more detail:

"Think of a "U" shaped piece of metal, could be a tube, or could be solid. That piece straddles the driveshaft with two returns, one at each end. Each of these returns locks onto a blade of the propeller. That's all. The propeller can't turn, and we would have engineered the strength of the piece to make sure the engine's power could not snap it in two."

Mark was smiling. Marvin added:

"Once we know the correct dimensions of the propeller, and the distances between blades and driveshaft, we can get it ready in a few hours. If possible, I would like to add a couple of clips on each driveshaft, one on either side of my blocking device, to make sure it does not slide up or down the shaft."

"Quite ingenious, I must say."

"Thanks, but it's also quite basic."

"Any risk?"

"The only one I can think of is that the torque of the engine is such that it breaks off the propeller blades to which the device is attached."

"Implications?"

"The ship could move, but her speed would be definitely limited."

"Is this realistic?"

"Frankly no. It could happen in theory, but I can't see it happening in practice. These propeller blades are very carefully engineered."

Mark had to conclude and ask:

"Now I see how that would work. To me, tell me if I'm wrong, the main challenge has to be to place the contraption. One contraption if there is one engine and one propeller, two contraptions if there are two propellers. And, by the way, we've got to be able to place them, as I'm pretty sure a ship of that size has to have two propellers, without being seen. How d'you deal with that?"

"A three-man submarine with a couple of divers."

Marvin went on to describe the needed action:

"The mini-submarine dives as far down as she can, given the condition at the bottom of the sea. Its small size and the depth at which it sails, it should not give a large enough Sonar image to be picked up by the target. When under the Russian ship, the submarine would gradually rise toward the surface, still staying deep enough to avoid being noticed and identified. Once she is less than 100 feet below the water surface, the two divers exit and swim toward the ship. They have to take their time doing that because of their decompression needs. At any rate, they place the device on the screws, and dive back down to the mini submarine."

"Any specific requirement?"

"Absolutely, the ship must be at anchor. I wouldn't want the divers to approach the propellers if they are rotating."

"I see. Let me get you pictures of the propellers and drive shafts."

"Great. We can then manufacture the devices and send them to INS *Protector*. I know they have a mini sub in their hold."

■ ■ ■ ■ ■

True to his word, Marvin was able to make his propeller stopping device right on schedule, once he had received pictures of the Russian cargo ship's screws and driveshafts. As expected, the ship had two driveshafts, each connected to a different engine. Though he was not sure what the exact power of each engine was, Marvin had the device manufactured to withstand twice the most likely power output of the engines. He also took into account the thickness of the metal where the blades connected with the axis of the propeller, as that would also determine how much power the blades should withstand before breaking off. While it made the device somewhat heavier and larger than probably necessary, Marvin had decided that this was the safest route. Indeed, as the divers would be operating in water, the weight of each device would not represent an unsurmountable obstacle for them; objects are lighter in water than in the air as they benefit from an upthrust equal to the weight of the water it volume displaces. With a wink in his eye, he added:

"Thank you, Archimedes!"

Marvin took advantage of the Eurocopter X3, the world's fastest helicopter, which the Israeli Air force had purchased precisely for its speed—it reaches a top speed of more than two hundred and fifty miles per hour. It looked somewhat different from typical helicopters: it had the same central rotor as all helicopters, but also featured two additional propellors, one on each side of the aircraft. The speed of the aircraft made the trip from Palmachim Air Base to the INS *Protector* substantially shorter timewise, which would allow "Operation Standstill" to be completed sooner and thus the risk of the ship sailing away diminished sooner as well.

The size of the two devices had required somewhat of an odd maneuver. Getting the devices into the mini submarine had proven impossible. It was then decided to use a couple of hooks attached tightly to the outside surface of the mini submarine. It would then effectively drag the devices underwater rather than carry them inside. The contraptions had to be secured tightly, as any movement might have damaged the mini submarine. The hooks were each connected to a cord which went through the airlock and was tied firmly inside the small hold of the mini submarine. Once on location, the airlock let the two divers exit while the pilot of the mini submarine untied the cords. Both divers swam toward the ship's propellers, breathing a big sigh of relief when they could verify that the propellers were indeed not moving. Their only complaint, afterwards, was that the devices were indeed quite heavy, even with the help provided by the operation taking place underwater. Marvin had provided for a wider shaft diameter than actually needed, but the idea was that it would make placing the devices on the shafts easier. The divers still needed to secure the clips that would prevent the devices from moving along the shafts.

When they returned to the mini submarine and were finally able to talk, they noted that they were particularly happy that they had been able to place the devices on the driveshafts without banging into them. They had indeed been warned that the greatest risk was that any sort of sound reverberating into the inside of the Russian ship would cause the sailors to question what was happening. They might then either send divers to check or decide to test whether everything was right with respect to the propellers. They might also activate their active sonar to pick up anything that might be nearby. That was, in fact, the reason Marvin had suggested placing the clips on first, as he was sure that this could be done with no risk of making any noise. Once the clips were in place, they could slide the device between them, do it totally silently and tighten the clips afterwards.

■ ■ ■ ■ ■

Captain Dayan's message to Yael Orbach was short and sweet: "Devices in place."

Yael replied that the next move would be for him to talk to the senior American officer on location to inform him and plan the next phase. He added:

"We are entering what is probably the most dangerous phase of the mission . . ."

■ ■ ■ ■ ■

Josh called "the voice" to inform the smugglers that he was ready to accept up to one ton of processed opium. The voice seemed definitely happy to hear the news. In fact, if truth be known, the voice had been told by the head of the smugglers in Erbil that the diamonds had proven to be even better than expected. Thus, the voice was more talkative than usual. Josh was delighted to note that change and asked:

"I was somewhat worried when we last exchanged our merchandise that someone shot at us. I'm pretty sure it could not be one of your people as the shooting started before the pickup truck had departed."

The voice replied:

"We were indeed surprised as well. We also assumed it could not be your people, but still worried. The lesson is that the location we selected probably offered too many entry and exit points."

"Do you have any solution in mind?"

"Not yet. Surely, I will take more people along. I know you had more people as well as the shooting stopped quite suddenly. You must have had someone there to cover you . . ."

Josh replied that indeed he did, but laconically added:

"But frankly, I wouldn't have had anyone if the shooters had come from the opposite direction."

Josh paused and offered a thought which would help him gauge the extent of the possible cooperation with the smugglers:

"Maybe we could agree that we pick a spot with only one entry and one exit and commit for one of us to guard one while the other covers the other. I do not have enough people to cover both."

He was delighted when the voice replied:

"Interesting idea, but how can we be sure?"

"I assume that you mean be sure that this is not a trap for you. If that's what you worry about, note that it's as much if not more of a trap for me."

The voice made what sounded like a grunt and said:

"Fair point. When will you be ready?"

"I need about thirty-six hours of notice at most."

"I'll call you back."

∎ ∎ ∎ ∎ ∎

Yael Orbach called Captain Dayan back:

"Invite the Russian submarine to surface again. We need to ascertain her intentions. The Americans are with us with respect to the suspected arms delivery. We've agreed that we are going to stop the two suspected ISIS boats. We've also agreed that INS *Destiny* is going to sail toward the Russian cargo ship and ask to inspect its cargo. A Kovesh is circling over the area with a torpedo bomb and a depth charge. Either could be used if needed, though we would prefer not to."

Captain Dayan immediately followed the orders he had received. The response from the Russian sub was unfortunately not constructive. Mike Dayan replied that he was disappointed and informed them that an Israeli frigate would approach the cargo ship to tell them that they needed to inspect its cargo. He added:

"Any adversarial move on your part will make your vessel a legitimate target."

The Russian submarine replied with even more aggressive language, which Captain Dayan chose to ignore. *After all*, he thought, *we have warned them . . .*

"Com officer to Captain Dayan . . ."

"Yes, what?"

"The Russian submarine is moving back toward the scene and told the cargo ship to be ready to move away."

"Thanks. Keep monitoring."

INS *Javelin*, the missile boat, started to move closer to the action, being now ready to intercept the ISIS supply ships approaching the scene. It ordered them to stop. When they failed to stop, the first rocket was fired. It landed near enough the first supply boat to make him slow down to a crawl. At the same time, the sailors on the two supply ships could see INS *Destiny* approach the Russian cargo ship.

■ ■ ■ ■ ■

Aboard the Russian submarine, the communication officer called the captain to announce that he could see another submerged submarine in the area. The captain asked:

"Israeli or American?"

"Can't tell, transponder shut down."

"Big or small?"

"Same size as the one that has surfaced."

■ ■ ■ ■ ■

Captain Dayan asked:

"Where are the two Orcas?"

"Close enough to the ISIS supply ships to take care of both of them."

"Be ready but hold any fire until my command."

■ ■ ■ ■ ■

Meanwhile, Albert Hoets called Countess Renate again to let her know that more diamonds were on sale from the same earlier jeweler. She called David to check the prior instructions were still valid and he confirmed:

"How much is for sale? Whatever the amount under 100 carats is acceptable. Do not buy more as we know they only received 100 carats in the last exchange."

"Hold on for a second David. Let me call Albert on the other line . . ."

She came back on the line within less than a minute:

"Albert says the offer is for 80 carats, diamonds between 1 and 2 carats."

"Let's go. We'll exchange them for 100 carats of investment grade diamonds."

He mumbled to himself that someone was taking a 20% cut somewhere. Countess Renate replied:

"Albert will be delighted. Thank you."

David added:

"By the way, Countess, could you please tell Albert to be on the lookout, as we're missing twenty carats. Must have gone through another channel. Would love to know where they are. Also, I assume it is the same seller as the first time, correct?"

"Will verify all and let you know."

■ ■ ■ ■ ■

The voice was back on the phone to suggesting to Josh an alternative location for the exchange. Josh replied that he would first need to have someone investigate the place, adding:

"I should be back to you within less than twenty-four hours."

He then called Mark to ask that Mehmet plan his next flight, this time to Erbil, adding:

"Got enough diamonds for the next exchange but would love to have him available to take the opium back to Israel."

"No problem. We have it under control."

CHAPTER.26

Josh found the road which the voice had suggested for the next transaction. As indicated, it was about 500 feet before the bridge over the Great Zab River, still off Highway 80. He turned right into it, looking for a road on his left about a mile further on.

The team had noted that the voice and his associates were not venturing far from the territory Josh and his colleagues assumed the smugglers controlled. The proposed location, which was close to a local soup kitchen, was less than two miles away from the place where the last exchange had taken place, on the opposite bank of the Great Zab River and on the opposite side of Highway 80 as well. Yet, despite the relative proximity, the geography was somewhat different.

Josh had sent Daniel and Nathan ahead when they looked at the map in the store. The map had given them an idea which would allow the team to have as much control of the situation as possible. Daniel and Nathan were going to take the road immediately before the one indicated by the voice. The map had showed that the road selected by the voice allowed an exchange to take place in a relatively secluded location. Interestingly, the place could only be accessed from one of two directions. From the north, there were two ways to get there.

From the south, on the other hand, there was only one way to get to the location: the road which Daniel and Nathan would be patrolling. There was still an outside chance that one might try to access the proposed exchange spot though a couple of trails, but as they were both literally across two fields, any car driving on these unsealed trails would immediately signal their presence with a cloud of dust, beside the fact that they would be clearly visible. Neither field had any tree on it or around its periphery.

Nathan and Daniel did a complete inspection of their end of the road. They concluded that there would be a perfect spot for Nathan to "set up shop" with a long-range rifle equipped with an infra-red visor. From there he could literally pick-up anyone. He actually noted:

"From there, I can shoot at anyone including people coming from the other end of the road."

He decided that he would bring two rifles, one armed with tranquilizer bullets and the other with real ones, thanking his lucky star for having asked *Mossad* to give him a larger supply of tranquilizer bullets. Daniel would patrol the area on foot ready to help Josh if needed.

Mike looked around the other end of the street while Josh was focusing on the exact exchange location. The full stretch on which the exchange would take place was less than 500 feet long. The full left side of the road followed the property line of a couple of houses, with a double row of trees, and small bushes in front of them. The lot next to the houses and to their southeast was vacant though quite large; nobody could possibly hide there in the daytime. Mike and Josh agreed that people in either house could not see what was happening, as the chosen spot was in fact offset to the northeast of the houses.

When the four associates got back together, they were about to agree that the location was totally acceptable when Mike asked a question:

"What if the location was picked by the traitor? What if either or both of the houses were owned by ISIS or ISIS sympathizers?"

Josh reacted immediately:

"Dammit. Unfortunately, this is quite possible."

Nathan asked:

"How can we make sure?"

Josh had to reply that there was no way they could in such a short period of time and possibly no way even if he had more time. They were again about to agree that Josh should mention his worry to the voice when Mike came up with a variant of his first question:

"What if the traitor was the person you call the 'voice'?"

Josh had to concede that this was possible as well. At that point, all four of them decided that they had to revise their original plan. The locations they had picked for each member of the team during the exchange had to be reconsidered. However, they also had to agree that they had little choice but to go ahead. Josh summed it up:

"Virtually all bets are off if the voice is the traitor. However, I've been very careful not to tell him how many people were on my team. Further, we know that there is a small bushy area just southwest of the house. One of us can hide there and from that hiding point, he can monitor any development at the house and yet be close enough to the action. Every one of us needs to be ready with enough fire power . . . By the way, we need to rent a pickup truck as we need to carry one ton of opium: we can't pack that into our trunk!"

He paused and added:

"Goes without saying, but we all need our Kevlar jackets. I had Kevlar Keffiyeh liners made to protect the top and sides of our heads. Let's wear them as well. Sorry if it's too hot. Thank God, it will be at night!"

The voice looked satisfied when Josh called to say that the location was OK with him provided the exchange would again take place a couple of hours after Isha prayers, i.e., around 2:00 a.m. Josh did mention the fact that the only weakness of the spot was the proximity of two homes together with a large vacant lot on which several trucks full of enemies could easily hide. The voice did not flinch, simply stating:

"We know about that and will plan around it."

Josh thought to himself:

Sure you will, but so will we.

■ ■ ■ ■ ■

As planned, the evening prior to the exchange, around 10:00 p.m., Josh and his team went to the general area where the delivery was to be made. They drove three different cars so that each individual could be optimally positioned. The four hours they had until the exchange gave them plenty of time to inspect the environment and get into position. Once in position, they could easily check and react to any change in terms of expected new arrivals, as well as unexpected interlopers. Mike used a northern route that made him go substantially west and north of the road where he would expect to encounter anyone. It took him to a small, apparently relatively new development comprising around a hundred homes a couple of miles from the center of Kalak. This, however, allowed him to arrive near the exchange spot without much of a chance of being identified. Nobody would reasonably assume that one would use that detour and he met virtually no one, not a surprise given the time late in the evening.

He parked his car right in front of the soup kitchen and walked the remaining 300 feet to his assigned spot. It was almost pitch dark with just a sliver of a moon in the sky. He briefly turned his flashlight on to make sure he was exactly sure of his next steps. He continued toward the target location walking on the road behind the two homes they had noted, to their north, and then along the road on which the exchange was going to take place. Being as early as he was, he believed that he was the first one to arrive. He used his infrared monocular to do a complete 360 degree sweep around searching for anything that would release heat. Finding none, other than what probably was a small cat or a big rat, he placed the monocular back into his cargo pants pocket, under his tunic. Looking at the two homes that he was tasked with watching, he noted that all the lights were out. He thought to himself:

Clearly, this does not mean that everybody is asleep. For all I know, they're watching us from here. But at least I see no activity. Anyway, I can shoot at quite a number of potential enemies from here.

He did not use his monocular to check the house. Indeed, he knew that glass acted very much like a mirror for infrared radiation. If he pointed a thermal imager at a window, he wouldn't see anything on the other side of the glass. However, he would get a nice reflection of himself in thermal. He decided to sit down on the ground and calmly wait.

Daniel and Nathan were in another car and also took somewhat of a circuitous route, along the bank of the river, to get to the location. During their inspection tour, they noted a small wooden area bisected by a small trail. The head of the trail closest to the target was far enough from it to afford a lot of privacy, while being close enough that a marksman such as Nathan would have a perfect line of sight to any point to which he needed. Daniel got out of the car and positioned himself about a couple hundred feet west of Nathan. That allowed him to control the two ways which both the smugglers and any possible other enemy could use. With Mike controlling the northwest end of the road and Nathan and Daniel its southeast end, all three thought they were in control.

Josh, driving the rented pickup, stopped about three miles short of the target location. He had not wanted to let his associates get near the target alone, but, on the other hand, he had no desire to be seen arriving as early as the other three. In particular, he wanted to avoid offering anyone the opportunity to construe a link among all four of them. The different routes and apparent times of arrivals pointed much more to a coincidence than a connivance. Yet, from where he parked his car, along the wall of a house and all lights out, he knew he could still watch the target location in the distance and thus be able to react if the action started earlier than anticipated.

Less than an hour before the exchange was scheduled to take place, all four members of the team, who had earbuds with short-wave radio equipment to communicate with one another, noted the arrival of a pickup truck quite similar to the one that the smugglers drove the last time around. It stopped at the northwestern intersection of the road where the exchange was to take place; the one that brought it from Highway 80. Josh said into his mike:

"I guess they're here to observe what's going on. Watch him carefully, but don't assume he's by himself. The last time, they came with two cars. The voice said he would have more support. I would expect at least another two cars, if not more."

Josh and the team did not need to wait too long before they saw a couple of cars, seemingly following each other, driving from the main road past the target location and stopping a couple of hundred feet further. Using his infra-red binoculars, Daniel was observing the developments and quietly reported:

"One . . . No make that *two* of them are walking in the direction of the vacant lot."

Josh replied:

"Thanks. Keep watching them."

Daniel later reported that the two men had taken position in the vacant lot, adding for the benefit of his colleagues:

"They seem to be sitting down. Wait, the other car is driving back toward the exchange point. It's passing it by and parking less than 100 feet away."

Suddenly, Mike came on the team's radio. His warning was heard by everyone on their ear buds:

"Watch out guys. One car just turned into the road where Josh was supposed to make the exchange. Hold it. It's stopping and parking. It has to be less than a couple hundred feet from what we think is the smugglers' pickup truck."

He paused and without giving anyone else the opportunity to respond continued:

"Another car is on the main road and slowing down. Sorry, my bad, it is not turning here. Hold it, it is turning into the road that reaches just east of the exchange point diagonally. Bet you that's ISIS."

Looking at his GPS signal on the tablet he had with him, he confirmed:

"The second car is the same as last time. It still has its bug."

Nathan replied: "I see it coming. It has stopped for now. They shouldn't pose a problem. Have got a straight shot."

Josh started his engine and started driving in the direction of the target. He slowed down as he approached the road on which he was to turn left. He did and his headlights briefly allowed him to see first the unidentified late arriving car and then the pickup which he recognized as that of the smugglers. He kept going holding a sheet of bullet resistant carbon material to the left of his face and upper body to make sure that any sniper located on the left side of the road could not hurt him, thinking:

Extra protection in case the Kevlar isn't enough.

Arriving at the agreed upon location, he parked on the right-hand side of the road and, just as he had during the last exchange, waited for the same ritual to unfold.

The smugglers' pickup truck drove and stopped just behind him. They went through the same routine as for the prior exchange, though what one might call the "verification round" was quite short. The last few packs of processed opium were being loaded into Josh's pickup truck when a couple of very muffled rifle shots were heard. Nathan had, in agreement with the rest of the team, chosen to use a silencer; he had used tranquilizer bullets, but he also wanted to make sure that no one knew where the shots were coming from. The smugglers that were hiding in the vacant lot next to the two houses saw the two suspected ISIS men seem to collapse to the ground. They immediately came out of hiding to be ready to help their colleagues in the pickup truck. They were not quite at the road when a couple of other shots rang out. These were coming from inside one of the two houses. The two smugglers managed to escape, but the shots gave the car with the other ISIS terrorists the signal to attack. They got out of the car and started brandishing their automatic rifles. They did not know that Mike had them in his sight, as did Nathan. Two shots, one with a muffled sound and the other with a loud detonation rang again and both individuals fell to the ground, in a sudden need to sleep off the propofol in the bullets.

The smuggler's pickup truck rushed away, but the other two cars stayed behind ready for a fight with anyone in the house. Josh drove away as well, in the direction of Nathan and Daniel. Daniel jumped onto the passenger seat of Josh's pickup while Nathan stayed in his commanding position. A few more shots resonated from the house but were suddenly silent when they must have seen four of the smugglers approach, though they were sufficiently well-protected using the natural cover to make it impossible to shoot at them. Nathan decided not to intervene, as did Mike who felt that it was not "his" fight. Nathan returned to his car as rapidly as he could, quickly threw the two guns in the back seat area and drove away, all the while telling Mike what he was doing. Upon hearing the message, Mike also abandoned the fight and walked calmly back to the soup kitchen where he found his car and drove away.

■ ■ ■ ■ ■

Josh drove directly to Erbil's airport when he was joined by Mike and met Mehmet. The P.180 was parked quite near the terminal, yet in an area that was sufficiently innocuous that the team could transfer the ton of processed opium into the plane. Mehmet had asked for a full refuel as he was waiting for his associates. Once the transshipment was made, he asked permission to take off, which was immediately granted. He had announced that he was flying to the southwest to Beirut. He and Mark had agreed that there might be at most another opportunity to use the Bagdad, Amman, Tel Aviv stratagem, but it did not seem prudent to try it again so soon. For an Italian registered plane to fly from Erbil to Beirut, the way seemed clear. In fact, Mehmet had checked and confirmed that there were four such commercial flights per day for that route, and back. Thus, he "borrowed" the flight plan of the Middle East Airlines, Lebanon's flag carrier, plane covering that route. He fully intended, once over the Mediterranean just north of Beirut, to ask for a flight plan change and fly directly to Palmachim Air Base. If push came to shove, he might even ask for some fighter escort over the Mediterranean.

CHAPTER.27

Abu Musa (Josh) called on his friend Ibrahim, a Kurdish leader whom he had met soon after arriving in Mosul. He had been impressed by Ibrahim's generally constructive thoughts, despite his strong focus on fostering at some point in the future an independent Kurdistan republic that would straddle the current Iraqi-Turkish border. Josh, of course, never told Ibrahim the truth about who he was, although he did indicate that he was sympathetic to Ibrahim's long-term goals.

They met at a coffee house in Mosul on Josh's pretext of asking him for a favor. Josh was honest with him when he said that he had been in distant contact with a group of Kurdish people with whom he had had, as he euphemistically put it, "business dealings." Ibrahim initially asked for a few details on the identity of Abu Musa's contact. Josh had told him that what Ibrahim was asking was something that he could not disclose, for both his and the other side's security. Ibrahim was too much of a gentleman and too well-educated in Middle Eastern customs to keep asking for more details. Yet he seemed originally surprised as it was an open secret within the Kurdish community that northern Iraq was one of the routes through which processed opium reached northern and western Europe. He apparently would not have guessed that Abu Musa was involved in that trade, though, given what Abu Musa had just said, he now firmly believed he was.

Josh first provided some background, explaining that he suspected that a subgroup based somewhere between Mosul and Erbil had probably been infiltrated by ISIS. He said that he did not feel he could talk to his usual contact, whom he called "the voice", because he did not know who might or might not be involved. Careful that the voice himself might be the spy, he wanted, he said, to be extra careful. He added that he had learned that a very senior member of the group with which the voice was eventually dealing was based in Erbil. He asked Ibrahim if he knew who that person was, to which the answer was unfortunately exactly as one should have expected:

"There are many people who meet that description, my friend. Can you say anything more?"

"Well, I can, but I don't know how much of this is fact. What I am about to tell you was told to me by someone else . . ."

"Can you disclose who?"

"Afraid not. You know the game, don't you?"

"I do."

"I am told that the gentleman to whom I am referring may be living in a large house, on a side street opposite the tower in Erbil's Citadel . . . I don't have a real address though. Is this still too vague?"

Ibrahim smiled broadly and simply said:

"This narrows the list a lot. Let me make a few calls. Can we meet here tomorrow, same time?"

"Sure. You don't mean that you could arrange a meeting here at such short notice?"

"You're right. I would be very surprised if the gentleman I am thinking of was ready to come here. I also suspect he would not want to meet you at his actual address—too much risk. Let me see what I can do and then let you know, hopefully by tomorrow."

■ ■ ■ ■ ■

The following day, as promised, Ibrahim was waiting for Abu Musa (Josh) at the same coffee house. He greeted him with a warm smile saying:

"The meeting you requested can be arranged."

Josh was of course delighted and asked for details. Ibrahim explained that the mission had been a bit more difficult than originally expected. He conceded that he knew someone who might have done business with Abu Musa, now that he knew what Abu Musa's main business was, but said:

"Unfortunately, the gentleman was not involved with anyone operating from a base somewhere between Mosul and Erbil. I had to look further."

"So?"

"Well, the gentleman you want to meet does not live where you thought he did. He said that he has conducted some business activity from a place that fits the description you gave. But he certainly does not live there."

He added that the gentleman would not allow anyone who conducted business with him to see where he lived. The place which corresponded to Josh's description was likely only a warehouse. Ibrahim said he speculated that a couple of associates of the gentleman may well also live there, probably to guard the premises. Josh interrupted:

"You know, that makes a lot of sense. I should have thought of that earlier."

"Anyway, the gentleman is prepared to meet you, but not face-to-face. He has specific requirements which he hopes you will accept."

Josh simply replied that unless there was too much of what he called "unilateral risk" for him, he was willing to meet just about any condition. Ibrahim replied that it all went without saying and provided all necessary assurances.

■ ■ ■ ■ ■

The following day, Abu Musa drove to Erbil, with Mike along with him in the car. They arrived near the entrance to the Citadel and parked the car at the main gate. They walked about a hundred yards till they were in front of a relatively nondescript house. It was neither big nor small; it was just like the other houses in the neighborhood. Josh and Mike noted the green shutters that matched the green door, with two flowerpots, one on each side of the door. Someone was immediately at the door after they knocked, using what looked like a small copper hammer that banged against a metal plate, probably made of copper as well, as it had oxidized and turned greenish. They were ushered into a sitting room, to the left of the small hallway. There, Mike was asked to stay while he was joined by someone, whom he assumed to be an associate of the gentleman. They both smiled at each other, but the impression was clearly given that no conversation was expected. Josh was asked to walk to a door at the back of the room; once it opened, he was invited to enter. Mike believed that the room was right behind the sitting room where he was but could not be sure as he had not been able to observe Josh after he walked through the door.

Josh was surprised to see what surely looked like a white sheet hanging from the ceiling. It seemed to be separating the room into what he believed were two halves or at least two parts. The associate pointed him to a seat in front of the sheet and against the wall to the left of the door through which he entered. He noted that the associate closed the door behind him with somewhat more noise than he would have expected. Josh thought: *this must be a signal of some sort.*

Immediately after he had heard that noise, right on cue, a voice on the other side of the sheet greeted him:

"My dear friend, Ibrahim, tells me you are a friend of his and that your name is Abu Musa."

"That is correct, sir."

"Any friend of his is a friend of mine. Welcome to this humble room. As you can imagine, I do not live here. I am only using this room for this interview. I hope you will forgive me for the spartan nature of the furnishings. Also, forgive me as well for not disclosing my name."

Josh thanked him for his hospitality and willingness to meet. He noted the civility of the dialog, thinking that the individual really sounded like a gentleman and not like a rough and tumble smuggler. He then proceeded with the topic at hand and said:

"I asked to meet you if you were willing to meet me in order to share with you a suspicion which bothers me."

"Ibrahim told me that you suspect that there is a spy within my network . . ."

"I did not appreciate this was your network, sir, but, since you are saying it is, the problem is exactly as you expressed it. I cannot point to anyone in particular, but there have been several instances where people which we suspect might be related to ISIS . . ."

"ISIS? Really? How do you know they're involved?"

"In truth we don't. It's just a suspicion. However, whoever they are, they seem to be working against you. I know they are not part of the network of the friend of mine which your group has met."

"I see. Let's keep calling them ISIS though neither of us knows for sure."

"Thank you. At any rate, first, someone sideswiped my friend near a store which he rents in Mosul."

"Sideswiped?"

"Yes, he told me he managed to avoid it, but his impression was that the car was aiming for him. My own suspicion, frankly, was that it was just a gesture of intimidation."

"I understand and would agree with your assumption. Any other issue with that incident?"

"None really except that my friend was not in a place where anyone ought to have suspected him."

"Intriguing. Wonder why. Anything else?"

Josh continued with the description of the two deliveries of merchandise in exchange for diamonds. The man asked:

"Your friend told you all that?"

He paused and then surprised Josh by saying:

"I don't know who you are, but something tells me we may well be on the same side. So why don't you drop the pretense of your friend. I'm pretty sure your friend and you are one and the same person. So, let's talk frankly. I wish I could remove this sheet, but that would be imprudent for you and for me. So, what else happened?"

"Have you heard of the incidents during the two deliveries?"

"What incident? Two incidents?"

Josh suddenly realized that the gentleman may actually not have been told anything, opening the way for the traitor to be anyone in the group from Kawrugosik. Before answering the last question, he had to ask another one. He said:

"Sorry that I am not answering directly, but would you expect your associates to report to you that they were shot at?"

"Of course, I would. You shot at them?"

"Of course not. A third party which I assume is not related to your group and which I know is not related to me shot at us in both instances, after the full exchange had taken place. They're the ones we suspect are related to ISIS."

"Very strange. Very strange. Something does not compute here."

He paused for a few seconds and continued:

"Assume the shooters are indeed enemies, your enemies or our enemies, or both. Why would they wait for the exchange to be completed?"

Josh replied with his voice betraying a lack of confidence in his own view:

"Because they might fear that the car I drive would leave with the diamonds?"

"Grant you that, but if that is what they're after, why not attack you as soon as you arrive?"

"Fair enough. So, they're not after the diamonds only and they're not either after the merchandise as they could just as easily attack your pickup truck."

"Let me ask you a question before I keep going; ostensibly someone disposed of the threat. Who?"

"I have a couple of associates who covered me."

The gentleman was wracking his brain. He asked:

"Would the enemy as we've agreed to call them have known that?"

"By "that" I assume you mean the fact that a couple of associates were covering me. Correct?"

"Absolutely."

"I cannot believe the enemy could even have guessed it for the first time, unless everyone does it here. But they could have figured out that I wouldn't be alone the second."

"Why is that?"

"The second time, they had to know that two of their people had been tranquilized during the first exchange."

He paused and added:

"However, as I just said, we used tranquilizer bullets because we didn't want to kill anyone. The victims should not remember what happened . . . Yet . . ."

"Let me ask around . . . Just a few questions. I want to keep trying to understand from your side. I'll go through Ibrahim to set up another meeting with you if I find out anything. On your end, tell him you need to talk to me, give him a number on which I can call you and you can expect my call within a few hours."

██ ▓ ██

Josh's phone rang. Ibrahim was calling Josh:

"Abu Musa, the gentleman you met yesterday would like you to call him."

Josh thanked Ibrahim and dialed the number he had been given. A voice which Josh recognized said to him:

"Thanks for calling back so quickly. The more I think of your issue, the less I understand. The only possible explanation, which I don't like and does not convince me much, is that someone is trying to intimidate you or us, or both."

"Why would they do that?"

"I have a vague idea but cannot discuss it at this point. I'm sorry to say that but I do not know you well enough to take the risk to tell you something which might help explain the issue."

Josh replied that he fully understood the gentleman's predicament but did not see how they both could move forward without that piece of knowledge. The gentleman surprised Josh with his next proposal:

"Would you be willing to play along and set a trap for the people of Kawrugosik?"

"I would certainly consider it, but it would have to be something I understood fully."

"Let us meet where we last met tomorrow morning, just before Dhuhr. Be alone, as I will be."

"See you then."

Josh knew that Dhuhr is the second of the five prayers which Muslims must pray daily. It is said after dawn and before midday.

██ ▓ ██

Josh found himself again in the gentleman's meeting room, with the sheet still hanging from the ceiling.

"You're very punctual."

"I try. So, what do we need to consider?"

"I want to test the people in Kawrugosik. I propose we proceed as follows . . ."

The gentleman proceeded to outline his plan, which Josh thought seemed quite workable. Josh asked a few questions on specific details to make sure there would be no mistake at the wrong time. They agreed that the meeting with the voice and his people would take place at a specific meeting point, which, this time would be suggested by Josh. He expected the voice from Kawrugosik to accept it, if only because Josh had accepted the last two locations. They agreed that Abu Musa would turn down any other meeting location. They agreed that the exchange would call for another ton of merchandise in exchange for 1,000 carats of diamonds at the usual diamond/heroin exchange rate.

■ ■ ■ ■ ■

Meanwhile, in the Mediterranean Sea south of Cyprus, the Israeli missile boat, INS *Javelin,* had moved to be smack in the middle of the channel which the suspected ISIS boats would have to navigate to approach the Russian cargo ship. A radio message was sent to them to ask them to stop and turn around. The two boats did not reply and further seemed to ignore the command. Using his Sonar, Captain Metzger who commanded the INS *Javelin* sent a message to Captain Gratzinger on the INS *Dragon* submarine:

"Fire a blank torpedo ahead of the first Syrian boat."

The first of the two boats slowed down; sailors could see that she went off the plane with her bow lowered into the water as she started sailing at minimum speed. The second boat followed suit. Yet, they were both still moving forward albeit at a very reduced speed. Captain Metzger called his own gunners:

"Fire anti-ship missile just ahead of the first supply ship."

The rocket splashed less than a hundred feet in front of the first boat, which, this time, stopped. Yet, it was still not turning back. Captain Metzger noted that the two Syrian ships were now quite close to each other. He asked Captain Gratzinger to fire a live torpedo toward the second ship, assuming that her sailors could be rescued by the first ship. He would then avoid any human casualty and yet deter any further movements on the part of the suspected ISIS ships.

At about the same time, INS *Destiny* had reached the Russian cargo ship whose captain ostensibly was surprised when he fired his engines to find that both propellers seemed in effect to be stuck. He certainly did not know what might be causing the problem, but the time for analysis had passed. He could not avoid his ship being boarded. The com officer on INS *Protector* informed Captain Dayan that a distress message had been sent from the Russian cargo ship to the Russian submarine. Captain Dayan asked:

"Any reply"

"Not yet, sir."

CHAPTER.28

MOSUL AND ERBIL, IRAQ, BEIRUT, LEBANON, TEL AVIV, ISRAEL AND ON THE MEDITERRANEAN SEA

Josh dialed the voice, seeking to arrange the next exchange of merchandise against diamonds. They agreed that he was prepared to accept one ton of merchandise against 1,000 carats of diamonds. Josh asked for the exchange to take place near Bn Pirez, along a stretch of road due west of town. Initially, the voice was quite surprised by Josh's choice:

"Not the easiest place to get to . . ."

"I know, but in view of what happened the last two times, I wanted to make sure that there really were only two ways to and from the target location."

"Why so close to Erbil?"

"Why not?"

The voice eventually agreed, most likely thinking that he had to be more familiar with the general environment than Josh. After all, the proposed location was at most ten miles from Kawrugosik as the crow flies and about fifteen miles by car. The road on which the exchange would take place ran almost perfectly north and south, alongside a piece of currently undeveloped farmland. The south end of the road went straight into town after a right-angle curve, while the north end also had a very sharp left-hand curve which eventually went back to the north end of the village. In short, whether going in or out, vehicles would have to transit through Bn Pirez. After hearing Ibrahim's friend recommend it and looking at it on the map, Josh noted how smart the choice was. A few strategically located associates would be able both to provide any necessary warning and to ensure that no one could get away who was not supposed to get away.

The exchange was set for a bit earlier than usual, but still after Isha, 1:30 a.m. as the prevailing darkness should provide for the necessary privacy. The smugglers' pickup truck arrived as planned and, as in the previous two instances, stopped short of the planned exchange point. Not surprisingly to them, Josh's pickup truck arrived next. It drove past the smugglers' pickup truck and stopped just in front of it. The smugglers walked from their truck to show one of the merchandise packets to Josh. His window was lowered, he looked at the package and approved the transaction. The smugglers continued to move the merchandise from their truck to Josh's.

Suddenly, a series of shots started to ring out. At least two dozen people jumped out from the undeveloped farmland at both ends of the road. Their targets were a couple of cars which had just arrived from Bn Pirez. Very quickly, the two cars were stopped and whoever was not killed was captured. The smugglers were surprised to see Josh's pickup truck drive away. They had not finished unloading their cargo and, more importantly, did not receive the diamonds they were expecting. Something surely did not compute. The smugglers were, however, stuck and had to drive back to Kawrugosik with no diamonds and some of their opiates still on the bed of the pickup truck.

Meanwhile, the situation in the Mediterranean was close to the boiling point. The torpedo fired by INS *Dragon* hit the second suspected ISIS supply boat. The first boat raced to rescue their comrades, thus sailing away from the Russian cargo ship.

INS *Destiny* was now right alongside the Russian cargo ship which, with no use of either of its propellers, was literally dead in the water. Captain Schneider called the Russian cargo ship on the radio asking for permission to board, in terms that were strong enough that the Russian Captain understood he did not have any real option. He agreed to allow a few members of Captain Schneider's crew to board, while still asking for the help of the Russian submarine. The captain of the Russian submarine knew at that moment that there was no way he could fire at the Israeli frigate. Whether using a missile or a torpedo, any direct hit on the INS *Destiny* was bound to bring the Russian cargo ship down as well.

Yet, he sent a coded Sonar signal to the Russian escort ships which were still too far away to be of any threat. The cable was intercepted by INS *Protector.*

"Com Officer to Captain Dayan . . ."

"Shoot."

"The Russian submarine is asking for instructions."

"Not unexpected. Let me know when you have a reply."

Sailing as it was still at the surface of the sea, Captain Dayan called Yael Orbach in Tel Aviv. Yael patched Simon Rabinowitz, the head of Mossad, on the call. They briefly discussed the situation. Then Simon heard Yael order:

"Have a Kovesh speed toward the Russian submarine. Do not use a torpedo, but just a depth charge. Let me know when ready to fire."

Captain Dayan came back on the phone to tell Yael that the submarine had been ordered to fire a torpedo at INS *Destiny.* He added:

"They are more keen to hide what is in the cargo ship than for the lives of their own people."

Yael simply ordered:

"Fire a depth charge so that the Russian submarine feels a strong impact but is not sunk."

He picked up his other phone to call the senior officer in charge of the American carrier strike group, who was on the aircraft carrier, *USS Truman,* Admiral Smith. He briefly explained the situation to him. Admiral smith replied:

"I'm sending a strong message to the submarine. Any attack on INS *Destiny* would be considered reason enough for us to target the Russian submarine."

The depth charge exploded 100 feet below the surface of the water less than 100 feet behind the Russian submarine. Any hit much closer could have inflicted serious damage to the submarine, which everyone was trying to avoid so as not to trigger real naval combat. The distance and depth chosen for the depth charge to explode were such that there would be some damage to the submarine, probably to its propulsion system, but not enough to create damage sufficient to incapacitate or sink it. The Russian submarine elected to surface not so much to comply with the request Captain Dayan had previously made, but in fact to inspect the ship and assess any damage. A Russian officer from the naval force that was still a few hours away from the action lodged a formal complaint to Admiral Smith who simply replied:

"Please contact our Israeli friends, no member of this strike force has yet been involved in this incident."

The Russian officer was not satisfied with the reply and threatened a retaliatory strike, indicating that he saw the U.S. strike force as a part of the enemy. Admiral Smith fired straight back:

"I wouldn't if I were you. You are vastly outgunned. Do you want to start a formal U.S. /Russian confrontation?"

The Russians remained silent.

Captain Schneider seemed almost out of breath when he called out to Yael Orbach:

"We found MIRV missiles indeed, but two of them seem equipped with a nuclear tip. Cannot assess how powerful they are."

That had to be the one thing the Russians were so desperate to hide: the nuclear dimension. Yael immediately called an emergency meeting of the Israeli War Cabinet. The delivery of nuclear weapons to ISIS was in fact a massive escalation which needed an urgent response. The War Cabinet met by zoom as there was no time for everyone to travel to a common place. Thankfully, *Mossad* had developed an encoding/decoding protocol which made any interception of the call virtually impossible. The decision that came out of the meeting involved two different strands.

The first had Moshe Shamir, the Israeli foreign minister, summon the Russian Ambassador to Israel, whose offices were located near the beach on Hayarkon Street in Tel Aviv; that was less than four miles from the Foreign Ministry on Yitzhak Rabin Boulevard in the center of town. The "request" was couched in sufficiently strong language that the Russian Ambassador dropped what he was doing and was immediately driven to Moshe Shamir's office. The conversation was tense but brought very little news. The Russian Ambassador simply denied the whole story, claiming to have no knowledge of any of it. He persisted in his denial when Moshe showed him pictures that clearly depicted both the Russian origin of the missiles and the nuclear signs affixed to the tip cone. He also had other pictures, showing the ship, though the fact that she was not registered in Russia afforded several ways out. Oddly enough, the Russian Ambassador chose the least likely of them all, calling the photos "staged." Moshe Shamir had been a diplomat for a long enough period of time to know that there was no point pushing further, then. Rather, he was satisfied that the

Russians were now officially aware that Israel knew of their intentions and that they had captured the missiles.

The second was that INS *Destiny* would tow the Russian cargo ship and bring her to port in Haifa. INS *Dragon* and INS *Javelin* were going to provide an escort, with the U.S. carrier strike group offering a secondary protection curtain, should the Russians send a submarine to attempt to torpedo the convoy. The official motive of the "arrest" was the fact that the ship had carried and attempted to deliver prohibited cargo.

■ ■ ■ ■ ■

David Heller had travelled to Beirut to meet with the diamond dealer whom Albert Hoets had recommended. He brought along Moshe Lantzer with him to help and dig further if they were able to obtain any leads. Eli Boez, the dealer, seemed cautious at first, but appeared to warm up when David made it crystal clear that he and Moshe were in no way related to any law enforcement organization. As David indicated:

"We're trying to find out what is happening to the diamond trade in the region. Albert told us that a change was taking place. We're just trying to understand it. What you do and how you make money is for you and the Lebanese authorities to discuss."

He paused and calmly added:

"And they won't find out anything from us!"

Eli, while still being ostensibly carefully choosing his words, said that the major change he had seen in the recent past was related to the provenance of the diamonds that were on offer. He added:

"Up until recently, I received offers to buy diamonds which I believed were primarily of Russian origin, though there were a few that came from South Africa and even fewer that were conflict diamonds. I have kept avoiding conflict diamonds as the penalties are much too serious to take the risk."

David had to ask:

"How would you know the provenance of the diamonds unless they carry a mark, which I am told Russian diamonds do not have?"

"I can't disclose all the trade secrets, but there are clear signs in terms of quality, cut and even color. I should add, to be fully honest, that there are at times certificates of provenance. But in the end, you know, it's really a question of experience."

"Where are those you've recently seen from?"

"So far, absolutely no idea. The one thing I can say about them is that they seem to be of higher quality, much more consistent in terms of "D" or "E" color, practically no inclusions and the cut is quite high quality. If you told me they were cut and polished in Antwerp, I'd have no difficulty believing it."

Moshe Lantzer ventured a question which he knew could backfire but was well aware that it had to be asked. The fact that he was asking it rather than David was meant to serve as a shield protecting him.

"Thank you for sharing with us the ultimate provenance of these diamonds. Are you able to identify whether the new diamonds come from the same sellers as the prior ones which you think are from Russia?"

David was very impressed by his associate's question, which he thought was particularly well-phrased. Eli did not seem offended and replied:

"I am sure you would not expect me to share with you the whole chain with names and addresses . . ."

He paused and smiled at David and Moshe. Then he added:

"But I can say two things which may help you. Please never reveal who gave you this information."

Both *Mossad* agents nodded so Eli continued:

"The first is that I have very strong reasons to believe that the ultimate seller is the same. It would be very unusual for different sellers to follow the same distribution chain."

"From this you would deduce that the ultimate seller is now getting his diamonds from a different source. Is that correct?"

"Absolutely. Or at least, that's my assumption unless somebody proves to me that it is not so."

Seeing David and Moshe smile, Eli continued:

"The second thing I can tell you is that I am pretty sure the chain starts in Iraq, though I don't know where. Actually, I stand corrected. I know the diamonds come to me from Bagdad. That's where my seller is. But I don't know where they are before they get to Bagdad."

"Not even a guess?"

"A guess? Always possible. But what for? You see, the real issue is what is the merchandise exchanged for these diamonds. If you assume it is some opioid, you would guess that they have to come from northern Iraq . . ."

"Mosul, Erbil?"

"Quite possibly, but there are other cities in that same area. I have been told that the Kurdish resistance finances itself by selling opioids that it gets from Afghanistan through Central Iran."

"Now what if it is not a payment for drugs?"

"Then we can hardly say anything. There can be multiple places, pretty much all around the region. The main thing people would be buying would be arms of any sort. We know that there is a Russian dimension to the puzzle: the earlier stones seemed to be of Russian origin. Remember, in the arms trade, Russia is a seller, not a buyer. So, the local seller, the one who received Russian diamonds, has to be selling something local. Can't think of anything much other than heroin . . ."

He paused again for a second and concluded:

"However, the chain could be quite a bit more complex. Imagine that you combine the two options we've just discussed. People sell opioids for diamonds, use the diamonds to buy arms from some local source, which in turns needs to find a buyer for these diamonds.

That's where I and a few colleagues here come in. Though other buyers might be in India or further away in Belgium for instance."

Moshe looked like he was going to say something when David decided that the contact should be managed. So, smiling broadly, he made a sign of his hand which Moshe immediately understood. David thanked Eli profusely and gave him a contact phone number which he could call if there was anything he wanted to tell him. He added:

"The number is in Belgium because I assume that would be the most convenient for you."

"Thank you indeed. Nice to have met both of you."

CHAPTER.29

Josh called Mehmet to ask him when he could fly into Erbil. He added:

"This is just a roundtrip. I will have about a ton of merchandise for you and do not expect any other purpose."

■ ■ ■ ■ ■

The call from the gentleman smuggler did not surprise Josh. The plan for the trap they had discussed fully provided for it. The gentleman asked Josh to drive to the house in Erbil. There a couple of the gentleman's associates would count the amount of merchandise which Josh had received during the "fake" exchange and would top it up to get to the one ton that had been contracted. In turn, when that was done, Josh would hand over the 1,000 carats of diamonds the smugglers expected.

Josh had decided that he would send Daniel and Nathan to the rendezvous as he was not ready to disclose his real identity, an obvious risk if he was expected to help the smugglers top up his load of merchandise. Indeed, helping the smugglers would have involved getting out of the truck, revealing his substantially larger than normal height. It would not have been natural for him to stay in the truck: how would he knock on the door? He had considered the idea that he would call the gentleman from outside of the house. But rejected it. Yet, unless and until the gentleman was ready to reveal who he was, Abu Musa (Josh) preferred to keep as low a profile as he could.

Nathan got out of the truck before he and Daniel had arrived at the house. In fact, he alighted while they were still on the plaza surrounding the tower of the citadel. He had a rifle with tranquilizer bullets hidden under his cloak. He went and hid on the plaza on the other side of the tower relative to the street where the house was. He certainly did not pull his rifle out at the outset but was ready to shoot at anyone that might seem inclined to hurt Daniel. It turned out that this was not a necessary precaution. The gentleman smuggler had arranged the exchange in good faith and his people carried it out in good faith as well.

■ ■ ■ ■ ■

The voice was surprised to receive a call from what he used to call "headquarters" in Erbil. The gentleman smuggler had indeed decided to ask the Kawrugosik group to bring the diamonds they would have expected to receive from their delivery. Their usual *modus operandi* indeed involved headquarters providing a set amount of merchandise to the group and expecting payment as soon as the delivery was made. With the benefit of hindsight, this explained why Josh and his team had found out that the truck had gone from Kawrugosik to Erbil in the early hours of the morning following the first exchange.

The voice was quite worried as the aborted delivery the prior night had prevented him from getting paid, despite having delivered a good part of his cargo. He was himself quite unhappy when the two associates who were in charge of the delivery came back without the diamonds and with at least two thirds of the cargo of opium missing. He could not understand what had happened, given the fact that, for the third time in a row, some other group had shown up to disrupt the exchange. He wondered whether headquarters were in fact those that were on purpose disturbing the exchange to bypass him and his team. The phone call therefore made him all that much more uncomfortable, thinking:

What if that's the coup de grace?

He explained the situation to the caller, avoiding any mention of his suspicion that headquarters may be behind the attacks. The caller was not impressed and said that the voice had to come to Erbil and explain himself. Though the caller had said that the voice should come by himself, the voice still decided that he would take a couple of his most senior associates with him, if only for protection.

■ ■ ■ ■ ■

David was somewhat excited when he noticed that the call on his cell phone came from Belgium. He picked it up and recognized Eli's voice immediately. He asked:

"What may I do for you, my friend?"

"Not really sure, but I wanted to pass on an intriguing twist to the diamond saga."

"Really?"

"Yes."

Eli went on to explain that he had received a call from another friend of his, from Beirut, who had also received a few of these "new diamonds." He went on to say that his friend was calling him because he had also noted that the diamonds were sufficiently different from those he was used to receiving and that he wanted to have what he called a second opinion. What surprised Eli the most was when his friend asked whether there was any chance that the diamonds were synthetic. David interrupted:

"Synthetic?"

"Yes, man-made if you prefer."

Continuing his story, Eli said that he had asked his friend for some time to carry out all the tests he could. He then surprised David:

"I know you can only see that my call is from Belgium, but I am in fact in Tel Aviv as we speak. I went to the laboratory of the International Gemological Institute there . . ."

David knew that the International Gemological Institute is the prime certification authority for both diamonds and colored stone. What he did not know is that the IGI maintains twenty laboratories around the world, the closest to Beirut being in Tel Aviv. David smiled thinking that Eli was thus most likely not more than a few miles from *Mossad*'s headquarters. He still elected to let it slide, thinking:

He does not need to know.

At the same time, David was concerned that, given Eli's question, someone had identified the diamonds as synthetic. That would jeopardize the whole plan. He was therefore quite careful as Eli continued, indicating that he had just received their report. He said that the stones he brought were deemed of excellent quality but did not fit any of the characteristics which synthetic diamonds typically have. David breathed a deep sigh of relief, which he hoped Eli could not hear on the telephone. Eli explained that synthetic diamonds often displayed the same physical, chemical, and optical characteristics as natural diamonds; in particular, they typically exhibited the same fire, scintillation, and sparkle. He said that even more sophisticated tests such as with magnets to detect traces of iron or nickel, fluorescence or even the very difficult detection of "grain" or "growth patterns" might allow a better understanding. The point he was making was that these tests had been carried out. They did not point to the stones being synthetic. Yet, Eli added:

"The one thing that the IGI deemed surprising was the microscopic inscription on the girdle of each stone: the letters "E" and "W" in Hebrew."

David had to ask, somewhat tongue in cheek:

"What does that mean?"

"Well, the point is that we don't know. Most synthetic diamonds have a mark on the girdle to say that they are manmade. But usually it is something clear. Here, this is a mark which they have never seen before."

"What do you conclude?"

"At this point, I don't have any conclusion. I asked them if it could be the signature of a cutter as both they and I noticed that the cut was exceptional. A master cutter undoubtedly. Now, why would a cutter start to sign their pieces? Who knows?"

"Indeed. Has it ever been done?"

Eli went on:

"Not to my knowledge. But there's another thing . . ."

"Another thing?"

"Yes. All of the gems I have seen so far have what we call "Hearts and Arrows" cuts."

"What?"

Seeing he had lost David in that level of detail, he explained:

"These stones are cut so precisely that their facet reflections overlap when viewed in a reflective scope. We've always believed that this precision is typically associated with Excellent-Ideal cuts of superior quality. Only a real master cutter can achieve such a high level of precision. Yet, I have never seen one signing his diamonds on the girdle. Wonder if that's some sort of a clue?"

David thanked Eli for the explanation adding he understood only a part of what Eli had said. However, he offered the only thought he could muster in a desire to encourage Eli to stay the course:

"To me, this has got to mean that there is a second source for these diamonds. Everything you've said points to them being exceptional. What are the odds that there would be two sources?"

"I tend to agree with you."

"Will you keep accepting them?"

Without any sort of hesitation, Eli replied:

"I will for as long as Albert Hoets keep buying them."

■ ■ ■ ■ ■

David immediately called Countess Renate:

"Countess, I just heard from Albert's friend in Beirut."

"Excellent. Anything interesting?"

David went on to summarize their conversation with a particular focus on the issue of the diamonds being real or synthetic. He explained that the diamonds seemed to have fooled the IGI again, as Albert had already tested them in Antwerp. He emphasized the need for Eli Boez to continue to accept the diamonds from the smugglers, concluding:

"Doesn't seem like he is ready to turn them down as we speak, but I believe that a call from Albert assuring him that he will continue to buy them from him would be very useful."

He paused to take a breath and added:

"The well-being of our four agents currently in Iraq depends on the smugglers having no reason to suspect anything with respect to the diamonds."

"Did you tell me why this might be a risk?"

"Eli Boez now knows that the Hebrew letters "E" and "W" are carved on the girdle of the diamonds. That doesn't surprise us as we had asked Albert to program his robot cutters to use that special mark. Precisely so that we could identify them. But the IGI pointed Eli to the inscription. That was in fact the only observation they made . . ."

Countess Renate replied that she would talk to Albert and ask him for some help with Eli.

■ ■ ■ ■ ■

The Russian ambassador visited Foreign Minister Moshe Shamir again, this time at his own request. The message was simple. He wanted the sailors and the Russian cargo ship released into his custody. Moshe, who had had the opportunity to discuss the issue of the ship with Yael and Simon Rabinowitz, was at the same time quite courteous and very stern.

"Mr. Ambassador, as you know from our last conversation, we have proof that the ship carried nuclear material; not only do we have the two nuclear tipped missiles, but, more importantly, we swept the ship with Geiger counters. The traces of radioactive materials are unmistakable."

"Could have come from an earlier voyage."

"Totally possible, though we didn't know you used cargo ships to deliver nuclear missiles to your overseas bases . . ."

He let it sink for a few seconds, though the Ambassador's face remained totally motionless. Moshe added:

"You also know that we have in our possession a number of MIRV missiles, two of which are the ones which unquestionably have nuclear tips."

"Don't know where they could possibly come from."

"I should add two things that might help your memory. First, we have been tracking the ship ever since it entered the Dardanelle Strait. We have her on film taken by arial drones. I would be happy to have a copy made for you. I should also tell you that we have good footage of the other ship, the one that sailed first through the Istanbul Strait, and of her attempted delivery to a couple of smaller supply-life boats. I am sorry to report that those two sank after the cargo was transshipped, but we were thankfully able to retrieve the cargo at the bottom of the sea."

The ambassador was of course not ready to confess to anything but shifted in his chair and seemed a little less at ease. He asked:

"Were there alleged nuclear tipped MIRV missiles in that first cargo as well?"

"Glad you asked. There may have been but if there were we did not find nor retrieve them."

The Ambassador seemed to relax a bit while Moshe continued:

"Second, we have incontrovertible evidence that the ship had direct communications with one of your submarines. We intercepted at least a few of those and have both oral recordings and translations for those who do not speak Russian."

The ambassador simply cleared his throat but did not say a word. Moshe concluded:

"We surely would not want to create a worldwide incident by sharing this evidence with the world. Would we?"

The ambassador remained stone faced. Moshe continued:

"We may well, eventually, need to share the evidence, but as of now, would it not be best if we kept it away from the United Nations? Wouldn't it be better if it stayed between us?"

The Ambassador's behavior changed. He smiled at Moshe and asked whether the sailors at least could be promptly returned to their families. Moshe replied that he would personally make sure that they could be fully debriefed, making sure that he did not use the word "interrogated." He said that they would be released afterwards, assuming that they were forthcoming. He added:

"We will be happy to offer them to have a representative of your Embassy present when we ask them what they know. You can be assured that we will respect all rules contained in Article 17 of the Geneva Convention."

The ambassador understood that there was little more he could ask. He thanked Moshe and left.

■ ■ ■ ■ ■

Meanwhile on the Mediterranean Sea, Captain Dayan was able to observe the Russian submarine being towed behind one of the Russian frigates that had finally arrived. He was able to confirm that, as originally suspected, the depth charge had caused some damage to the ship's propulsion mechanism.

CHAPTER.30

MOSUL AND ERBIL, IRAQ AND TEL AVIV, ISRAEL

Josh and Mike were at Erbil airport when Mehmet's P.180 plane landed. It taxied to a discreet point on the tarmac, near other cargo planes. They drove up to the plane after Mehmet had received permission to have them do so. They quickly unloaded the merchandise and drove away from the plane. Mehmet asked for some fuel, although he was ready to fly if there was not any available. The airport provided the extra fuel requested. After paying for it, he left and took off in the direction of Bagdad. His last flight from Erbil to Beirut had indeed had a slightly less comfortable passage than desired. Initially, he thought he was in luck. With the wind coming from the east, he had to keep flying past Beirut and thus over the Mediterranean to land to the east. However, he had not obeyed the last few instructions from the air traffic controllers who had asked him to descend to a lower altitude and consequently to reduce his speed appropriately. He had kept going until he was told that he was not welcome in Beirut anymore. Thankfully, he was quickly in international air space and the threat of being intercepted was no longer a serious risk.

After landing in Tel Aviv, he had discussed the issue with Mark. They went through every permutation they could imagine and rejected all of them as either too risky or too complex. They even considered the option of having Mehmet land on the *Harry S. Trumann* aircraft carrier, but that was nixed: way too complicated. They also discussed the option of simply not taking any more of the heroin out of Iraq, rather using Mehmet's plane just to fly the agents out. In the end, it was thought that a repeat of the first strategy, a flight officially to Bagdad, re-routed to Amman and then Tel Aviv might work a second time. The agents could always be flown, officially, back to Ankara.

■ ■ ■ ■ ■

The voice was decidedly uncomfortable when he arrived at the safe house which also served as the depot from which he and members of his group would come to take delivery of the opium which he would then sell. He was ushered into the same room where Josh had been invited to sit, but, this time, there was no sheet separating his seating area from the one where the gentleman smuggler and two of his acolytes were already seating: a nice sofa with four matching armchairs around a coffee table, with a nice Persian rug on the floor.

Very calmly, in an almost detached manner, the gentleman asked the voice what had happened. The voice repeated the explanation he had given on the phone. He was quite surprised with the next question:

"Why didn't you tell us when you were attacked the first time?"

The voice mumbled something incomprehensible and then, finally, acknowledged that it had been his own decision, adding:

"The first time was quite a surprise, and I was simply a bit confused. Frankly, I didn't know who was behind it and just wanted to see how it would develop. I assumed it might have been an isolated accident."

The gentleman interrupted:

"I can accept this answer, although I am astonished you were not surprised when the enemy seemed to have been shot by someone who was not in your party. If my information is correct, you had people with you and another car waiting to make sure that your buyer was not following you."

The voice was stupefied to hear the description of the event. He knew that it was totally correct and that he, for one, had not shared any of that with anyone outside of Kawrugosik. The gentleman continued his questions:

"What about the second time? I might accept that you might have been surprised again, but a pattern was emerging, don't you agree? I'm sure you don't need me to give you chapter and verse about what happened, but still four enemies were shot down that time . . ."

The voice was now definitely beyond discomfort. He was worried that he might in fact be there, sitting at his own trial. He knew very well what the penalty usually was in these trials. He was himself at a loss to explain what had happened, because the attack, there also, had started after he had received the diamonds from Josh and thus had begun to drive away. Suddenly, he looked directly at the gentleman and said:

"There must be a traitor within my people . . ."

Calmly, the gentleman replied:

"Would seem so to me."

He paused and added:

"Particularly when I note that a car attempted to swipe your buyer in the street behind his shop . . . even earlier on from what I've been told."

The voice could not resist asking:

"How do you know all this? How could you find out who our buyer was?"

The gentleman ignored the two questions, only replying:

"I need to know who the traitor is and to have him brought here without delay. Your mistake has cost us quite a bit of money and I do not like to lose money . . . I don't want it repeated. No, in fact, let me state it more definitely: it shall not be repeated. Understood?"

The gentleman's tone of voice had dramatically changed, and so had his facial expression. He was clearly conveying an ultimatum and no smile would be forthcoming.

■ ■ ■ ■ ■

Meanwhile, Josh asked his teammates to help him clear out the two shophouses he had rented. He was still not sure who had tried to sideswipe him before the first delivery had taken place. Yet it was clear to him, by then, that the stores were a source of potential danger. They did not serve any purpose anymore.

Josh and the team first went to the back door of the first store. Josh inspected it from top to bottom, comparing what he saw to a picture he had taken earlier. He wanted to make sure that he would not miss the slightest scratch that would not have been there earlier: any such scratch could be an indication that someone had tinkered with the door. Finding absolutely nothing that appeared untoward, he motioned to his team to accompany him to the back door to the second store, which he still firmly believed was totally unknown to either the smugglers or to the suspected ISIS enemies, despite the fact that it was in front of that door that he had been sideswiped earlier. He inspected the door as thoroughly as the back door to the first store and went in when he was satisfied that everything looked as innocuous as could be ascertained. He asked the others to wait for him near the back door to the first store. He briefly looked around the second store and was not surprised to find nothing that needed his attention. He went through what the group had come to call their "attic gallery." His main concern was to ensure that the back door to the first store had not been booby trapped, however it would have been done, even if it had not left any trace on the outside of the door.

Their plan had assumed that there was another risk beside the booby trapping of the back door: what if someone had penetrated the store and was waiting for him or them? Of course, he and his team knew that they were probably in the "belt and suspenders" mode; the recordings from the cameras inside of the first store had not shown any movement, thus no one getting in or getting out. These were motion activated and the recordings, which were sound activated, wouldn't have failed to start had there been someone in the store. Yet, they were well aware that one should never ignore any detail or underestimate the enemy. As planned, when Josh was in the attic of the second store, he sent a signal to Daniel who knocked on the metallic back door. Despite the fact that they were operating just after midnight when the whole shopping center was deserted, there was no need for loud banging. They just wanted it to be sufficiently noticeable so that anyone inside the store would naturally walk toward the back door or, at the very least, move. This would trigger both the motion detectors and the cameras. Josh would, at that point, be in a perfect location to tranquilize the individual if there was anyone, particularly if the individual had moved toward the back door, as one might think he would have instinctively done.

With no indication of any move in the first store, Josh went down the ladder and, again but this time from the inside, inspected every square inch of the door. Being satisfied that it looked safe, he invited his associates to move away from the door as he opened it from the inside. He breathed a definite sigh of relief when nothing happened. Josh asked Daniel, with his uncanny ability to lose himself into the background, to take position across from the back entry to the first store, armed with a gun with its silencer. His role was to make sure that no one would come and surprise the team either while they worked in the stores or, worse yet, as they exited them for the last time, with their packages.

Nathan and Mike came in to join Josh who proceeded to return to the second store through the attic gallery, while Mike took his position in the first store. Josh collected everything that they had brought in, handing them over to Nathan who was going back and forth with what little stuff had been moved to the second store, mostly inflatable mattresses for them to sleep when they were as they called it "on watch." He handed them to Mike who piled them up near the back door. Josh combed the second store virtually inch by inch to make sure he had left no trace; he then went back into the ceiling space to join Nathan and Mike. He was quite careful to hide the passage between the attic of the store and that of the store next door.

He repeated the operation in the first store, although his first focus was on the security cameras he had installed. While the removal of the cameras that were inside the first store was a totally trivial operation, he was well aware that the one challenge he would face was when the time would come to remove the camera that was above the front door but outside. That would indeed be the first time the front door of the store would need to be opened. What if the enemy had somebody watching it?

■ ■ ◪ ■ ■

Though disappointing on the surface, David Heller was not terribly surprised to have proven virtually unable to get anything out of the interrogation of the crew of the Russian cargo boat. Yet, an interesting tidbit came out. First, the team learned that this was the first such voyage, although nobody in the crew seemed to know anything about the nuclear tipped devices they were carrying. While each of the sailors and the captain had been kept in isolation from one another, they all had the same general message. Was it a case of excellent training or were they simply telling the truth? They had been carrying arms to Syria for some time, because they had been told the higher ups felt that going through Turkey was not possible. They knew that other, heavier arms had been brought in by plane into Syria, specifically into the Khmeimim Air Base controlled and managed by Russia in Syria. They were surprised when, as they were about to depart and after the other, the first cargo ship had already left, they were asked to take on a couple of additional cases. They were told those were quite fragile. They were the novelty.

David immediately made the assumption that this might have been the first time that nuclear-tipped missiles had been delivered to a foreign client of Russia. In the meantime, Marvin and his team had very carefully dismantled the nuclear-tipped missiles and discovered that the amount of nuclear material was enough to cause serious trouble, but not enough to be perceived, from the outside, as being a real "nuclear explosion." As Marvin had added:

"Wouldn't expect a mushroom cloud with that thing. Was just a dirty bomb."

CHAPTER.31

MOSUL AND ERBIL, IRAQ, ANTWERP, BELGIUM, BEIRUT, LEBANON AND SOMEWHERE IN THE AUSTRIAN ALPS

Josh opened the front door to the first store, as it was the last task he had to carry out before loading everything into the truck in the alley and moving away. A couple of shots rang out in the night. He immediately closed the door and moved away from it and the window. Daniel ran into the store to find out what had happened. Josh told him in as few words as possible and sent all three of his associates outside. Daniel would monitor the west end of the alley, while Mike would monitor the other end. As the back doors were recessed into the wall, each of them offered the men a place to hide while still being able to shoot at anyone coming their way. Mike went out of the first store as well, but rather than staying in the alley, he first walked into the second store and took his position with a loaded rifle. He and Josh had agreed that Josh would open the front door once more. If, as expected, another shot or two was fired at him, Mike was to fire in the direction of the shooter.

The ploy worked only up to a point, as Mike did shoot at the window on the opposite side of the shopping mall plaza. However, there was no way of knowing whether he hit anything. The team decided that it was not crucial for the camera on top of the front door to be removed; they were totally standard and had been bought in Mosul. At most there might be a couple of fingerprints, but those would not be valuable if they were there. Josh took on the task of loading into the truck everything that they had piled together. Mike was keeping watch on the plaza from inside the second store while Nathan and Daniel were monitoring the alleyway. Once the truck was ready, Nathan and David climbed into the back to be ready to shoot at anyone trying to follow them, while Mike who by then had come out of the second store climbed in the passenger seat, equally ready to shoot at anyone coming toward them from the front.

Their goal was to drive back to Josh's "official" apartment which they believed was still unknown as he had not brought anyone with him there.

■ ■ ■ ■ ■

Back in Kawrugosik, the voice was very agitated. He needed to find out who the traitor was within his team, though he could not let out that he knew there was someone that ostensibly had been telling ISIS – or whomever the enemy was if it was not ISIS – what they were doing. He decided to try setting his own trap. He brought together his small team, there were only eight of them in total, and spoke about the need for someone to deliver to what he called headquarters the opium that was left from the last aborted exchange. He also mentioned a couple of other tasks which were equally unexciting but would require up to four associates to drive in the direction of Erbil. Kassim Mustapha immediately volunteered for the first task, though he asked if he could first run an errand. The voice had no trouble accepting his offer and decided then that he was going to accompany him to Erbil. That left two team members to protect the compound, which should not be an issue, as the voice was still convinced that ISIS or whoever the enemy was did not know its location.

The first team to drive in the direction of Erbil was given an address outside of the Citadel, to the east of the main gate. They were asked to stay there and wait until they were called by the voice. The second team was given an address that was in the same general vicinity, but on the other side of the gate, though neither team knew where the other was going. Both were to arrive at their destination about an hour before the voice expected to arrive with Kassim Mustapha at what had turned out to be the warehouse.

The first team took up its position and for at least forty-five minutes observed everything going on around them, seeing nothing of interest. Cars, people on foot or riding donkeys, a few with livestock, principally chicken, sheep and goats, entering or exiting the Citadel, as there was the usual market in the back of the Tower Plaza. Similarly, the second team was wondering what it was that the voice really expected from them. The situation was indeed a bit more complicated for them as both members of the team had at least once gone to load the truck at the smugglers' warehouse. They were asking each other why the voice would be asking them to be near what they knew as the warehouse and yet stay hidden away from it.

Kassim's errand did not take as long as he had intimated it should. This allowed him and the voice to leave early and thus to arrive early near the main gate of the Citadel as well. Both teams were quite surprised when they recognized the pickup truck of the voice entering the main gate. Discipline kept them on location, though the temptation to follow the voice's truck was very strong.

I I ▪ I I

Josh picked up the phone and heard the voice of Ibrahim's friend:

"Abu Musa, I believe we have some unfinished business. Would you be willing to meet with me to discuss it?"

"Certainly. I must first bring a couple of friends to the airport and should be able to meet you after that."

"I would not wish to impose but wonder whether your associates might not be willing to come along as well. I would like to meet them. I must tell you a couple of stories and they might very well be interested."

Josh felt somewhat confused. First, why would the gentleman be interested in Josh's associates? How did he even know that there were associates? Suddenly, he remembered that he had mentioned a couple of associates when describing the earlier ambushes at the time of each of the prior deliveries. He asked:

"I might be able to convince them to postpone their flight, but I am pretty sure that I will not be able to prevent them wearing their usual side arms."

"Provided you are not upset if my people do the same, I am totally comfortable with that."

They agreed on a time in the next ninety minutes. Josh and the team discussed the proposal and were at a loss of the why of it, but they all decided that well-armed, they would surely be in the strongest position. Nathan added:

"I seem to remember that you said twice "a couple" of associates. Does that mean that this is all your contact knows?"

Josh nodded. Nathan continued:

"Why don't we give them just what they expect?"

"What do you mean?"

"Simple. The three of you ride in the cabin of the truck while I remain hidden on its bed. I can set up one or two rifles with bipods with me under a blanket."

Seeing that his colleagues seemed to agree, he added:

"Thus, I can pick anybody up if it comes to that?"

Josh agreed that the idea looked excellent, though he had to add:

"Great unless trouble is waiting for us inside the house. Then we'll die knowing that you will get them when they come out."

Everybody had a light laugh, but it surely seemed just a tad too much like gallows humor.

■ ■ ■ ■ ■

The one thing which the gentleman had not told Josh was that he and the voice had talked. The voice had informed the gentleman of his plan to flush out the traitor. He had explained:

"Kassim will be with me. He had never been to the warehouse and yet had very often volunteered for the trip. Could be a sign of commitment but could also be a hint that he is looking for the address, potentially to reveal it to the enemy . . ."

"Agreed, but isn't that a big jump from diligence to treason?"

"Can't deny it. I am also sending two other teams of two, in two different cars, to be near the main gate of the Citadel. One group, team two, seems unlikely to include the traitor as they both have been to the warehouse before. If finding its address was their goal, they should have acted already. The other team is less sure, as I have never sent them to the warehouse."

"Is that all your forces?"

"No, two people are back at the compound, but they are blood related to me. I trust them."

"Understood, but a risk, nevertheless. Agreed?"

The voice conceded the point.

■ ■ ■ ■ ■

Albert Hoets called his friend Eli Boez:

"Eli, what is this story about synthetic diamonds?"

"Where have you heard that?"

"Someone I know and you know. David Heller. He was telling me earlier today that you might be worried that the diamonds I've been buying from you are synthetic . . ."

Eli immediately apologized. Clearly, he did not want to lose the one buyer whom he knew to have appreciated the hearts and arrows diamonds earlier. At the same time, he had found out about the microscopic signature and that raised a valid question. He explained to Albert that another jeweler in Beirut had come to see him with questions about the diamonds. He indicated that the jeweler was getting his diamonds from a different source, which made him wonder. Albert simply replied:

"So, we now know that there are at least two sources who have access to these diamonds. Correct?"

"Yes. But my contacts tell me that my colleague's source is Erbil, and so is mine . . ."

"How many jewelers are there in Erbil?"

"Many, but, as you know, our sources often have another characteristic."

"What do you mean?"

"They exchange merchandise, often opiates from Afghanistan, for diamonds. My seller is deeply involved in the Kurdish resistance, or I should say the Kurdish Regional Government. I know they use the money I give them in exchange for their diamonds to buy arms and maintain the resistance. So, I'm comfortable with the deals."

"And the other?"

"I don't know, but I know my source only deals with me. In fact, it is a condition I set for buying their diamonds. I didn't want any competition in the market as I was selling them."

"So, you have to assume that some other group is involved in drug trafficking and is paid in similar diamonds. Where does that lead you?"

"Could there be a single source behind the whole thing?"

"I see, you are asking whether your source has broken its promise."

Eli conceded that this was one of his questions. The other, however, related to the mark on the girdle. He asked:

"Have you ever seen anything like that?"

Albert replied that, in all honesty, he had never seen anything similar, adding that the only similar marks he had seen were on synthetic diamonds. Eli came right back:

"Could that be a new mark in that same market?"

Albert found himself in a tough position. Given what he knew he could not mislead his seller and look at himself in the mirror. At the same time, being a member of the Shadow Experts, he could not reveal what he knew. He remembered that David had told him point-blank that the diamonds were indeed synthetic. The dilemma was serious. The only way he found around the conflict was to reassure Eli saying:

"Eli, everything is possible. Yet, I believe I've done my homework, and on that basis, I am still willing to buy these diamonds from you at the wholesale price we've agreed upon."

He paused and added:

"So, in short, you're taking no risk accepting these diamonds, since you know I'll buy whatever you show me."

He paused again and concluded:

"However, I'm asking you not to take any diamonds other than from your usual source. I would not want to have to buy the diamonds from other local jewelers. Assume that your seller has kept his word and only buys these marked diamonds from him."

Eli thanked Albert and committed to him that he would indeed not buy these diamonds from anyone else. He still had to ask:

"But what can I tell my colleague?"

Albert fired right back:

"The truth. You had questions. You went to your own buyer. The buyer told you he was prepared to keep buying them at a price which assumed they were genuine. But your buyer has a limited absorption capacity."

He paused and concluded:

"He should understand that you will not buy them from him. I'm sure he'll ask you for my name. I'm happy to talk to them but cannot guarantee him the same deal. You came first, you have priority."

■ ■ ■ ■ ■

Albert immediately called Countess Renate to bring her into the loop. She reassured him that he had followed exactly the right path, saying that she was of course going to fulfill her end of the bargain. She took the opportunity to congratulate him on the way he had been able to assist his friend, fulfill his role and not compromise the current mission.

CHAPTER.32

MOSUL AND ERBIL, IRAQ, ANTWERP,
BELGIUM, BEIRUT, LEBANON AND
SOMEWHERE IN THE AUSTRIAN ALPS

Josh took Nathan's advice and proceeded to the warehouse in Erbil. He parked his pickup truck, as he had the prior time, on the opposite side of the plaza. Knowing that Nathan was hidden under the blanket on the bed of the truck, he did not back into the parking spot, but rather drove into it. Nathan, though feeling somewhat hot, was still comfortably installed under the blanket. A couple of strategically placed miniature holes in the blanket allowed him to see most of what would be happening on the plaza. Josh had taken the precaution of lining the blanket with the team's Kevlar jackets as well as he could. He did not want Nathan to be a sitting duck.

Josh, Daniel and Mike stepped out of the truck and went straight for the door of the warehouse. There, a major surprise awaited him and his associates. The door was indeed opened by his friend, Ibrahim. Josh exclaimed:

"What are **you** doing here?"

Ibrahim smiled broadly at his friend and replied:

"All along, I have been the person on the other side of the sheet or on the phone . . ."

"How come I didn't recognize your voice?"

"Voice box trick. Don't tell me you don't know about that?"

Slightly embarrassed, Josh conceded that he did know. Yet he asked:

"Why this game?"

"There is something you need to know. We were the ones who shot down the plane that brought the diamonds. The plane flew further than we expected after we shot it and unfortunately, by the time we got there, I guess the diamonds had burned. Pretty big loss for us. We were expecting close to $100 million . . ."

"Wow! But why did you shoot it down? Why not simply ambush the plane where it was expected to land?"

"We did not want it to take off as soon as he might see us."

"I can see that, but that's a big loss."

"You can say that again. We were planning our next move when our guard was attacked and someone, you as I now know, delivered a box with the sample."

"Sorry for your guard."

"Grateful you used tranquilizer guns and not real bullets . . ."

Ibrahim, aka the gentleman, paused and continued:

"Your offer gave us the opportunity to keep plying our trade to finance our people."

"Wait, I don't understand . . ."

"I can see that. There's one piece you still don't know. We had decided to stop dealing with our prior buyer when we finally discovered they were a front for ISIS. We still don't know where they are, but we are determined to find out and deal with them."

Josh smiled and simply added:

"We might be able to help . . ."

Josh's offer was interrupted by a knock at the door. Ibrahim motioned to Josh, Mike and Daniel that they should step into a room next door, as he had to take care of some business.

■ ■ ■ ■ ■

The three associates did not hear exactly what was being said, but they could note that the conversation did not seem to have any particular urgency. Josh, however, tried to listen a bit more carefully, telling his two colleagues that he recognized at least one person:

"One of the persons talking is the voice, the smugglers' leader in Kawrugosik . . ."

A vibration ring on his phone prevented him from finishing his sentence. It was Nathan who was warning him that there was trouble brewing:

"A couple of cars full of people with arms just arrived at high speed on the plaza, followed by two other cars. The armed group is trying to go in your direction. The two other cars are maneuvering to be between them and the warehouse."

He stopped and added:

"Wait a minute, someone is opening the door to the warehouse. Oh, be careful; a dozen people are coming out of the door, running to the two cars that were trying to block the enemy away from the door. Now they're shooting. So far nobody seems to be hit, but it's bound to happen."

Josh asked:

"Do you have a gun with a silencer with you?"

"Both rifles have silencers and I have a handgun with silencer as well."

"Don't be obvious, but do not hesitate to shoot at those you call the enemy. I think I have a hunch as to what happening."

Still hidden under his blanket, which provided an extra layer of sound deadening, Nathan shot a couple of enemies, using the tranquilizer rifle; as the bullets had less powder, they made even less noise when they were shot. He could tell that the enemy could not understand what was happening. They had ostensibly not seen where the shot had originated, but they could see a couple of their numbers down. Seconds later, Nathan took aim at a couple of individuals who were furthest away from "the action" and similarly brought them down. So far, these were the only visible victims of the skirmish. Someone among the enemy yelled something and Nathan could see all of them move backwards toward their cars. He could not resist taking another couple with the tranquilizer gun, which hastened the departure of the remaining half dozen. They jumped into their cars and drove away offering a perfect target for Nathan who fired twice at one of the wheels of each car. He was pretty sure that he had a couple of hits. The cars kept going, but it was obvious that at least one of their wheels did not have a fully inflated tire.

Inside the house, Josh clearly heard his friend Ibrahim ask a very pointed question to Kassim Mustapha. Though he had not done anything to attack him or even the voice while the fight was going on outside, it clearly seemed that he had something to do with the fact that the enemy had located the warehouse. Josh saw something which led him to scream:

"Ibrahim, move away, fast!"

Though that was enough to save Ibrahim, it did not prevent Kassim from triggering the suicide vest he was wearing. Both he and the voice died in the explosion and the warehouse was damaged, though the destruction was limited to the front room of the house.

The four other smugglers who were outside ran toward the warehouse but could only note the obvious. Josh, Mike and Daniel raced to the room where Ibrahim had managed to escape and saw that his injuries were mere scrapes. Ibrahim said:

"Thank you, Abu Musa? Thank you."

He paused for a second and added:

"Much too close for comfort. You saved my life. I owe you an eternal debt of gratitude. You can count on me. I'm here any time you need me. A simple call away."

Shifting gears, he mentioned:

"By the way, the suicide vest he was wearing was not nearly as powerful as it could have been. I have to guess that he had removed some of the explosives so that the vest was not obvious under his cloak."

Josh smiled and told Ibrahim that they did have some unfinished business when he felt he could handle it. Ibrahim stood up and though somewhat shaken appeared ready to listen. Josh took him aside and gave him a rundown of the address of the ISIS terrorists in Tal Afar. Calling Mike to him, he asked him to give as good a description of the environment there as he could. Mike described the house from which he had seen the airport guard emerge, while he let Josh describe the main house. They added that a house near the point where the second exchange had taken place was suspect, providing sufficient details that it could be located. They then shook hands with Ibrahim and with his three comperes drove away in the pickup truck. Destination: Erbil airport, where he dropped Nathan, Daniel, and Mike in the care of Mehmet.

EPILOGUE

First of all, I would like to thank all my colleagues who were willing to share details of conversations in which I did not participate. Without their recollections, this book would not have been possible.

The two enemy cars which left the Erbil Citadel with at least one flat tire each did not go terribly far. They were rapidly stopped by friends of Ibrahim and the four terrorists captured. I am told that they confessed to their connection to ISIS, although I am afraid that I cannot vouch for their interrogation having complied with the rules prescribed by the Geneva Convention. Their confessions concurred with those made by the terrorists tranquilized on the Tower Plaza in the Citadel.

One thing is for sure, nobody had a chance to warn the rest of the group in Tal Afar who had to have been surprised when the cars they expected to bring back news of a successful mission arrived. The surprise was even greater when the assault which was given by Kurdish troops came in full force. The news is that the compound was wiped out and everyone who was there was either captured or killed, save of course for women and children.

I am told that Ibrahim met with Abu Musa (Josh) a week after the events and gave him all the information he needed, without Josh needing to reveal his affiliation as a *Mossad* agent. In fact, I can confirm that he is still there in Mosul. He did tell Ibrahim that he did not want to have anything to do with the drug trade which he realized

Ibrahim could not stop until Kurdistan was formally established. He saw his mission as only a mixed success as he could not wipe out of his mind the fact that these drugs kill thousands if not millions of people each and every year.

In Tel Aviv, we actually considered the mission much more successful. We established the nefarious role of Russia in arming insurgents, and its callous willingness to introduce nuclear weapons, albeit weak ones into these regional conflicts. Our government has yet to produce the proof of the nuclear transfer: it is a good sword to maintain above the head of the Kremlin. The proof Moshe Lantzer uncovered that Russia also used Russian diamonds to finance terrorist activities such as the ones we encountered allowed us to get Russian diamonds to be treated like "blood diamonds" and thus avoided in a number of countries.

The drop in supply helped stabilize the global diamond markets which had initially reacted quite negatively when the origin of the "E & W diamonds" was revealed: the Weizmann Institute and its star chemist Samuel Eisenstein owned up to the fact that the stones were synthetically produced. The market had indeed, initially at least, not welcomed the news that synthetic diamonds would now potentially fool the most respected and technologically advanced certification institute. Yet, in the end, the fact that no one has yet managed to package that much value in so small a volume together with the natural beauty of diamonds means that there will remain a market for them. At the margin, though, I cannot help myself thinking that it could well be synthetic whenever I see someone wearing what looks like an abnormally large diamond.

I recently visited with Samuel and was quite surprised when he showed me colored stones in which he had even managed to replicate the normally random impurity which jewelers often call "silk." I am told that the Internal Gemological Institute is developing microscopic new tests to differentiate real from synthetic stones given the incredible progress being made by chemistry.

Signed: D.H.

www.ingramcontent.com/pod-product-compliance
Lightning Source LLC
Chambersburg PA
CBHW051139030726
47504CB00004B/943